BORDERLINE
TRUTHS

BORDERLINE TRUTHS

Maurice J.O. Crossfield

CROSSFIELD
PUBLISHING

CROSSFIELD PUBLISHING

www.crossfieldpublishing.com
books@crossfieldpublishing.com

2269 Road 120, R7, St. Marys, Ontario, N4X 1C9, Canada

Copyright © Maurice J.O. Crossfield, 2017

Second printing 2022

ISBN: 978-1-990326-10-3 (Pbk.)
ISBN: 978-1-990326-24-0 (ePub)

All rights reserved.

Printed and bound in Canada.

Editing: David L. Pretty, Isabel Armiento
Cover art: Carl Lightbody, Lawrence Stilwell, Magdalene Carson
Design: Magdalene Carson RGD / New Leaf Publication Design:

Library and Archives Canada Cataloguing in Publication

Title: Borderline truths / Maurice J.O. Crossfield.
Names: Crossfield, Maurice J. O., author.
Identifiers: Canadiana (print) 20220447616 | Canadiana (ebook) 20220447624
    | ISBN 9781990326103 (softcover) | ISBN 9781990326240 (EPUB)
Subjects: LCGFT: Novels.
Classification: LCC PS8605.R682 B67 2022 | DDC C813/.6—dc23

For my mother, Genevieve Perron-Crossfield
Life is a creative act

Acknowledgements

A writer simply cannot work in a vacuum, and as such there are a number of people who have helped me bring this story to light, and as such deserve my heartfelt thanks. First, foremost and always is my True Love, Sarah Biggs, whose grace, creativity and talent are brought to bear on all things. She is my heart's home. To Susan C. Mastine and France Jodoin, who read early versions of this story and who have consistently cheered me on my sometimes-tortured path. To my editors, Isabel Armiento and David Pretty, who challenged me to be a better writer and made my prose sing. For my kids, Julien and Gabe, who make me want to show them the best of myself, to always stretch and grow, and embrace the limits of possibility. To Tina Crossfield, who has helped keep me on track, and put so much effort into having this all make sense. And to my ancestors, storytellers all, most of whom enjoyed a good laugh at the end of a tall tale. I am humbled by all of your love and kindness.

Once again, a special thank you to my former colleagues at the *Sherbrooke Record*, that mighty little paper that shaped my writing, my worldview, and my love of the Eastern Townships of Quebec.

Maurice J. O. Crossfield

BORDERLINE TRUTHS

Prologue

As the life slowly bled from his body, he wondered how everything had gone so fatally wrong.

In that moment he reflected on his father's temper, which could ignite into a firestorm from out of nowhere and cause trouble for all around him. It was this same inherited blind anger that had led him to his current desperate situation.

They thought he was dead when he was hauled into the trunk of the car. Hell, *he* thought he was dead. But life held on, still unwilling to let anyone, or anything, dominate him. As his mind cleared, some deep, ever-angry part of himself refused to let go. It was the same strength of will that kept him going in the ring and during those Griffintown street fights when he was collecting for Charlie McKiernan.

But now he knew that McKiernan was dead, the Irish mob was out for his head and the two men he'd vowed to kill were now toting him away in the trunk of a car. They thought they'd killed him, but they were wrong...and he was going to make that their final, fatal mistake.

He could feel the blood pooling underneath his head and run his tongue along the jagged edges of his broken teeth. As soon as he was done with these two pricks, all he needed to do was find someplace to hide out while he healed up. *All in good time.*

Passing in and out of consciousness, he caught only scraps of conversation from the front seat. Occasional words, but not enough to figure out. When the car stopped at one point, he could smell the exhaust, hear the rumble and feel the warmth from the leaking muffler below the floor pan. That low, silk-smooth rumble lulled him to sleep.

He barely noticed as the trunk opened and the two men hauled at the rope around his torso, straining at the effort. The rope cinched his chest, and he came fully awake. He instinctively kicked out, that deep internal fire willing his body to make a last, definitive stand and eliminate those who sought to dispose of him.

But the body was unable to answer his mind's call to action. Legs and arms thrashed but failed to gain purchase. Then he felt the bullet's final sledgehammer blow to his chest and the night erupted into the last light he'd ever see.

"It's going to be a long, hard fall," he heard Stubby Booker say in the far, far distance. "Blow you to pieces in the dark."

And then, finally powerless, he felt the husk of his shattered body tumble into darkness. Darkness as eternal and deep as damnation.

1
Thin Ice

So, there I was, sitting at my desk, staring at my name tag: Dave the reporter. I've been an accessory to murder, my dead father isn't talking to me anymore and I'm keeping all of this a secret from my wife.

Been a bit of a rough ride these last few months. To be honest, I've hardly been sleeping lately, and when I do, I'm ripped back into wakefulness by the nauseating pop of Farstall's elbow, bright lights beating down on me and cowering behind my car while being shot at. I still dream about my dad, but while he used to talk to me, now the dreams are silent. He doesn't speak, and I can't seem to say a word. Can't bear to look him directly in the face.

I really don't know why this came up again. After I left the sand pit and dumped the car at Homer's scrapyard, things kind of settled down. It was rough for a few nights, with bad dreams and waves of anxiety. I could usually blot most of it out with a few beers in my belly and then fall into a sort of dark rest. And gradually, things relatively returned to normal. Naturally, Jen had questions, but I managed to answer them as truthfully as I could without saying something that would ruin my marriage.

This was the brief, clean version that I gave to Jen: believing that Stubby Booker was responsible for my dad's death, I set out to confront him. I was angry and out to get even, though I wasn't sure just what that meant. Booker and I met up and he explained himself more- or-less to my satisfaction.

I left out the part where I got abducted and then left on the side of the road with a pistol, a box of bullets and a murderous rage boiling inside me, hatching mental plans to shoot him. I also left out the part where Stubby and I met at a sand pit and were promptly shot at by disgraced cop Reggie Farstall, and how Stubby saved my ass while I cowered in the dirt behind my bullet-riddled car.

As lies go it was pretty thin. Especially when you add in the fib about how my car died and I managed to find an old Vauxhall Viva as a replacement the same day. No mention of the holes in the hood or the fact that I dumped it at Homer's scrapyard on Stubby's orders. She never saw the car, and I never offered up the information.

So yes, even though I'd been skating on thin ice, Jen seemed to take it all in stride. Perhaps in part because she'd been dealing with the aftermath of being attacked at our home in Brigham, which had been burned down hours later. Completely shell-shocked by that point, we were so caught up in ourselves that we didn't give much thought to the other. At first we briefly relocated to an apartment in Granby, but then found something a little better in Cowansville. It was a small duplex, half of a house really, located on a back street. There was room for our dog King to run in the back, and most importantly, the proliferation of nearby neighbours made the place feel safe.

Even though our living space was smaller, the distance between us had grown. As winter settled in, we just focused on getting by. On some weekends, Jen would take the bus to the city while I stayed behind with King. That's when I usually watched hockey and drank myself to sleep. Still harbouring some resentment over the secrets that had come to light after my life was in danger, I went in to see my mother only occasionally.

Tensions were building at the *Granby Leader-Mail* as well. With every new death notice that came in, readership was dwindling and we were haemorrhaging subscribers. Ad revenues were down, and open talk about seeking jobs elsewhere was often heard in the newsroom. When Steve Farnham left to go to Toronto, he wasn't replaced. We just took up the slack, and no paid overtime was offered. The paper getting thinner, as if it was suffering from some slow, wasting disease.

That sense of anxious gloom could be felt out in the community as well. The separatist Parti Québécois had become a rising force, while Premier Robert Bourassa and his governing Liberals were increasingly hated by the entrenched Anglos thanks to Bill 22, which made French the sole official language in Quebec. The Union Nationale, which once held an iron grip on the vitals of Quebec society in the era of Maurice Duplessis, was now collapsing, despite continued strong support in the Eastern Townships. Change was coming, and the community I wrote the news for was anxious.

This had a lot of English-speakers talking loudly and openly about leaving. After all, anglos had grown accustomed to calling the shots. If you were a Francophone in a manufacturing town, you could be sure of three things: your boss was probably English, he likely didn't speak a word of French and you would never have his job. The writing was on the wall, and since it was in French, many Anglos couldn't even read it. But deep down they knew what it said: the age of Anglo dominance was drawing to a close.

Those feelings were reflected in the *Granby Leader-Mail's* letters to the editor, as well as the decline in readership. Advertisers were also finding it increasingly effective to reach out to the French-speaking majority and eschew the dwindling Anglo contingent.

By the spring of 1976, this atmosphere of crisis had firmly settled in at the *Granby Leader-Mail* and the paper's fortunes were being discussed in hushed tones. Every printing contract lost sent tremors through the old building, shaking paper dust from the rafters, which hung in the air like cigarette smoke blended with the faint tang of furnace oil. Every new contract won felt like a minor reprieve, but it was muted by the suspicion that the end was only a matter of time.

Fortunately, there was plenty of news to cover. In the spring of 1976, things were ramping up in tiny town of Bromont, formally known as West Shefford until the 1960s. Bromont was playing host to the equestrian events for the 1976 Olympics and the world's collective gaze was on Quebec. Montreal, in particular, was being viewed through the dual optics of a world-class city and a hive of political corruption. Politicians were bought and sold, Olympic construction contracts included kickbacks on top of kickbacks, and it quickly became clear that *all* Canadian taxpayers were going to have to flip the bill to play host to the world. Not even the Olympic Lottery, with its primetime televised draws and three grand prizes of $1 million, could cover the financial shortfall.

Not to be outdone, the CN Tower, soon to be the tallest building in the world, was nearing completion in Toronto. And, in the US, media-heiress-turned-kidnapping-victim-turned-terrorist Patty Hearst was sentenced to seven years in prison for armed robbery.

The Olympics also gave the region a case of Royal Family fever, as people kept watch out for Princess Anne, who was competing for England in show jumping. This kept our photographers quick-drawing their cameras at the slightest sign of royalty or their security detail. At the time, we tried our best to nail down an interview with a Royal, but is wasn't in the cards. Instead we reported on people who caught a glimpse of a member of the Queen's household.

The hooligan element came out as well, with several people trying to make off with anything Olympic-related that wasn't nailed down. This ranged from innocuous things like traffic cones all the way up to broadcasting equipment. And, over the course of the equestrian events, dozens were arrested trying to sneak onto the grounds without tickets.

For me, and many of my colleagues, the Olympics provided an opportunity to get out from under the dark cloud that hung over the office. "I'm just going to see what's happening over at the Olympic site," I'd say. I made ample use of my press pass, sometimes using the access it provided to just nose around. There was no shortage of stories, including a multitude of personality profiles on volunteers, trainers and even the horses themselves. Yes, *I interviewed a horse.* Granted, its trainer provided translation, so if the article contained miss-quotes or inaccuracies at all, it was entirely his fault.

Mind you, on a few occasions, these trips also included a little back road exploration. Out of sight of the office, out of mind of the boss. Unreachable. Just the way I liked it.

Exploring roads and rivers had become my preferred hobby. I'd motor past thriving farms and abandoned wrecks where settlers once sweated and toiled in the hopes of building something better, something uniquely their own. All of this was within virtual walking distance of the world's collective gaze as they watched the equestrian elite spur their mounts to Olympic glory and the A-list royalty gazed down from their segregated section of the stands.

All this was taking place not far from where Anthony Bakerstein's body was found last fall.

And, as much as I enjoyed rubbing shoulders with big league reporters, it didn't take much to draw me away. Increasingly, I preferred doing stories about the locals, especially the old-timers. People who lived life close to the bone, and whose efforts were rarely recognized for how real and how human they were. In other words: non-Olympic subjects that the bigger papers didn't care about. My best moments were often sitting at a kitchen table with a cup of (usually instant) coffee, talking about everything from milk prices to what trouble the local town councillor was trying to stir up.

Sometimes the best part of the interview was *after* the notepad had been put away, something you didn't get living in Montreal. Maybe some reporters did, but I never experienced it at the *McGill Daily.* It was those precious moments when guards were lowered and trust was given, and you got to see who these people really were, and what they really thought.

When I was growing up in Montreal, my mom and I pretty much kept to ourselves. It felt like we'd barely unpacked before dad fell from the high steel, a seismic event of tragedy that cemented our relationship and built a wall up around the two of us. The neighbours didn't know us, and since my mom wasn't talking to anyone about it, they didn't get to know who we were. Hell, *I* didn't know who we were.

After everything that happened, I did have to do some explaining to do to my mom. I had to sanitize the events; explain that, *no*, Stubby Booker hadn't killed dad, and, *no*, he wasn't trying to kill me, and, *yes*, we were both safe now. To this day, I doubt she believed any of it, but any leaks in my story were likely smoothed over by a healthy dose of a parent's willful blindness to see flaws in their child. If she had any doubts, she kept them to herself, like she always did. For me, it was just another layer of lies, more verbal bobbing and weaving as I tried to keep all the stories straight, including all of the fibs I told myself.

Sometimes a man has to lie to himself just to get by.

* * *

One of the things the Olympics brought to our part of the world was the closure of many small back roads that crossed the border. These roads had been in use since the first settlers arrived, and the government had never paid much attention to them. The Canadian and American border patrols would cruise by now and then, mostly to make sure the signs asking people to check in at the nearest customs crossing hadn't been completely obscured by brush... or stolen. One time I heard a story about the police impounding a car that had a large hole in the floor that had been patched with a road sign. Good heavy gauge metal, those signs.

On a sunny early summer afternoon, with the Olympics only a few weeks away, Fernand Dubois, local spokesman for the Quebec Police Force, took to a podium erected at the end of Valquirit Road in Frelighsburg to introduce the honoured guests. First up was a tall, pale and bespectacled RCMP sergeant named Moffatt, complete with close-cropped red hair and a Mountie-issue ginger moustache. On one side of him was Heward Grafftey, the Progressive Conservative Member of Parliament for Brome-Missisquoi, known in some circles as the "Gnome from Brome." On the other, representing the Quebec government, was Liberal Glendon Brown. Rounding out the stage was Frelighsburg mayor Wayne Enright.

Behind them was the centrepiece of the press conference, an excavator at work, digging up what had previously been a road to and from northern Vermont.

"Security is of the utmost importance when you are hosting an international event like the Olympics," said Moffatt in his incongruously-thick French accent. "We will be taking every precaution to ensure that these games will be safe from disruption, both for the athletes and those attending the events. This will allow the world's best athletes to showcase their skills to a global audience."

Frelighsburg's mayor followed up with a short speech of his own. Mayor Enright spoke of his town's long association with the border, how many of the locals had family on both sides of the line, and that these unmarked crossings were now becoming a thing of the past. The price of progress was increased security, and there were too many of these tiny roads for the authorities to keep an eye on. Even though he didn't say it outright, I got the distinct impression that he wasn't a big fan of all the goings-on.

In theory, anyone using these roads was supposed to report to the nearest customs offices. Signs were put up to point the way, and the vast majority of locals from both sides of the border observed the honour system, and it seemed to work quite well if you asked them. Most residents knew the customs officers anyways, so reporting in gave them a chance to catch up on the local gossip.

Beyond digging up the roadways to ensure people only crossed at legal ports of entry, both Canadian and US authorities would also be stepping up patrols. Sergeant Moffatt assured one and all that no one would be getting in or out of the country unnoticed.

Sometimes it's the little details at press conferences that mean so much. The whitewashed officer's face had barely pushed out those bold words before I heard a gentle exhalation of breath to my left. I turned my head to see an older gentleman, obviously a farmer. He looked at me and winked.

Then came the standard question-and-answer session. Yes, things would be safer. No, terrorists wouldn't be getting in anytime soon. No, there'd been no specific threats yet, but you can't be too careful. Let's not forget the 1972 Olympics in Munich, when the Palestinian terrorist group Black September killed eleven Israeli athletes and a German police officer.

Then things broke up, with photographers being escorted down the hill to get shots of the excavator digging up the road, and the CHEF radio reporter getting some tape from the dignitaries.

I opted for a slightly different approach, turning my attention to the farmer, who was now making his way towards a rusting brown Chevy Impala.

"I noticed you didn't seem very impressed by all the hoopla," I said to his back. He turned, revealing a slight smile that hung below deep, green-brown eyes. His ruddy skin was a testimony to a long life spent in the elements.

"They put on a nice show," he said. "I figured since they were close by, and I used to be on the town council, I'd come and see what all the fuss was about."

"You don't seem convinced that all of this effort is going to increase border security."

"It's nothing more than a pain in the arse for those of us that live in these parts," he said. "If anything, it's going to cause more trouble than it solves. And now I've got to take the long way around just to go see my Aunt Verna over in East Berkshire."

He paused for a moment, staring at the ground next to the Impala's front tire.

"I'll go put some coffee on. You finish up here, and when you get back to the Richford Road, turn right. My place is the third farm after the Mine Road. We can talk better there, and I need to let the dogs out before they wreck the place."

2
Crowbar hotel

Not even the sticky heat of a July day could make it past the security door and into the pervasive cool of the cellblock at the Sweetsburg Jail. As the door lock buzzed and the lawyer stepped inside, he could feel the change, his sweat-damp polyester suit clinging to his body. It wasn't an expensive suit. It didn't even fit particularly well, but that didn't matter. He wasn't paid to wear a good suit, he was paid to be a smart lawyer. And George Carson was a very smart lawyer.

Through a second security door and down a dark hallway, he blinked behind steel- rimmed glasses as his eyes tried to adjust to the dim light. He'd been down this hall dozens of times, almost as many times as the pair of provincial guards escorting him. They unlocked an interview room, leaving the door open while they went and got his client. He went inside and dropped his notepad on the table. He'd left his briefcase back in the car, reasoning that there was no need to have the guards rifling though it for no reason.

The door swung wide and a short man with thick eyebrows entered, shackles on hands and feet. Denim shirt, jeans. The lawyer smiled, greeting an old friend.

"Hey, George," said Stubby Booker. "Give me the news."

"Hey, Stubby. How are they treating you here? Any trouble?"

"Only that I've been stuck in this shithole for the last month. Is this what I'm paying you for? Dumb questions?"

There was a pause in the conversation as the guards removed the shackles. Then they left the room, locking the door behind them.

"This case has been a little trickier than usual, and the Crown has been fighting everything tooth and nail. They really think you killed Farstall. So much so that they made a few mistakes along the way."

"What kind of mistakes?" Stubby asked.

"Enough for an appeal. Like the reference to that time years ago when McConnell disappeared, so they nailed you for obstruction. That's over twenty years ago, so it should never have been brought up."

"But you were overruled on the objection," Booker said. He'd remembered every detail of the trial and re-examined the evidence and testimony in his mind, ever watchful for something, *anything,* of use.

"Yes, but I dug through some jurisprudence and there's a similar case that was thrown out for just such an error. Obstruction two decades ago doesn't mean obstruction now. It's enough. With that and the arrest procedures, we'll get you an appeal. We've got a hearing with the Quebec Court of Appeal Tuesday of next week to see if they'll hear the case. Trust me, they'll hear it. And as soon as they give us that, I'll have you out of here the same day."

"What if I lose the appeal?"

"I'm arguing against both the conviction and the sentence. Worst case, you'll end up serving weekends. You won't do anything close to the two years less a day the Superior Court sentenced you to. But I don't think you'll even get that."

"You sure?"

"I've been your lawyer for many years now, Mr. Booker, and I think we've done pretty well by each other. Trust me on this. You'll be released on the usual conditions...check in weekly with the police once a week, can't go to bars, the usual. The fact that you have a business to operate that employs several dozen people will work in our favour."

"All right. But, look...I'm getting a little antsy here. The guards have been *less than kind* this time around. Keep grumbling that I'm a cop killer. I don't much care for it."

"Do you need me to speak with anyone? I've got contacts with the guards and the inmates."

"I can handle myself," Stubby said. "You just get me outta here, and I'll make sure it's worth your while."

"It always has been, old friend."

* * *

Stubby was escorted back to his cell. Being away from the world had given him plenty of time to think. These days he was mostly feeling tired. Tired of the constant stress, always looking over his shoulder and trying to stay a step ahead of everyone else. In the early days of his incarceration, he mainly just slept. That was, when he was allowed to. There was one guard on the night shift, a real prick, who would run his night stick along the cell bars when he was making his rounds. Enough to wake him up and remind him of where he was in the dark of the night.

In the outside world, Stubby Booker was feared. He had a reputation as a brutal murderer, *and you stayed out of his way*. He was the kind of guy who wouldn't hesitate to eliminate you if you got in the way; like the mafia and Hell's Angels all rolled into one. Hushed, but widely-circulated, stories had him stealing things, beating people and robbing banks. By these same accounts, he'd murdered at least a half-dozen people, maybe more, and dumped their bodies down old mine shafts, sunk them into lakes or burned them up, never to be found again.

Truth be told, he'd only ever murdered two people. He *had* ordered a couple of people eliminated last year, to deal with some loose ends, but only when he saw no other option. He didn't much care for killing , it's was too messy, too complicated and it usually created more problems than it solved.

Confined to a cell all day, it's easy to picture oneself as nothing more than a small-time thug. But he quickly quashed this thought, which threatened to leak into his foundational sense and rot out his self-perception. Stubby wasn't feeling remorse; that was an emotion he didn't really understand. He just felt tired of all the bullshit. At night he dreamed of going fishing with an old friend, but all of his old friends were either dead, in jail or were now giving the notorious Stubby Booker a wide berth because of his larger-than-life reputation.

Now here he was, in his mid-fifties, acutely aware that he had fewer days ahead of him than behind him, sitting in a jail cell where every passing day it felt as if one more grain of sand in the timer of his life was being taken away. Slowly, he was starting to realize that it was time to get out of the business.

First, he'd have to have enough...but how much was enough? Was there ever such a thing as "enough?" Coming from nothing, he'd always lived by the simple philosophy that more was better. He sure as hell wasn't going to hang it all up and go work at Canadian Tire for minimum wage, or slave away his remaining days busting his ass working on a farm. No, retirement had to mean complete independence, and never having to worry that a cop, or a competitor, would try to take a shot at him.

As he whiled away the days in jail, Stubby Booker rested, meditated on his retirement plans and fantasized about what he would do to that fucking night guard who kept waking him up just to be a prick.

3

History lesson

I pulled into the yard of a white, tumble-down clapboard house and was greeted by a pair of dogs. One was obviously a border collie and the other was a large, black beast of indeterminate lineage, but the tails were up and waving for both and the barks were absent of menace. I parked next to the wraparound porch, just as the big shaggy one planted his muddy paws on the hood. I was thoroughly sniffed over by the time I made it to the woodshed and up the three stairs to the door.

Wilson Butler greeted my knock with a wave through the warped glass window, entreating me to come in. His was a typical farm kitchen, with the everyday electric appliances lined up against one wall, while the wood-fired cook stove still held a place of pride near the kitchen door. It was May and Wilson had a fire going, a warm reminder that the old ways still held sway in this household. Parked next to the stove was a daybed, clearly a place where a noontime nap could be had before heading back to the fields. A short stack of magazines and newspapers, including the *Family Herald*, *Sherbrooke Record* and the latest *Granby Leader-Mail*, lay at the foot of the daybed next to Wilson's rocking chair.

"Come on in, make yourself at home," Wilson said as he rose from his chair. "Coffee or tea? I've got instant."

"Coffee sounds fine, thanks," I replied. "Nice place you have here."

"Lived here pretty much all my life, except for when I was in the war. After that I trimmed trees in the city for a bit, but I got sick of all the climbing. So, when my old man decided that he'd had enough of milking cows every day, I came and took over. He built that little place across the road and up a bit, still within sight so he could watch the cows."

During my visit, he explained how he kept busy with any number of things to get by, whether it be collecting milk and eggs, harvesting maple syrup in the spring or fixing farm equipment for his neighbours. His dad still helped where he could, unable to shake the addiction that is farming despite being nearly ninety years old.

"So you're Dave Junior," he said. "I knew your dad. Not well, but I used to see him around sometimes."

"Oh really? He died when I was a kid," I said, always eager to learn something, anything, about him. "Do you have any stories that you could tell me about him?"

He gave me kind of a half-smile, then looked at the floor. "Like I said, I didn't know him all that well. Mostly by reputation. He'd climb up somebody's silo or a church steeple, and before you knew it word would get around. Or he'd be tearing up the roads in his old Buick, gettin' all the old timers up in arms with the noise. I saw him on the back roads 'round here once or twice, probably coming up across the line."

Something in the way he said that caught my curiosity. As I looked at him through narrowed eyes, he just smiled back and said nothing.

"Anything I should know?" I asked.

"Maybe another time."

With that the conversation shifted, a tacit agreement between the two of us to let the matter lie.

"So, earlier you said that closing off the border crossings were going to be a pain in the arse," I ventured. "That it's going to cause trouble. What's it really going to mean...other than you having to drive the long way around to see your aunt?"

He looked at me as he rubbed his chin thoughtfully, his little finger pointing out at a sharp angle from its companions, probably the result of some accident that didn't warrant a trip to the doctor. His eyes seemed more green than brown in the yellowish light of the kitchen, but they held a glint of mischief.

"Put your notepad away," he said. "Let me tell you a story."

Intrigued, I did as I was asked, shifted in my chair and leaned forward in anticipation. In response, Wilson cleared his throat and launched into an epic tale that kept me riveted to my seat.

"People around here have been hauling just about anything you can imagine back and forth across the line since before there even was a line. Even the Abenaki passed back and forth here, moving with the seasons. When the first Loyalists came up to these parts, they didn't even know exactly where they were. One of my ancestors thought he'd made the trip and staked out a spot where he built his house, all safe from them American rebels. Of course, Vermont wasn't one of the original thirteen, and there wasn't anyone for miles anyways. So he started from scratch, built his cabin and put down roots. Fought through those first hard years and made a go of it.

"One day the surveyors come through, and he learned he'd been on the south side all along, and he was actually an American. Story goes he was pretty mad, but not mad enough to pull up stakes and move again. That's where Verna, my ninety-two-year-old aunt, now lives.

"In those early days, the Loyalists, and later the ones who came for the free land, needed the basics to survive. Now if you look at a map, the nearest place for anything was either Missisquoi Bay, where most of the earliest Loyalists ended up, or Montreal. But to get to Montreal from these parts you had to make your way through virgin forest, swamps and across about a half-dozen rivers. You can do it in an hour and a half now, but back then it might take you the better part of a week. Picture that with oxen or horses, or often on foot, carrying whatever you could lug. Imagine trying to coax a team of oxen through woods with no roads. You might get lost, which would add on a few extra days. How do you get a team of oxen, pulling a load of supplies, across the Richelieu River? Come out in the wrong place and God knows what you'd find. And what about if you tried it during the spring melt? Impossible!

"Easier to head south, make your way down in a day or two, get what you need and then be home before the wife even missed you. That is, if she ever did."

I smiled as Wilson enjoyed his own joke far more than he should have.

"Flour, cattle, chickens, horses, tools....you could get everything you needed. This was the sort of stuff you needed if you were trying to make a go of it. In fact, many who didn't have the gear just didn't pull through. Over on Russell Road there's a little cemetery, and you can see that the husband died on December 19, 1835, and the missus died on December 20. Though it might sound like she died of a broken heart, it was more likely that she died of disease or starvation or she froze to death. Life was pretty hard in those days.

"As time went on, going to Vermont for things was just what you did. Even when the roads opened up and the trains came, it just made more sense to buy stuff in Vermont. People knew where to get things, even wives, which were in short supply around here. And not a customs officer in sight! Little roads, like that one they dug up today in front of all you folks, started to snake across the border. Nobody around here ever gave it much thought, they were just paths that developed naturally. If someone found an easier way to get where they needed to go, they'd blaze a trail and, before long, everyone was using it.

"In the early 1800s, counterfeit money was the thing. It wasn't illegal to counterfeit American money, so long as you didn't try to spend it up here. Over in East Dunham there's a road that used to be called Cogniac, but they call it Hudon now. *Everybody* was making funny money up there. Hell, even the man who represented Missisquoi in Quebec City was in on it. Just look up Seneca Paige. He was a member of government, a justice of the peace and one of the biggest counterfeiters around. They'd print it up here, take it down there, bring back real cash...or even gold.

"Then it was booze, of course. At different times, towns on either side of the line would get 'temperance fever' and go dry. Of course, those places were never really all *that* dry, they just moved the drinking indoors and out of sight. And, of course, wherever there's a dollar to be made...there's someone willing to make it.

"Back when I was little, too little to know much about it at the time, there was a cat house built right on the border called Queen Lil's. Montreal train to Boston used to stop there for the entertainment. Place was full of women and booze and whatnot...including Queen Lil herself. She always seemed to know when the police were coming. When the Mounties would show up, all the girls would be sitting on the American side, looking all proper. But then, when the State Troopers raided the place, all of the alcohol, and most of the patrons, were up north and out of reach.

"One day, Queen Lil settled up and cashed out. Just like that. Her and the man she married became sheep farmers on the Vermont side, not far from where she plied her trade. Never arrested, lived a nice quiet life, church on Sunday and all.

"People got caught sometimes...like it was a game. Didja see that farm up at the corner of the Mine Road? Smugglers lived there. They barely made any effort to make it look like a working farm and even let peckerbrush grow all over the junk that piled up. Eventually the Mounties seized the place, and a few years later this hardworking French family moved in. When they put the plough to the soil they immediately started bringing up glass. Turns out the smugglers would go by with a single furrow plough to turn the sod up, then they hid their bottles of booze in the ground and folded the sod back over. *Tidy.* That's why the police never found anything when they raided the place.

"All to say that bringing things like food, supplies, booze and even people, across the border has been pretty much an open secret. It's just part of life, part of who we are and how we get by. When I drive down the back road to see Aunt Verna, I see the sign telling me to report to customs. Almost never do though. Unless I come across a border patrol car, then I wave and make a good show of it. If I need a piece for a mowing machine, am I going to drive a half an hour to the machine shop in Cowansville, or ten minutes to Richford?

"But it's not us folks along the line that customs has to worry about, and they know that. Last ten, fifteen years it's been outsiders, or people working for outsiders. Lots of them. Strangers heading for or coming from Montreal, runnin' big trucks full of everything from cigarettes to drugs to TV sets to God knows what. That or draft dodgers. A lot of them came up and stayed, sneaking back to visit their people whenever they thought they could get away with it. If you sit up on the Pinnacle at night you can see the lights going back and forth. Some are just regular folks, but some aren't. Customs can't be everywhere, though you gotta give them credit for effort."

"Who's running truckloads of stuff across the border in plain sight?" I asked, finally able to get in a word edgewise.

"Hard to say, as they aren't the type to stop to talk. But rumour has it we've got the mafia, the Irish, maybe some motorcycle gang types. I don't think I move in the right circles to know for sure. All headed for the city would be my guess... or from the city down across the line."

He paused to drain his coffee cup and then pulled a pack of cigarettes from his shirt pocket. Players Navy Cut, unfiltered. He offered one, standard practice, but I declined. Never quite got the taste for it. He fished a book of matches from a dish on the kitchen table, a chrome and melamine affair. He then settled back into his rocking chair before lighting up.

"You might want to check with the game wardens. They see lots of stuff around here. They're looking for poachers and the like, but that means driving a lot of back roads in the middle of the night."

"So, can I use any of this?" I asked.

"I believe you can...isn't it what you newspaper people call 'background'? Best leave my name out of it, though. I gotta live here, and I've been on my own since Hazel died. I've already had some odd-looking critters giving me funny looks just for passing by at the wrong moment. And, as you probably noticed, my dogs aren't much for protection against burglars and ne'er do wells."

"But this is really good information."

"Hey, anyone can find out information if they phone around," he replied, talking through the smoke. "But, since you didn't grow up around here, I figured I'd give you a little history lesson. It's not just stories, young man. The thing people always forget about history, and newspaper stories, is those are real people we're talking about. It's as real as it gets."

4

Three suits

Stubby Booker had three suits. The first was his dark grey "going to court suit," used for legal proceedings. The style was a bit dated, the tie was a little too narrow and it fit loosely. After he'd primped and preened, this suit made him look a little older, a little more out of shape and, as such, relatively harmless. Stubby used it to present himself as someone a little down at the heels who wanted nothing more than to show respect and admiration for the people and institutions of the justice system.

Then there was his "funeral suit" which was dark charcoal, almost black. This was typically accessorized with a black fedora, to be removed at the right moments of protocol, and a black wool overcoat if foul weather called for it. If he deigned to go to a funeral, he would make every show of respect to the deceased and their families. But this look also had a slightly menacing air, just in case someone in attendance doubted who he was or what he was capable of.

But today, a week after his release pending the appeal, it was time for "the good suit." An expensive cut, tailored to accentuate his broad shoulders while concealing his gut, this dark blue pinstripe was top of the line, a suit fit for someone who was in charge. Someone worthy of respect. A leader who got things done. An equal.

Hair slicked back, face freshly shaved. Aftershave and cologne. God, how he hated cologne, but those damned Italians seemed to bathe in the stuff. And they sniffed it out on others, like dogs who checked for drugs at the airport. He'd brought it over from his house in Roxton Pond to the Magenta Road in Brigham, to the farm that no one knew he owned and where he kept his Cadillac, waxed and spotless, in the barn.

Today it was time for an afternoon trip to Montreal. He'd hung his jacket up carefully in the back of his car, with the air conditioning on at full blast to counter the hot July day. 'Never let them see you sweat,' he mused to himself.

He didn't like these trips to the city, but he'd been summoned. It didn't happen often, so it usually meant something important was afoot. As he drove, he ran over the possibilities in his head. Maybe they just wanted to make sure that he hadn't given up any information while he was in jail. But they knew him better than that. He didn't talk. *Ever.*

The guns he'd bought for the People for an English-Speaking Quebec had already been paid for. Despite his time in court and in jail, the cigarettes, construction materials and booze kept flowing north across the border as per usual. Sure, the recent "discovery" of the unmarked border crossings had been problematic, but alternative routes had since been found. There were always alternative routes. He'd even overseen a number of shipments south, mostly hashish, without incident. As far as he could figure, the Italians had been getting what they were asking for.

Like any good Cadillac-driving, suit-wearing, middle-aged man, Stubby followed the speed limits along the Eastern Townships autoroute, making sure to drop the right amount of quarters in the toll booth slots and taking care not to pull away too quickly and set off the alarm. His pulse quickened slightly as he crossed the Champlain Bridge, anticipating the meeting ahead. He was unarmed, sticking to the philosophy that if you feel you need a gun to meet with someone well-connected, you should probably not be doing business with them. This was another gesture of respect, formally acknowledged by the thug at the door during the pre-meeting pat down. There would be no shooting your way out of a mafia don's offices anyways. Up Atwater, left on St. Antoine, left on Walker and left again through the alley to the chocolate factory. Then up the stairs that couldn't be seen from the street.

"Welcome, Mr. Booker," the tall, tanned, well-dressed man said as Stubby entered the office. He rose to meet his guest, waving him to a deeply-cushioned leather chair. Though the rich smell of chocolate from the factory below filled the air, this room, with its polished wood and tasteful bookshelves, felt more like a study in an English manor house. It seemed like the sort of place where great men discussed great things, and enjoyed the social niceties of Scotch and cigars once business had been taken care of.

"So, now that the Olympics are over, we're finally getting things back to normal," Vince said, returning to the soft embrace of his leather office chair. "And I have some concerns that I'd like to discuss with you."

"I'm sure we can handle any concerns you might have," Stubby said. Like his overall appearance, his voice was clipped and cleaned, ready for business. His Township drawl had been replaced with clear, urban English.

"Your willingness to accommodate was never in doubt," Vince replied, his tone calm and reassuring. "Even during that difficult period last year, you were as good as your word. Sure, you drew a little unwanted attention to yourself, but everything stayed above-board for us."

Vince took a long pause and re-lit his cigar and Stubby fought the urge to shift in his seat.

"But there may be a problem," he finally said. "As you know, a lot of those little backroad border crossings out your way have been taken out. You and your people know the area, so you've been able to adapt, but I'm hearing some grumbling from the Irish. You see, they run a lot of drugs from the Port of Montreal down to the States, mostly coke these days, and they like to use the same crossings your people do. They're *concerned* that there are too many trucks and not enough border crossings. It attracts attention, and I don't need to tell you that attention is bad for business."

"But can't you handle the Irish?" Stubby asked. "I mean, I

work for you, and my business benefits your business. You guys run the show, don't you?"

"We might run the show, but the Irish run the port," Vince replied, staring at the glowing tip of his cigar. "And, bottom line, we need that port. If the Irish clamp down on it, everybody loses and the Irish get to call the shots."

"But what about me? What about the services I provide?"

"Valuable, yes, but not like the port. We don't get along all that well with the Irish, but we need their help so we can bring in what we need to do business. Goods, money, people, all go in and out of the port every day. And we're not talking truckloads, my friend, we're talking shipping containers. Lots and lots of shipping containers. So, yeah, the Irish might not be as big as we are, but they have the port all locked up and we gotta play ball. If we keep 'em happy, we all benefit."

"So you're just cutting me loose? I have shipments lined up for the next month. People need to take delivery. People need to get paid. All because those Mick bastards don't want me to step on their toes? I've dealt with the Irish before, and I've held back on them since you and I began working together."

"Sadly, Stubby, you're a large fish in a small pond. Put you out in wider waters and you'd get eaten alive. Look, I can do everything in my power to keep Dunie, McKiernan and the boys calm, but they're having problems with the youngsters. There's a new generation coming up...the West End Gang, and these lunatics are looking to assert themselves by any means necessary. All they wanna do is prove something and they're starting to mark their territory."

"My territory is not theirs to mark," Stubby replied. He could feel his hands gripping the arms of the leather chair. He told himself to relax, play the game...*breathe*. "I can take care of things."

"All I am saying is that there's something ugly on the horizon. As long as you're available, we'll still do business with you. We're willing to be flexible if there's a disruption and even help out where we can, but we can't start a war with the Irish. So my suggestion to you is to be careful, find what alternatives you can and watch yourself. I heard someone say 'keep your shit wired tight' the other day, and that's the best piece of advice I can give ya. Remember: this is bigger than you."

The room fell silent as Stubby considered his options. He didn't like what he was hearing and there were a lot of angles to consider. It was likely that Booker's operation might have to slow down, focus on more legitimate income streams and make a lot less money at a time when cross-border trade was booming. He chafed at the thought.

"There's another thing," Vince said. "One of those young Irish is McConnell's son."

"McConnell?" Booker gave the olive-skinned man a puzzled look.

"Don't be coy now, Mr. Booker," Vince said. "You know who I'm talking about. When officer McConnell disappeared out there in the country all those years ago, he left behind an infant son. Now he's grown up, working for them and living out your way. And if he finds out about you he might be wanting to get even."

5

Frank Junior

Frank McConnell was named after a father he never knew. He was barely a year old when his dad, a junior detective recently transferred to the Eastern Townships, disappeared. Everyone said that he'd been murdered, but they never found his body. A distraught mother of an increasingly-rambunctious toddler held out hope for awhile, but when it became clear that her husband wasn't coming home, she pulled up stakes and moved back to the old neighbourhood in Montreal's Griffintown.

Young Frank was raised by a working poor mom and her extended family. She had known a brief period of prosperity in those few short years she was with her husband, but when he disappeared, middle-class life came to an end. The widow McConnell and her son were among the poorest of the working poor, hanging their laundry out on the back balcony inside-out to hide the stains and make the patches show a little less.

A stepdad, George, came later, but was almost never around and he never seemed to care much. A port stevedore turned truck driver, he would disappear for days on end, coming home to sleep off the miles, or often as not, dry out from the latest bender. He provided little, other than occasional abuse, followed by contrition. A cycle that repeated.

Like all young boys who lose a parent, Frank idolized his dead father. A man who could do no wrong. The very essence of tough, putting the bad guys behind bars. An image built up on detective comic books and TV shows. And, because there was no body, no closure, he daydreamed sometimes that his father was still alive, still out there somewhere, waiting to come home and throw George's deadbeat ass out into the street. But in his darker moments, when bravado escaped him, he knew that his dad wasn't coming home.

As he grew, he also picked up on his Irish heritage. Or at least what he thought it meant to be Irish. Red-headed and hot-tempered, he was quick with his fists, often taking on kids older and bigger than himself. Soon he was running with an older crowd, a feisty ten-year-old hanging out with twelve and thirteen-year-olds. Desperately poor, it was his way to stand out from the crowd, maybe take what was his when circumstance might usually dictate otherwise.

"Hey, that guy over there, he thinks you're a fag," one of the older kids would say, just for the hell of it. And with that, Frankie would take off, punching the unsuspecting kid in the head before he even saw him coming. Then the real beating began, lasting until Frankie was tired out, or the big kids pulled him off. The big kids all stood around and laughed, sometimes giving him a cigarette for the show. A reputation was born, and with it came pats on the back and dramatic retellings.

With the exception of his mother, whom he also idolized, young Frankie took out his rage on those around him. His rage at never having a father, at being poor, at having a stepfather who was dismissive, who treated his mother like a servant. Who beat him when he heard word of the fights. Then there was THE BELT. *That fucking wide leather belt.* While other kids would shrink away at the prospect of a beating, Frankie stepped into it, bottling it all up into a concentrated extract of rage. "Pain goes away," he'd say. For him it wasn't false bravado, it was a fact of life. A way to survive.

Not that he wasn't without his charms. Loyal to his friends and always quick with a joke, he was popular among the Griffintown kids. A natural athlete but too poor for organized hockey, he played back-alley baseball and street hockey. He dabbled in boxing, but found it had too many rules.

He boosted his first car at age fifteen. Nothing spectacular, just hotwired an old Plymouth sedan left unlocked on the street. Took it for a joyride around the city, leaving it with one wheel up on the sidewalk near the corner of Sherbrooke and Walkley over in Notre Dame de Grace. Not a bad trip for his first time behind the wheel. His adventure complete, he scavenged enough change out of the glove compartment to pay for a bus ride back home.

He liked driving, but the only chance he'd get to practice was if he could steal something. So, with school a fading memory, he advanced his driving training with more car thefts. Before long, he was supplying fresh cars to storage shed chop shops, never to be seen again. The big kids were bigger now, blending into various jobs and groups and providing him with much-needed contacts.

Then, one summer day, while he was wandering the streets in downtown Montreal, he saw George stepping out of a three-ton international truck and into a tavern in the Faubourg àm'lasse. A cool place for a cold glass of draft on a hot July day. A mainly French neighbourhood near the port, Frank reasoned that his stepdad had no reason to be there. This was really all the excuse he needed.

The truck was unlocked, and the wiring under the dash was easy to figure out. The four-speed manual transmission on the column with the straight-cut gears was a little harder, but soon he was off, lurching up the hill towards St. Catherine. Laughing to himself at how his stepdad would probably get fired for drinking when he was supposed to be working.

He made it up onto Sherbrooke, but the gears continued to frustrate him. By the time he was in front of the Sir George Williams University building, he pulled over, content that the truck was far enough away that his stepdad wouldn't find it. At least not before the shit hit the fan.

Frank had no sooner stepped out when two men in suits had his arms behind his back, slamming his face against the box of the truck. He struggled, but a brass-knuckled punch to the kidney dropped him to his knees.

"Get in the car," came the command.

"Who the hell are you?" Frank said through gritted teeth.

"Never you mind," came the calm response. "Not like you have a say."

He was hustled over to a waiting Buick sedan, shoved forcefully into the back seat. As he turned to see his abductor, Frank felt the sharp, cold steel of a .38 against his cheek, turning his head away. If he was going to live, he had to bide his time. Pain goes away. *Breathe.* He glanced through the front windshield to see another man get into the truck, pulling it out into traffic.

Frank and his escorts were now heading back down towards the water along Guy Street. Left on Ottawa through Griffintown, to a corner where parts of the old neighbourhood were being bulldozed to make way for the new Bonaventure Expressway. Stopping in front of a building that, upon second glance, housed a tavern. Frank prided himself on his knowledge of the neighbourhood, but he'd never noticed this place before. And only a few blocks from his mom's cold-water flat.

Inside, the cool air chilled the sweat running down his back. As his eyes adjusted to the gloom, he saw Charlie McKiernan sitting at a small, round table, with a beer glass filled with water next to an ashtray that gently cupped a pipe. He was engrossed in a cribbage match against a large, heavy set man who kept his eyes on his cards. Frank instantly recognized Charlie McKiernan. Everyone in Griffintown knew Charlie. A man to be respected, or feared, or admired...usually a bit of all three.

"So, you like boosting trucks," McKiernan said, not looking at him, still focused on his hand.

"Fifteen two, fifteen four and a pair is six," the fat man said quietly.

"I didn't know it was yours," Frank said.

"But you knew who was driving it, didn't you?"

Frank stayed quiet.

"I said, you knew who was driving it, didn't you?" A question that wasn't a question.

"Yes, sir."

"I know you like stealing cars. In fact, I know you're pretty good at it. So, what were you going to do with that truck?"

"I just wanted to get him in trouble after I saw him going for a beer when he was supposed to be working," Frank said, deciding honesty might, at this moment, be the best policy.

"Why would you want to be doing that, Mr. McConnell?" McKiernan said, further clarifying the fact that he knew the youngster standing before him.

"Because he's an asshole, sir. He treats my mother like dirt, he never helps out, he never brings any money home. He's drunk more often than not."

"Fifteen two, fifteen four, fifteen six and two is eight and two more is ten," McKiernan said to the cribbage board. He pegged his points and turned to Frank, looking him in the eye for the first time.

"So, he doesn't treat your mom well, eh? That's too bad. She's a good woman, your mom. Yes, I know your mom. Knew your dad, too. Good man. *Loyal.* Treated her like gold. I respected her wishes and stayed clear after your father died. I didn't know George was such a shit."

Not knowing what to say, Frank stayed quiet. He'd have more questions before long, but they hadn't quite settled in yet. "He *is* a shit, sir," Frank said finally.

"So now we have to figure out how to straighten this out," McKiernan said, almost under his breath. He reached for his pipe, scratched a wooden match on the tabletop and let the sulphur burn off before touching it to the blackened bowl. The air immediately filled with the sweet aroma of Borkum Riff. The room stayed silent, with everyone waiting to see what Charlie was going to do. Frank came to the full understanding that they were all with Charlie.

"Did he ever hit your mom?" McKiernan asked.

"Yes, sir. More when I was little. Now he's just drunk all the time."

"I'll tell you what, young man. I think George has worn out his welcome. And since you stole one of my trucks, you owe me. But , more importantly, you owe your mother. To square things up, here's what you're going to do. First up, your stepdad is likely now out of a job. So tomorrow, when your mom goes to work, you're going to have a little talk with him. At the end of that talk, he's going to come to his senses and realize that the best thing for him to do is to pack his things and leave town."

"How do you want me to do that, sir?"

"Make him see the sense in that however you see fit. Just make sure he leaves and never comes back. *But don't kill him.*"

"I understand, sir," Frank said.

"Now, if you don't take care of this, we'll make sure to take care of both of you. Handle it right, and then come back and see me. We'll see where things go from there."

So the next morning, as his mother was heading out the door, Frank McConnell was taping his knuckles. He remembered that from boxing. He bided his time to make sure she wasn't coming back. Then he smoked a rolled cigarette down to the butt out on the fire escape.

Stepping back inside, he pushed open the door to the bedroom George and his mother shared. George was asleep, his body trying to process last night's alcohol. Frank Junior dragged his deadbeat drunk of a stepdad out of their cold-water flat, down the hall and into the back alley. As neighbours looked on, he proceeded to beat George to a bloody pulp, first with his fists and then with a baseball bat he'd hidden behind a trash can. The message was delivered, loud and clear.

Frank looked up to see his neighbours flocking to their balconies. Their shocked expressions. Those bastards who had heard George dishing it out for years, but chose to do nothing. Chose to close windows and turn up radios to drown out the noise. The thought enraged him even further.

"I'm Frank McConnell and no one will ever lay a finger on my mother or take advantage of her ever again!" he shouted. "And none of you cowards ever saw this!"

And with that one beating, Frank Junior's reputation in the neighbourhood was well and truly set in steel. No-one ever mentioned the beating to his mother, or gave any indication as to why George had left so suddenly. Or where he'd gone. And no one ever laid a finger on her in anger ever again.

It was 1971. Frank McConnell was 17.

6
"Deer Police"

Once the Olympics wrapped up, the whole region went into a bit of a news slump. There were a few stories about the aftermath, but then the news cycle dried up. It happens. Sometimes there's just not a lot going on. It was back to town council meetings and cop shorts and increasing rumblings about an election coming up, though the date hadn't been set yet.

My visit with Wilson Butler kept creeping back into my mind. So, in my spare time, I did a little snooping around, perusing back issues of the *Granby Liar*, which made scant mention of anything related to smuggling and absolutely nothing about who was doing it. A couple of cop shorts, a guy caught with a pickup truck full of Marlboros, someone else with a kid in the trunk. Nothing further on either case, not even names to go on. August bled into September.

So, on the Tuesday after Labour Day, I decided to give the game wardens a shot. To keep the number of hunters under control, these regional fish and game clubs had formed across Quebec in recent years. All volunteers, they would patrol the back roads and the fishing holes, help issue hunting and fishing licences, and maintain some semblance of law and order in a region where government wardens were almost nonexistent. When things got more serious, they were supposed to call in the provincial wardens, who were typically few and far between.

"And the cops don't give a shit about this kind of stuff," said Jeff Williams, president of the Sutton Fish and Game Club, in a gruff voice. "So it's pretty much left up to us to deal with these guys."

I brought up the subject of smugglers part way through our conversation.

"Yeah, we run across some smugglers now and again," he said. "We're not out for that, so we usually just look the other way unless they out there blatantly jacking deer. None of our business, really."

"Would I be able to meet some of your wardens, maybe ride along to see what they do?" I asked. "I could write a story on a night in the life of a club game warden."

"Sure. I'll ask around, see if anyone would like to take you for a joyride. Be good to let people know what we do."

Two weeks later I was walking into the Abercorn Hotel, looking for Billy and Steve. When I spoke to Steve on the phone he said they'd be there, waiting for the sun to go down behind the Pinnacle.

"If you're lucky, maybe we'll get to see some bad guys," he'd said with a laugh.

The Abercorn Hotel had seen better days. As I walked in, I caught the faint smell of mould, like being in an abandoned building. While it was still daylight outside, you'd never know it from the bar room. Most of the light came from the faux, stained-glass shade above the pool table, while the cigarette machine and juke box gave off a faint glow from the far corner.

"The "Deer Police" are over here!" called out a broad-shouldered man with curly red hair and a red mackinaw. He was looking at me and waving a quart beer bottle. "We're just getting ready."

"Getting" ready seemed to consist of having a few rounds. Steve was mixing beer and vodka shots, while Billy was sticking to rum and Coke.

"Going to be a long night, so it's good to get a bit of a base coat on before we head out," Billy said. A beer bottle sat at his elbow. At the end of a sentence he'd spit tobacco juice into, like punctuation.

I pulled up a seat, a well-worn, wooden, round-backed affair with cracked green vinyl padding on the seat. I ordered up a Labatt 50, and when it arrived there was a shot of vodka with it. What the hell?

"A 50? Well, I suppose we won't hold that against you," Steve said. "At least it's not an O'Keefe."

"Or a Dow," I replied.

For the next hour or so we visited, while Steve smoked and Billy chewed and spat. There was maybe a half-dozen other people in the place, regulars who stopped by after work for a beer or two before heading home for the night.

"This place ain't what it used to be," Steve said. "A lot of Americans still come up here on the weekends. They come up, get drunk, pick a fight and then get escorted back to the border by the cops. Nothing too serious."

Though it was a tiny village, Abercorn had not one but two bars, the Abercorn Hotel and the Prince of Wales. During the US Prohibition years, several more drinking establishments opened and closed at various times. Vermonters came north to drink, while people from nearby Frelighsburg, with its militant Temperance Society, would slip over the town line under the cover of darkness for a pint or two. Or three. As you might guess, the bar named The Bucket of Blood was the roughest spot during prohibition, a bar just north of the line where Americans and Canadians, typically friendly when sober, would take out their frustrations on each other.

"The Bucket of Blood? You can't be serious," I said.

"No bullshit. Had a sign and everything," Billy said. "My old man showed me a picture once."

The Abercorn Hotel offered rooms and stayed above the fray in those days, for the most part. But, with the repeal of Prohibition in the US and a relaxing of attitudes, its fortunes declined. Most small towns in the region had their own bars now, and other than alcohol, Abercorn didn't have much to offer. It still had some big nights, but for the most part, the Abercorn Hotel had settled back on its haunches, letting the passage of time take its toll. Its rooms were rarely occupied or had long-term single male residents who took their meals downstairs in the bar while they watched the Habs, the Expos or the Alouettes, depending on the season. In late summer and early fall, migrant workers would take rooms for a couple of weeks, until the apples were picked clean and it was time to move on to the next job.

My second quart and shot arrived when I wasn't looking. Steve kept up a constant flow of conversation, talking about everything from how the combine he'd been driving much of the last month kept stalling out, to how he thought the Parti Québécois were likely to beat Robert Bourassa's Liberals.

"I tell you, if they separate there's going to be a revolution," he said. "People around here won't stand for it, and it's going to get messy."

"That'll never happen," Billy said during a brief lull in the conversation. "They'll bitch and whine, but nobody's going to listen to those fuckers. They don't stand a chance. Lévesque will lose and they'll go away. Fucking frog bastards."

Things had become tense between the language groups in Quebec over the last few years. The long-established status quo of French factory worker and English boss was in flux, and people had become resentful of "the other."

Neither Billy nor Steve were entitled English bosses. Steve was a full-time farmer, while Billy worked the land when he wasn't doing shifts at the Vilas furniture factory in Cowansville. But, between the shifting political and linguistic landscape and the decline of smaller family farms, they were frustrated that they no longer seemed to fit in the world around them. Relics of a different time, skating on the thin ice of change.

By that point, not only was I too drunk to engage in the political talk, the conversation had ramped up to the point where I couldn't get in a word in edgewise. After two quarts and two shots of vodka, my inner conscience was asking how I was going to keep my wits about me long enough to wring a story out of the evening ahead. I got up and, with the bar tilting slightly beneath me, made my way to the bathroom. It was a small, narrow affair, with a single stainless steel trough along one wall that emptied into a single drain, cluttered with cigarette butts that no-one cared to fish out.

I paused to look in the stained mirror, and the person looking back at me seemed different, disconnected. Yes, I was well and truly drunk.

My return to the table was greeted by another quart and another shot. "One for the road," Billy said. "It can get thirsty out there."

I knew this was trouble and I had to mitigate the damage. So, as we all toasted the evening, and Billy and Steve threw back their shots, I tipped my head back and dumped mine over my shoulder and onto the carpet.

Although there was no such reprieve with the beer, I was confident that it would work its way out of my system before the drive home.

We loaded into Billy's car, an ancient, cream-coloured Chevrolet Biscayne station wagon. I collapsed onto the back seat, grateful for the couch-like bench and the opportunity to gather my wits. Billy pulled around to the side of the bar and Steve got out, coming back a minute or so later with three unopened quart bottles handed out the back door.

"Roadies...before we head up towards the Pinnacle," Billy said. "Find a vantage point and see if we can see or hear anything. Deer jackers are a pretty sneaky bunch...but the "Deer Police" are on duty!"

With that, he punched the gas, pushing me back into the seat as we pulled out onto Route 139 and then veered right onto Claybank Road. As he negotiated the washboard road, I heard the clink of glass bottles next to me. I reached out a hand in the dark and felt what seemed to be a beer case. Some of the bottles were stubbies with caps, but a couple of taller ones had rags sticking out of the top. I'd like to remember that I smelled gas from the rags, but honestly I was too drunk to smell much of anything. Instinctively, I moved as far away from the case as I could. Steve cracked a window and lit up a smoke.

"Uh, guys, I'd prefer it if you didn't smoke while I'm sitting back here with a case of Molotov Cocktails," I said.

"Oh, sorry. Forgot about that," Steve said as he tossed the

cigarette out the window. It made a stream of angry sparks as it raked down the side of the car.

It was now completely dark, and I continued my inner mission to sober up enough to salvage a story out of this insane evening. I was still working on this when we pulled to a halt.

"This here is the border," Steve said, shining a flashlight on a rather modest concrete pillar. "Everything off to the left there is the US of A."

The view was nothing short of spectacular, with the dark and silent forms of the Appalachian Mountains dotted with the lights of farms and homes and the occasional set of headlights winding up the Vermont country roads.

We continued on, veering to the right as we passed the customs office, a tiny one-room shack with a streetlight in the yard. Another five minutes or so and Billy steered us off the road and into a farmer's orchard. He pulled the car around and there we were, the world stretching out before us for miles. He switched off the ignition, and we got out to take in the scene.

The silence thrummed my ears, with the only sound being that of late-season crickets, lulled almost to sleep by the cool air of a September evening. I could faintly hear the sound of a passing car on the road below.

"We like to watch out for any unusual movement," Steve explained. "Cars that stop for no reason, lights where there shouldn't be any. Or gunshots. If you hear a shot at this time of night, then something suspicious is going on."

We waited awhile in the darkness, with Billy and Steve looking and listening while I tried to leverage the cool air and darkness to achieve some level of sobriety.

"So what's with the gas bombs?" I asked.

"Those? Oh, you know, just in case," a voice said. I think it was Billy.

"For what?"

"You just don't want to be unprepared. You never know what might happen," Steve said.

"Like for going after poachers?"

"No, we have guns for that."

Okay, so there *were* guns in the car. *Great.* I began to seriously hope that we wouldn't see anything, just so I could sober up and go home.

As the night dragged on, Billy and Steve kept prattling on about various things. Billy started to complain about life at the Vilas plant, which he said was "going to hell in a handbasket." Even though it was one of Cowansville's main employers, labour strife and a decline in demand for its hardwood furniture were making the workers there very nervous about their future. I should have paid closer attention to the particulars, but I was concentrating on sobering up. Like that would help.

"Gonna leave us all sucking hind tit," I heard one of them say. I didn't know who; I was too busy trying to get my head together and my mouth felt like it was full of cotton. The only thing to drink were the take-out quarts from the bar, so I opened one up, figuring that if I sipped on it I could whet my whistle without getting more intoxicated. *Not the best tactic.*

I stepped around behind the car to make room for the new beer, leaving Billy and Steve to themselves. The tone seemed to be getting harsher, with them blaming their ills on everyone from Robert Bourassa to René Lévesque to the Molson family, who bought Vilas in 1967. It was nothing new; I'd been hearing this kind of talk a lot in recent months. It's all part of what people do: we get together and bitch. Sometimes things get a little angrier than others, but complaining is often how we build community with our peers.

Just as I was about to finish up behind the Biscayne, a rifle shot rang out just to the southeast of us. Maybe a half-mile off. It was followed by two more quick shots.

"Jesus! That's over on the Mine Road!" Billy said. "Let's go!"

And with that we piled into the car, Billy taking the wheel and roaring the big V-8 to life. Before I could get my bearings, Billy fishtailed to the right, slamming me up against the left rear window. Dazed by the impact of my head against the window and about four beers too many, I don't remember much of the next couple of minutes. I did, however, have the presence of mind to put my thumb over the mouth of my freshly-opened beer. By the time I got my bearings, we were in a hard left onto the Mine Road, the six-pack of gas bombs sliding up against my feet. Up front I heard the metallic click of a shotgun being loaded.

"There they are! Kill the lights!"

We ground to a halt just short of a pickup truck and Billy flipped the lights back on. There was nobody there.

"Fish and game club! What are you guys up to?" Steve called out. *Nothing.*

"Stay in the car," Billy said to me. "Put the dome light on."

"Why the dome light?" I asked.

"So if they start shooting you can draw their fire."

I didn't say anything, but there was no way in hell I was going to be the target. I gave them a few seconds and then quietly slid out the door, around the back. This was feeling too familiar, and not in a good way. Just as I was glancing around the passenger side of the car, two men appeared, one armed with a scoped rifle.

"You're not game wardens, *we're* game wardens!" came the response.

"Who's that? Step into the light so we can see you. Henry? Is that you? What are you doing here?"

"Billy? You're supposed to be patrolling the north side of the mountain tonight!"

"Well, you're not supposed to be patrolling *at all* tonight! What's going on?"

"Nothing. Just out driving. Figured we're all volunteers, so we'd volunteer a bit more."

"You have to clear that with the club. What's going on here?"

Steve turned on a sealed beam flashlight and began scanning the scene. The beam came to rest on a deer carcass in the ditch.

"You out jacking deer, Henry?"

"We just came across it. Nobody around, so we were checking it over to make sure it was dead."

"No, you're not. We heard the shots, you lying bastard. You're a club game warden and you're out jacking deer!"

"What's your problem?" came a shout from the darkness in front of the pickup. "Like you're all high and mighty. You're no more than a thief yourself!"

"That's bullshit and you know it! Right now, my problem is you two. Henry...Fred, step out around from behind the truck!" Despite the amount he'd had to drink, Steve was all business now.

"If I come around there, you're gonna have one helluva problem on your hands," Fred replied. "Now just get back in your car and fuck off before you get hurt!"

"*You're* the one who's gonna have a problem!" came the witty retort.

By this point, I was just drunk enough to know that I had nothing to add to the situation, so I stayed back in the shadows behind the Biscayne, watching everything transpire. Henry stepped into the light and took a swing at Steve. It caught him flush on the side of the head, but he just shook it off. Next thing I knew, they'd gotten a handful of each other's jackets, and punches were flying everywhere. Most missed, but a few haymakers connected, making me wince in reaction.

Then I saw Billy heading for Henry. Henry threw his rifle into the back of the pickup, clearing his hands for the fight he knew was coming. Billy dumped the sawed-off shotgun on the hood of the Biscayne. It slid onto the ground and went off.

The shotgun blast ripped through the night air, somehow managing not to hit anyone. But the scrap ramped up, with the four men locked into a hockey fight, pulling on lapels and hammering away. Then Fred gave a heave, and Steve bounced off the side of the Biscayne. Fred backed off, struggling to catch his breath.

That's when Steve got angry. He scrambled for the back door, began fishing in the darkness, and that's when I saw the flame of a Zippo. As the rag on a Molotov Cocktail flared up, so did the fear in the pit of my stomach. He turned and launched, and the gas bomb sailed through the air, hitting the roof of the truck. But the glass refused to break, and it bounced into the ditch, where it continued to sputter, intact, next to the vacant eyes of the deer carcass.

That ramped things up for a few seconds, with the cursing and the fisticuffs reaching a frenzied peak. But, like the Molotov, the fight soon sputtered out, with all four men dropping their fists to catch their breath.

"Now get the fuck out of here," Billy gasped.

"Fine. Fuck you too," Henry said.

"Leave the deer," said Steve through a cut lip and a bleeding nose.

"So you can put it in your own freezer? I don't fucking think so," Fred quipped in. "You stupid fuckers tried to set my truck on fire!"

With that, Fred and Henry dragged the deer into the bed of the pickup, and they sped away without a word. We were left on a dead-end road, with the silence settling into the blood thundering in our ears. Billy cracked up laughing, and with the adrenaline starting to burn out, we all joined in.

"Nearly broke this, the bastard," Steve said, producing a mickey of rum. He passed it around, and we all took a swig. It burned. I didn't care.

For the next while, we stood around, retelling the story that we'd all just experienced, as if the others hadn't even been there.

"I think I've got a loose tooth," Billy said. We all laughed.

"And you, you fucker," Steve said looking at me. "What are you going to write about this?"

"I have no idea."

* * *

I woke up the next morning in the back seat of my car in the parking lot of the Abercorn Hotel. The car wasn't where I'd left it. Apparently, I'd driven about thirty feet and decided to call it a night. I'd gently nosed the vehicle into a cedar tree and left it in drive with the ignition off. I was in the back seat, awash with sweat with the morning sun beating down on me. One window was open about a half an inch. I had the worst headache in recorded history and my mouth was full of sour sand.

Jen was going to be pissed. And the worst part is: *I couldn't blame her.*

As I gathered my thoughts, flashes of memory brought back reveries of rum, beer and being loaded back into the Biscayne for the ride back to the Abercorn Hotel. Then, as I was being helped back into my car, I remembered one of the boys saying, "We've got to get to work in the morning, so we'll let you take it from here."

Jesus Murphy.

7
Dave's day after

Honestly, I shouldn't have made the trip home from the Abercorn Hotel that morning. I was in no shape to drive. The car weaved when I least expected it, and felt a bit like it was weaving all the time. On my way back I pulled over just outside of Sutton to throw up. I thanked God for the cool morning air, the kind you only ever feel at 6 a.m.

"Are you okay over there?" came a voice.

I looked up to see a pair of police officers standing at the rear of my car, their flashers searing my brain. Sutton's pair of town cops, out on patrol together. Both tall. One heavy set, the other skinny like a basketball player.

"I think I'll be fine," I said through strained vocal cords and the acidic tinge of vomit.

"Maybe it was something you ate," said the heavy-set one. At this point, his scrawny partner lost it and burst out laughing, turning his face from me as he did so.

No part of this scenario was even remotely funny to me. Not only was I looking at an impaired driving fine, they might even tow my car. I was in enough trouble already.

"I'll tell you what," the heavy set cop said. "Take a few minutes to get yourself together and then take your time getting home. Once you're there, it's best to drink a lot of water after this kind of food poisoning. Get some rest."

Without another word, the two cops turned and got back into their cruiser. At which point I could hear further laughter. The blue and red flashers were shut off, and the car pulled quietly away.

Home. As much as I longed for my beloved bed, it wasn't a welcoming thought. Along with the bed would be an angry wife, fed up to the gills with all of the unanswered questions, topped off by a husband who didn't come home last night. After all she'd been through in the last year, she must have reached the boiling point.

The duplex, actually a house split in two, was in a good neighbourhood. Working class folks with good manufacturing jobs. Steady folk.

As I was climbing the stairs to our apartment, another wave of nausea hit me. I stopped, gathered as much strength as I could muster, and swallowed hard, willing the bile to retreat. God, I needed some water, if only to have something new to throw up.

Neither Jen nor King were there to greet me. Off to work at the library, seemingly as if nothing had happened. Jen had begun bringing King to work, and the pooch would spent his days stalking the stacks at the library, making friends and begging for occasional bites from bag lunches.

I knew that I'd better call her. The longer I put that off, the more hell there would be to pay.

After a couple of glasses of water and putting my head under the tap in the sink, I put the kettle on to boil. *Coffee.* It was going to have to be strong and sweet. Then, opting to step into the discomfort, I called the library. Jen wasn't there yet. I imagined raised eyebrows at the other end of the line as I hung up.

I was just stepping out of the shower when the door opened. King came running to the bathroom, happy to see me as always. Dogs are forgiving that way. He didn't care that I was nursing a guilt-filled hangover. My guts clenched. Time to really step into it.

The conversation began with my expressions of heartfelt remorse, then moved on to an explanation of the debacle the night before. She sat at the table, her face buried in her hands. I sat across from her, my own hands shaking. This was bad. *Very, very bad.*

"You shit. You rotten shit," she said, and then she cracked up laughing. "I don't think you should go out at night anymore. Bad things happen when you go out after dark."

Even if I crack the mystery of immortality, I'll still never understand women. Just when I was convinced that Jen would kick my sorry arse to the curb, and deservedly so, she starts teasing me.

"Seriously, I feel so bad about this. I mean, after everything we've been through. I had no idea they were going to get me that drunk, or that things would go sideways like that," I babbled out. "I feel really bad about the whole thing."

"First off, they didn't get you drunk. *You* got drunk," she said, her face turning serious. "*You* made a choice, and it's a choice you've been making more and more often lately. Don't go blaming others for this. No one held you down and forced it on you."

Yes, my drinking was another thing I'd been skating around. It wasn't usually enough to get fall-down drunk, just enough to sleep without dreams. To shut down the synapses and make my world a little smaller. Jen would go to bed and I'd stay up a bit longer, quaff an extra beer or two in front of the TV. I'd managed to convince myself that she hadn't noticed.

"I'm not going to police your drinking. That's not my job," she said. "But if you're going to start not coming home at night, don't expect a warm welcome when you wander in from whatever rat hole you've been hanging out in. Jesus, you don't even have much for friends around here, except for the people you work with, and they can't *all* be alcoholics!"

If only she knew...

All of this piled nicely on top of my hangover remorse, and the guilt at not having been truthful about the events that had turned our lives upside down. I knew I was eventually going to have to come clean, or risk losing what we had. But when you embark on a lie and let it gain a life of its own, how do you reel it back in without destroying the very thing you were trying to protect in the first place?

One of the classic defensive tactics of the hungover husband is to buy time. So I promised to work on cutting back on the booze, be a better husband and clean up my act in general. She seemed to buy it.

I wish I could have.

* * *

Jen didn't buy it.

She'd seen it develop in him, building over the months after his run-in with Stubby Booker. He was withdrawn, distracted. Even when he was in the same room with her, his thoughts were obviously elsewhere. He watched a lot more TV and took only a minor role in the workings of their tiny household. He didn't even tinker with the car anymore.

And then there was the drinking, which had been building up in recent months. Slowly at first, with an extra beer after dinner. Then two. In those moments he seemed to become a little more exuberant, a little more like the man she'd fallen in love with. Quick to laugh, quick to tell a tale. Warm, loving, attentive.

But, by the end of the evening, he was usually back in front of the television, staring but not seeing. She took to going to bed alone, with Dave arriving later, smelling of beer and sweat. Snoring the night away, only to wake up with a start following some dream of God knows what. From the thrashing that awakened her and the expression of fear in his eyes when he finally "came to," she knew he was having nightmares. But whatever was haunting him, he wouldn't fully say. Usually, it involved his father. On the nights when he drank more he'd say he didn't remember anything, but she knew the dreams were there just the same.

Jen had her own aftermath to deal with. Nightmares in the weeks after she was attacked at their home in Brigham. Sometimes the physical sensation of digging the man's eye out would come back to her unbidden, and she would have to stop what she was doing, take a breath and move on as if nothing had happened. She felt more vulnerable now than she ever did while growing up in Montreal, even with its bank robberies, FLQ bombs and muggings. Yes, those were crimes, but not crimes against her personally or against the people she loved. Violence can result in a seismic shift of perception when it becomes personal.

She began bringing King with her whenever she could. Good-natured and calm, he was a charismatic canine, welcomed wherever he went. She knew he had her back, and that's what she really craved. It was a level of certainty and protection that she hadn't been getting from Dave, even when he was there. When a wave of fear crashed into her, Jen would reach out for King, and the reassuring nuzzle of a wet nose would be enough to restore her sense of balance.

Jen knew that Dave had been through more than he let on. He'd set out to confront Stubby Booker over the death of his father, and it turned out to be a big misunderstanding? *Bullshit.* And the car mysteriously died the next same day and now he had a new rustbucket to drive around? *Not likely.*

The legend that was Stubby Booker came to her in bits and pieces. Watercooler comments and tales told in her circle of friends. In the eyes of his fellow Townshippers, Booker was larger than life. The man who robbed and cheated and stole, who defied the law and made sure that no one messed with him. He was the local mafia kingpin, the murderer who never got caught, the man who could take whatever he wanted with impunity. He had the cops on his payroll and the courts in his pocket. Always surrounded by the mythology that had built up around him over the decades, a weave of the factual and the fantastical that had become impenetrable.

Mostly, Jen lived with a low-level sense of fear, a fear that demanded constant acknowledgment just to keep it in check. A fear that bled so much out of her life that the thought of confronting Dave about everything that had happened to them was too much to bear.

So she made do. And waited. For what, she had no idea.

8

Junior gangster

George's blood had barely dried in that alleyway when Frank McConnell Junior found himself back in the nondescript tavern, watching Charlie McKiernan playing cribbage. He'd been summoned. Word got around fast in Griffintown in 1971.

"So, that's how you handle things," said McKiernan. "I guess George must have been quite a shit."

Frank merely nodded. He wasn't sure if he was there to be rewarded or punished. Either way, his future seemed a bit uncertain. He liked the feeling, the excitement of not knowing what comes next.

"How are your knuckles feeling?" McKiernan asked.

"Not bad. I mostly used a bat."

"That can be good. Save yourself some effort while still getting the message across. I knew a guy, used to be a boxer, did some work for me from time to time back in the day. Had mitts like concrete blocks. Used to joke that he couldn't swim because his hands kept weighing him down. By the time he was fifty, he couldn't turn a door knob without using both hands. Fingers all mashed up, knuckles that looked like a bag of alleys. Knuckles like acorns. Smart guy who couldn't even write his own name anymore."

"That's too bad, sir," Frank said.

"There's two lessons to learn there, kid. First, take care of yourself. No point in being the toughest guy in the room if you cripple yourself while you're at it. Pretty soon you won't be the toughest guy, and some young buck will take you out. Second, be careful when you do things in the heat of the moment, because that can send you down a road you never even knew existed. That boxer ended up alone, an alcoholic who had to use a straw to drink most of the time. Punch drunk from too many hits to the head, inside and outside the ring. Got beat on in jail, which shifted things from bad to worse. Ended up living on the street with people laughing at him. I looked out for him for a bit. I tried to put him in an old folks home but they didn't take drunks, and things got really miserable once he started to dry out. They put him back on the street, and one day he disappeared. Never heard from again."

McKiernan focused on the game, played his cards and pegged out. When he stood up, Frank was surprised at how tall he was. Even though he was heavy-set, he moved easily. He walked over to the window and looked out on the street to observe the cars drifting by and people going about their business.

"You're just a kid, so you really don't know how strong you are, or how smart. Life hasn't tested you yet, hasn't exposed you to the expectations, the disappointments."

"I can handle myself, sir," Frank answered, puffing his chest out slightly. His mind was racing, wondering where this was going, what the outcome would be. Beyond the fact that he'd been caught stealing the wrong truck, what other interest did this man have in him? He shifted, hitched up his jeans and adjusted his shirt. Cocksure gestures in the face of uncertainty.

"You think that. Every kid thinks that. Every kid thinks they're special. They have no idea how life can crush them. Or that it's not the crushing, but how you stand up after being crushed that really defines you. It's time for you to get an education."

With that, McKiernan turned, grabbed Frank by the throat with both hands, and slammed his back into the wall. Between the fact that his feet were now barely touching the stained linoleum and scarcely any air was leeching into his lungs, the boy was completely stunned. He thrashed about, but McKiernan's long, muscular arms kept Frank from finding anything to grab onto. The sudden speed, anger and strength sent a shot of fear through him. McKiernan might have looked slow and heavy-set, but he moved like a panther.

"I knew your dad. Pretty well, as a matter of fact. One day I'll tell you how well. I'd say he was a good cop. A bit hot-headed, but all cops get that way sometimes. I see that in you, Junior. We're going to train that out of you. Do a better job this time around."

McKiernan released his chokehold and Frank collapsed onto useless legs. Dizzy and disoriented, the young man coughed, gasped, rolled onto his knees and stood up. McKiernan picked up his pipe, calmly sparked it up and watched as the boy regained his composure. He smiled through the resulting filigree of smoke.

"Go home, get cleaned up and keep your feckin' mouth shut. Be back here at 10 a.m. tomorrow."

And with that, Frank McConnell Junior became a part of Charlie McKiernan's crew. He was paired up with an older man named Ellwood, whose job it was to make the neighbourhood rounds, collect various debts and protection payments and maintain general order in Griffintown. He had a kindly face, but the biceps that stretched his shirt taut almost to the point of splitting were evidence of his ability to handle himself. Ellwood's new task was to groom Junior, as he came to be known. Ellwood didn't say much, except when he was making his rounds. During this time he was friendly and outgoing with the clientele, making them feel listened to. If there was a problem, Ellwood would sort it out, providing tribute had been paid.

The first thing he did was make Junior upgrade his wardrobe. 'People are less likely to pay what they owe if you don't look serious,' Ellwood said. 'You don't need a suit and tie, but you need to look like you're doing your job, a professional.' Looking too much like a common thug just attracted undue attention. So, gone were the torn jeans and stained t-shirts, replaced by clean-cut hair, a collared shirt and a mid-length wool car coat when the weather chilled. It was enough to hide the tools of the trade and look big and serious, but not conspicuous enough to turn anybody's head. Leave the flashy stuff for the bikers, who always seemed to be trying to kill one another anyways. Even *they* knew how to spot, and avoid, the Irish.

McKiernan also got Junior into a dentist, his first visit since he was a young child. They pulled a couple of rotten teeth from his head and filled two others. He also set the young man up with a driver's license and sent him to a gym where he really learned how to box. As it turned out, the formal skill was far different from the street brawls he'd known as a kid. Junior resisted at first, remembering his earlier, unenthusiastic forays into the sweet science, but when he saw there wasn't a choice in the matter, he embraced it. His lanky frame filled out, the softness of youth giving way to a firmer, more capable young adulthood.

At night Junior would return home, usually dressed in jeans once again, although that particular pretense soon fell away. His mother asked few questions, in part out of a lifelong habit of not asking too many questions of the men in her life. 'Don't ask, and you won't be lied to,' his mother once said. Since whispers around the neighbourhood were rampant, she must have known. She'd certainly heard about George's beating. Clearly, she accepted the things she couldn't change and made the best of it. George was gone from her life, and she eventually learned to embrace the knowledge that she no longer had to live in the fear of the next drunken rage or the rent money disappearing.

In fact, though she was never really aware of it, Ma McConnell could walk through Griffintown in near complete safety. The Irish were looking out for her, and woe to anyone who considered stealing her purse or pushing her into a back alley. Keep in mind that this was a time when Montreal's murder rate was twice that of any other Canadian city.

As for Junior's new job, he had it pretty easy. Most of the time spent making the rounds with Ellwood was pretty straightforward. Walk into a business, pick up an envelope, maybe talk to the shopkeeper about the day's events and then move on to the next place.

"It's a pretty good system in this neighbourhood," Ellwood said one day while having a smoke on the corner of Basin and Gallery, pondering the ruins of St. Ann's Church. "Charlie takes care of the people, and they take care of him. If there's news, they get word to us. If there's a new cop around, or some drifter causes trouble, they let us know. In return, we take care of the problems. We didn't like it at first when the Ukrainians and Italians started moving in, but we learned to get along. Now even *they* come to us. Everybody knows their place, and what to expect. People like that. Doesn't matter who you are."

Ellwood explained how McKiernan helped out local charities at times, and provided his neighbours and business associates with turkeys at Christmas every year. He'd been a strong supporter of St. Ann's, but with fewer Irish Catholics around, and even fewer still going to church, its fate was sealed. Even Charlie McKiernan couldn't save it. Griffintown had become a shadow of the neighbourhood it had once been, and Charlie moved with the times. He spread his tentacles into the Port, first through the Irish dockworkers, then through their union and eventually into management itself. He became bigger than the little Irish backwater that spawned him. When people in Montreal spoke of "the Irish," they were really talking about Charlie McKiernan and his underlings.

For Junior, it all seemed pretty easy. That is, until one winter's day in early 1972, when he was making the rounds with Ellwood. They visited a little corner store, nothing to look at really, which was run by an angry, middle-aged man with parchment skin, jet black hair and a thick moustache. He was yelling in an accent that Junior couldn't place. He didn't see why he should be 'paying money to a rich man just so he could do business in a poor neighbourhood where nothing ever happened' and then declared that he 'wasn't going to pay anymore.'

Ellwood kept his voice calm, explaining that yes, nothing ever happened here...*because the Irish kept it that way*. The man said that he still wasn't going to pay.

"I think you will," Ellwood said, his voice low, neutral.

"I refuse!" the man said. "I get baseball bat, make sure you leave!"

In one quick, fluid motion, Ellwood grabbed the man's tie with one hand, pulling him forward over the counter. With his other hand, he grabbed a handful of hair on the back of the man's head and slammed him face first into the tempered glass display counter. Then he let go of the tie, moving that hand around to the back of the man's head, slamming him into the counter again with the force of both arms. The man fell to the floor, unconscious, blood streaming from his nose and mouth.

With that, Ellwood stepped around the counter and over the man, grabbing a pack of MarkTen cigarettes from the shelf. He removed the wrap, opened the pack and took one out. Using a pack of matches from the counter, he lit it up and dropped the match on the man as he turned, leaving a dime-sized burn on the cheap dress shirt and singeing the skin beneath. He walked out of the store, pausing in front to take a deep drag.

"I guess he doesn't want to pay," he said to Junior.

That night, two masked men smashed in the plate glass door, turning the place upside down and making off with the week's receipts. Meanwhile, Ellwood and Junior were at the tavern, playing darts while Charlie McKiernan watched Hockey Night in Canada on channel six.

9

Father and son

In my dream, I'm in the high steel. And, at first, the height doesn't bother me, since I'm only looking up. I'm pursuing someone who is climbing higher and higher. He's agile, working his way up through the steel girders, pulling himself up, scaling I-beams, grabbing cables as he ascends. He moves with practiced grace, no wasted effort, no hesitations, no missed steps. I can't see his face, and haven't stopped to wonder who it is yet.

Finally, he reaches the top. There's nowhere left to go. He turns. It's my father.

Suddenly, I realize where I am. I realize in that instant that this is where he died. I drop as low as I can get, clinging to the girder. My lifelong fear of heights surges back and now I'm frozen, terrified. *Don't look down.* As hard as I cling, I can't feel the beam. Where the fuck is the beam? Why is it so small? Everything I sense, and everything I don't, is ramping up the terror.

I see him talking, but I can't hear what he's saying. The mouth is moving, but I don't understand. He's scared. I can't remember ever seeing my father scared. He was the daredevil, the one they called "Slippers," because he could climb anywhere. Confident. Solid.

As I'm straining to figure out what he's saying, I realize that he's not talking to me. He's looking *over* me, at someone behind me. But I'm too scared to turn my head, convinced that if I keep focused on him he'll eventually help me get back to the ground. That's what dads do, right? They save their kids, don't they?

I glance away for a second. The city of Montreal surrounds me. I don't know what building this is, but it's higher than anything else I can see. It's early, and there are lots of city lights, but the sun is just starting to edge over the horizon. I try to bury my head into the beam, convinced that I will be overcome with the urge to let go.

It looks like my father is getting frantic. He's pleading with whoever is behind me. But it's like watching a TV with the sound off. I can't make it out. A look of resignation crosses his face. He glances down at me, and our eyes meet.

Then he turns, and steps off the girder into the void of the Montreal skyline.

And I wake up, my heart pounding, unable to get enough air. I'm in my apartment, and Jen is sitting up, watching me. I bolt up, dropping my feet to the bare linoleum, bracing one arm on the imitation wood paneling wall next to the bed. My nerve ends are on fire.

"Jesus, you were thrashing around quite a bit there," she says. "I was starting to get worried."

"Just a bad dream," I say. "Nothing to worry about."

I get up, make my way to the kitchen and draw a glass of water from the tap. It tastes like chlorine. God, Cowansville water is terrible.

I get back to the bedroom and tell Jen about my dream, as if she hasn't heard it all before. It's been three nights since my last drink. The first night was fine, but this is the second night in a row I've had this dream. I don't remember the last time I had it. Probably a month or two ago.

I don't want to see my dad like that ever again.

But I know I will.

10

Threats

Stubby Booker never responded well to threats, but this one had him puzzled, mainly because it wasn't really clear what was going on. And, he had to admit, it had been awhile. Maybe that was it. Maybe he was out of practice.

"So tell me again what happened so I can get this straight."

Stubby was in a corner room of his truck garage, the place where he took care of his day-to-day business: juggling figures, shipping, receiving and dealing with the small crew who knew as much as they needed to, and the larger team who provided the legal front. They didn't know anything more about Stubby's business than anyone else in the Townships. They heard the rumours, of course, but they did their legitimate jobs, got paid fairly and went home. No questions asked. The tacit understanding was: *silence is golden.*

As he sat at his desk, with the stub of an Old Port cigar smouldering in the ashtray, "Shaky," one of his night closer drivers, told the story once again.

"So I was on my run last night, coming across the line on the East Richford Slide Road. I'm just at the point where it wanders over the border and I'm watching for the opening we cut in the puckerbrush so I can peel off through the woods and head north. Suddenly, behind me I see this other truck and I'm guessing it was an international cab-over from the looks of the headlights.

"I'm wondering who this asshole is, 'cuz he can't be one of us. And he pulls right up behind, so close I can't even see his headlights anymore. I tap the brakes, just to get him to ease back, but I'm thinking that might attract more attention. He held back for a minute or two, but then crawled right back up my arse again. So, after that I just keep going, like everything's normal. I can't take the trail with this guy behind me.

"So I decided to take it easy and keep going down to the 105 like I'm headed for Richford. He follows along, just like he's with me. I'm watching for cops and border guards, but there's no one around. I get through Richford, the town's empty, and this guy is still behind me, so I decided to make a dash for it. The border at the Pinnacle was closed, but I ran it, and I could hear the alarm bells go off and see the lights flashing. Bastard was right behind me, so I heeled over hard onto Claybank. I was so busy fishing for gears and trying to keep upright that, when I looked in the mirror, he was gone. I took the back roads for a bit, up around the Three Parishes and down Alderbrooke, just to be sure no one was following."

Stubby picked up his Old Port, then put it back down.

"No Border Patrol? No Mounties?" Stubby asked.

"None. Not a sign of anybody."

"Well, there's that at least. Okay, go home. Take the next couple of nights off, stay put, don't go to the bars and *don't call here.* Come in Thursday evening...we'll decide from there how it goes."

In the quiet of his office, Stubby Booker considered the situation. Things were getting crowded along the border these days, with the road closures and all. The Slide Road had been a good find, a little Vermont dirt road that nudged up over the border that no one paid attention to. Then, one of his people found a spot where a sugaring road came south almost to the Slide. After a few evening's worth of work, his men opened up a slot just big enough to squeeze a ten-wheeler through when the ground was dry enough. There was enough rough brush around to cover things up, so the US Border Patrol wouldn't notice. And, even though the sugaring road came out behind a farm, a few cartons of Marlboros and a hundred bucks easily bought them free passage.

"Just don't come through in the daytime, don't tear the place up and leave me alone," the farmer had told Shaky. "I've never seen you before, had no idea, hadn't noticed a thing."

No handshakes, just a nod to seal the deal.

Stubby rubbed his eyes. Years ago, this would have raised his ire and he'd be ready for a fight. Didn't matter who or where, he'd take a couple of his best men along and straighten things out. Always ready to deal with it himself, as much to ensure the violent finality as to remind his people that he was the boss.

But now he was just tired. Tired at the thought of having to deal with this latest threat to his supremacy. The alpha wolf past his prime. Tired of the fight, but not willing to let it show. Letting it show could prove fatal.

Stubby thought back to the talk he had with Vince. The Irish would be crazy enough to do something like this. Some of them, anyways. He had to figure out who he was dealing with.

He never even thought of the McConnell kid.

11

Learning the ropes

By 1972, Frank McConnell Junior was a rising star in the Griffintown underworld. He trained for the ring, using his boxing skills on the streets to help Elwood collect various debts for Charlie McKiernan. It opened his eyes to an entire world he never knew existed. A world where almost anything was within reach, from back-alley sex to a shot of smack to the finest new clothes. It was all just there for the taking.

But that didn't mean taking whatever you wanted whenever you wanted it. There was order and there were manners. On one occasion, Junior decided he liked a coat from a store he was in with Ellwood while making the rounds. The shopkeeper, who was paid up and in the good books, looked to Ellwood, who gave no response. That is, until they got outside.

"Take it back."

"What?"

"We don't have these talks in front of the clientele. It undermines our authority," Ellwood said. "Take it back."

"C'mon, you know he's probably ripped us off for more than the value of this coat!"

"He's paid up, and so you take it back. Or you buy it."

"No fucking way!" "*Yes*, way... and watch your language. Take it back. *Now!*"

Junior gave Ellwood a look. They'd become close, like father and son, but when fathers and sons come to blows, the kid knows he's going to lose. Frank had all the muscle and sinew of youth, but Ellwood had an indomitable inner core of strength, born from decades of hard living and frustration. Add to this a surplus of middle-aged anger and the knowledge that he'd never let the unfair truths of life get the better of him.

Junior looked away. He glanced at his feet for a moment, straightened his shoulders and then shrugged the coat off.

"And no smart talk when you give it back. Be polite."

There were other rules as well, all with the aim of maintaining order. Chief of which was no drinking anywhere, except at McKiernan's tavern. Charlie's people could visit the neighbourhood establishments if they wished, but they had to stay sober. This became a sign to the owners of the various watering holes in the area. If a man came in but never drank alcohol, he was either connected or a cop, and most bar owners could peg a cop before he even made it to the brass rail. If he was connected, that meant you gave him the right combination of space and excellent service. And, if there was ever a problem, your bouncer made sure he was looked after, and the other guy was tossed into the alley. Maybe even roughed up a bit, just for appearances.

Charlie's nameless tavern was the place where his associates gathered to let off steam or have a beer at the end of a long day or night. The rules were simple there: don't disturb Charlie while he was playing cribbage and keep the noise down when hockey was on.

Frank was also surprised to learn how often quiet restraint was employed instead of the up-front violence he was accustomed to. Disagreements happened, conversations ended, and then people went home. But if folks were still at odds with Charlie's way of doing things, they might suddenly find themselves dealing with "accidents," burglaries or maybe a late-night mugging. This was usually carried out by petty thugs hired in back alleys who had no idea whose bidding they were doing. That way, if things went sideways, the police could never trace it back to the source. It was important to always keep the bottom feeders - the addicts, muggers and low-level thugs - at arm's length. The common wisdom was that they had no honour and would roll on anyone for another hit or to avoid jail.

There were times when this system was bypassed, usually when dealing with someone further up in Montreal's organized crime hierarchy. This might include a port official who was paying a bit too much attention to certain containers leaving the facilities, a pushy biker waiting for his monthly coke allotment for the downtown bars or an armoured car driver who didn't want to look the other way during a robbery. These guys were dealt with by people like Frank and Ellwood, usually behind closed doors in a dusty office somewhere. Fast, brutal, efficient.

But Junior chafed at the idea of simply being Charlie McKiernan's hired thug. He missed the thrill of jacking cars, but he also had visions of one day being above the fray and calling the shots. In short, he wanted to be the next Charlie McKiernan. But first he needed to prove that he could do more than rough up drug dealers and shopkeepers who didn't pay their rent. That's when he decided on the armoured car robbery.

Junior met a lot of people in his travels and, in doing so, he became highly skilled at sussing out people and situations and figuring out motivations. It also made him a very sharp judge of character. When he made the rounds with Ellwood, he tried to figure out why various people made the deals they made. For some it was protection, while for others it was peace of mind. Maybe it was a drug habit, a gambling problem or some more persistent, troublesome vice. Or maybe they just wanted to be in the know and on the good side of those who made the decisions.

In the winter of 1973, Junior met up with just such a man. Andy O'Brien was a con with a dream. Yes, he wanted to make the big score, but more importantly he wanted to be noticed. And, with the Montreal Irish mob's history of robbing banks and armoured cars, he figured a similarly-clean, well-executed heist would do the trick. He even had a contact: Rory Fryer, a disgruntled Brinks driver who was sick of working in the bank robbery capital of North America for barely above minimum wage.

Along with Junior and Fryer, O'Brien put the plan together. At the last minute he added a fourth crew member, Randy Dubeil. Dubeil, a cocaine addict and parolee who was deeply in debt to O'Brien, never really understood the plan from the outset. Jacked up and fast on the trigger, Dubeil opened the back door of the truck, spied the guard sitting inside with the cash, and promptly shot him. This wasn't a part of the plan, and with the unwitting second guard being a friend of Fryer's, things quickly unraveled. Fryer shot Dubeil, and in a knee-jerk reaction, O'Brien shot Fryer. Junior, who had stolen a Plymouth sedan for the occasion, barely got away with O'Brien.

Fryer survived, suffering buckshot wounds to his lower body. The vault guard survived as well, though only barely. Dubeil wasn't so lucky.

Despite all of his bitterness towards his job and wanting to take a piece of the pie for himself, it didn't take long for Fryer to crack under police questioning. O'Brien stayed on the lam for a couple of weeks, but the police had gotten enough information to track him down at his sister's apartment in a dirty, rundown neighbourhood just off St. Laurent Boulevard.

Fortunately for Frank McConnell, Fryer only knew that he was called Junior, and precious little else. And what he *did* know, he had enough sense to keep to himself. O'Brien knew enough to keep his mouth shut, preferring time in jail over ending up dead.

Charlie McKiernan wasn't impressed. Even though he slapped Junior around and put the fear of God into him, the young man knew better than to raise a hand to his boss. But McKiernan had come to like the feisty, red-headed kid, and having pulled off an armed robbery or two in his own day, he stopped short of really hurting him.

"But now we have a problem," he grumbled. "The cops will be looking for you. They might not know who you are, but they do know that there's a ginger-haired kid named Junior out there who's handy with stealing cars. We need to relocate you for awhile."

And so, well before the cops had even had the chance to properly question Fryer, Junior found himself shipped out to the country to lie low.

Junior knew better than to question it. To refuse this offer was to end up dead or in jail. Besides, it made sense. So, with barely enough time to say goodbye to his mother, he packed a change of clothes and, map in hand, set off for the Eastern Townships village of Frelighsburg. McKiernan set him up with a well-used Valiant, to be returned later during a truck-switching operation.

He'd never been off the island of Montreal before as an adult, and the open spaces made him anxious. Even though he'd been born at the hospital in Sweetsburg, he was still a baby when his father disappeared and his mother brought him to Griffintown. Sure, he'd seen pictures of the countryside, but this was his first time witnessing first-hand the St. Lawrence Lowlands give way to the first rises of the Appalachian foothills, with the open cropland blending slowly into the mixed farms and forests. He got turned around, first finding himself in the village of St. Armand, then Pigeon Hill, following the one and only road eastward from there to Frelighsburg.

His instructions were pretty basic: go to Frelighsburg and find a bar called the Quebec House. Get a room and wait for further instructions. Keep a low profile. Someone will contact you.

The room was a dingy little affair, featuring dark, fake wood paneling with the faux joints etched in black and a window looking out on the main street below. In the corner of the room was a forlorn black-and-white, rabbit-eared television set that got one American and two Canadian channels, one of which was French. That first night was a Friday, and he found himself watching late night movies with soft-core nudity on *Bleu Nuit*. In the quiet moments, he could hear the music and noise of the bar below, but he knew better than to go check it out.

He sat on the edge of the bed, flipping between the late-night edition of Pulse News on channel twelve and the more interesting sights on channel nine. When he saw the update on the armoured car robbery, he was glad that Charlie McKiernan was the only one at this point who knew where he was and what he'd done. Then he reached over and changed the channel, back to a scene of two topless women cavorting suggestively on a beach while a man with a bad mustache looked on, his open Hawaiian shirt revealing gold chains and a hairy chest.

In the mayhem of the robbery, Frank had mashed his shoulder into the door pillar of the getaway car, which was now deep beneath the water of the Lachine Canal. He couldn't lift it much above shoulder level. It would heal, he'd just have to baby it for a bit. Moments after lying back on the stiff, cold mattress, he was asleep.

A knock on the door brought him back to wakefulness. A quick glance at his watch revealed that it was 6 a.m. It was still dark outside. The flickering TV displayed a monochromatic Indian-head test pattern on the silent screen and cast strange shadows around the unfamiliar room. For a moment, Frank had no idea where he was, but a second knock nudged him into full consciousness and he went to the door.

"You Junior?" came the question through the door. Frank opened it a crack and glanced through to see a tall man wearing an army surplus parka and large, white, felt-lined boots.

"That's me. Who wants to know?"

"I'm Ted. I'm the guy who's supposed to bring you over to the house."

Ted looked harmless enough at first glance, though it was hard to tell with all the winter gear on. He was a big man, tall, with broad shoulders and his sun-burnt face looked like it had been carved by the elements. Feeling the cold from the hallway, Frank glanced back over his shoulder and could see that the window overlooking the street had frosted over in the night. Frank didn't like mornings, and he didn't like this one in particular. Without a word, he shrugged on his wool coat and his city-boy boots and followed Ted out to the parking lot.

En route, he dropped the room key on the desk by the door, and Ted put a twenty dollar bill underneath it. This tip would be taken as a command for the bartender/manager/owner to look the other way and keep quiet.

Frank had to pump the gas several times to coax the Valiant to life. The engine knocked, as one by one the cylinders shook off the frost and got to work. He used a chipped plastic scraper to clear the inside of the windshield, leaving a layer of snow on the dash. His hands were frozen and he cursed his thin leather gloves. Clearly, they were better suited for protecting the knuckles of a closed fist than actually keeping the cold at bay.

He followed Ted to the right, continuing on straight when the main street veered left. They climbed a steep hill out into the country, the road making its way through apple orchards and past farms. Still half-asleep, Frank was focused on little more than the taillights in front of him. Two miles up, they turned onto a narrow driveway that made its way through scrub brush before opening into a farmyard. There was a squat stone bungalow with a rough barn to one side and some sheds scattered about. Next to the barn were a pair of straight-body trucks and a flatbed, with block heaters tethered to the barn wall by extension cords. Various other farm machinery Frank couldn't identify had been parked in an area behind the barn. A shaggy, rough-looking dog announced their arrival, loping towards the cars, tail waving gently.

Following Ted, they stepped in through a side door and walked down a short, dark, narrow corridor leading to an even shorter and narrower door. Ted hunched lower and stepped inside as the dog pushed up behind Frank, eager for the warmth of the kitchen stove.

"Honey, I brought company," Ted announced to a short, square woman whose hair was tied up in a kerchief. She smiled, greeting the newcomer with the ease of an old friend.

"You came out from the city dressed like that? You'll catch your death…it's a good twenty below out!" she exclaimed. "Ted, we're going to have to get this boy some proper clothes!"

That was Diane. A traditional farm wife, built more for the innumerable hours of rural toil than for eye-catching beauty. A woman who was equally at ease driving a tractor, placing a load of hay, cooking dinner or sewing a quilt.

Introductions were made, and cups of steaming coffee were produced, including one for Rex, the dog, with plenty of milk. Rex finished his coffee in a few seconds, then made his way over to a carpet behind the kitchen stove, which was stoked high to drive out the morning chill.

"So you're Frank McConnell's son? We knew Frank. He'd come around here sometimes when he was on duty, just to see what was going on," Diane said. "He was always friendly. Not one of those cops who shows up and accuses you of whatever comes to mind."

"I don't remember my dad at all," Junior said. "He died while I was still little."

"I remember that. *Tragic.* You look like him...though you're thin as a rake. Not to worry, we'll get you fattened up!"

"I'm not even that sure what I'm going to be doing here, or for how long," Frank said. No one had explained anything to him.

"Well, first off, you're here for awhile, and you're here to work. *Boss's orders,*" Ted said. "You'll be on the farm here for the first bit, until we get your truck licence straightened out. Charlie says you drive, but until you get a proper truck licence, you're no good to him. That's already being taken care of... should take a week or two, maybe a bit longer. In the meantime, you'll start out in the woods with me and Heaver."

And so began a new apprenticeship in the life of Frank McConnell Junior. The city boy who had never been in the woods before was thrown into the life of a lumberjack. Ted cut firewood, sawed logs and produced pulpwood; a little bit of everything. This included managing a small army of drivers who brought truckloads of various things back and forth across the border for Charlie McKiernan. Ted was most at home in the woods, and he knew just about every cow path across the border within twenty miles. He also knew the skills Frank would need in order to become one of the team.

The first thing Ted did was get Frank some real winter clothes. A trip to the army surplus in Dunham was enough to get him some long johns, wool socks, a pair of coveralls and a plaid mackinaw jacket. Ted also found him a well-worn pair of felt-lined Sorels at the farmhouse, as well as some gloves and toques to get by.

Having proven himself countless times in the ring and on the mean streets of Montreal, Frank thought he was tough. But the life of a lumberjack was a different grade of tough. His hands were constantly numbed by bitter cold or the vibrations of his chainsaw. There was the constant threat of danger from falling trees, flying branches and hissing winch cables. Then there was the sheer effort of working in the cold, constantly climbing over deadfalls and rocks and wading through branches and waist-deep snow.

Breakfast was served while it was still dark, complete with strong, dark coffee and plenty of eggs, bacon, ham or sausage. Diane didn't fuss with making bread, so it was the store-bought cardboard fare he was familiar with, Gailuron. Just as the sun first cracked the horizon, they were off to the woods. He'd get there by sitting on the hood of a yellow John Deere skidder, hanging onto the side rails of the roll cage, trying not to burn himself on the exhaust pipe that emerged between his legs and belched black diesel into the crisp morning air. Heaver, who looked to be about Frank's age, rode alongside Ted, his legs inches from the flailing tire chains as they rumbled into the forest.

"Don't you say a word to Heaver about what happened in the city, the trucks or really about much of anything," Ted cautioned. "He ain't too bright, but he likes to run his mouth off to anyone who'll listen. He's strong as an ox...and just about as bright. Hard worker, though."

The days were long, but because of the physical toil, the cold and the wet conditions and constant feeling of being a fish out of water, they felt even longer to Frank. At night he'd nurse a slew of bruises and blisters and grit his teeth in pain as he massaged the feeling back into his borderline-frostbitten fingers and toes. He missed the city, with its familiar faces and comforts, and he also missed his mother. He considered fleeing back to the city, but quickly dismissed the notion. To go back to the city now would risk going to jail time and, even worse, it would piss off Charlie McKiernan. And he knew that nothing good would ever come of that.

By nightfall he had little interest in doing much of anything. That first Saturday night he sat down to have a beer and watch hockey with Ted, but he fell asleep during the first period. Ted gave his feet a kick when the game was over, and he crawled off to bed.

The next day was Sunday, a merciful day of rest and reprieve. Last weekend, he'd been too caught up in getting ready for a week of work that he hadn't bothered to pay much attention to his new surroundings. But, after a long, hard week and a good night's sleep, he decided to get a better look at his new home.

Followed by Rex, he walked out into the dooryard, an open area ringed by sheds, machinery and a modest-sized barn. A small group of beef cattle steamed in the morning sunshine, chewing their cud and watching this unfamiliar human. They crowded up to the gate next to the barn, jostling each other for a better look.

Behind the far corner of the barn sat a pair of trucks. The flatbed truck looked familiar, but the others were covered in snow. He climbed up on the side of the GMC 5000 to look inside, knowing that he'd probably be driving one of them soon.

"You won't be driving that one for a bit," Ted thundered, nearly causing Frank to jump out of his skin. He was a big man, but quiet as a mouse in his movements, even on crisp winter snow. 'He completely got the jump on me,' Frank admonished himself. 'Time to sharpen up.'

"We'll start you on the single axles, something like that one over there," Ted continued. "These trucks aren't very good on the back roads and trails we use, especially in the winter, so you'll have to learn a thing or two. We've got time, though. For you, the serious work will wait until the spring."

Ted gave Frank the rundown of how the system worked. In the winter, shipments (the word "drugs" was never mentioned) from the port were brought to the Townships to a dropoff point. There were a few spots which were all planned out ahead of time and always changing. Ted would bring the shipment back to the farm and everything would be repackaged into oblong boxes. Then, when Ted was loading the flatbed with logs, he'd cut a few that were only a few feet long. He'd use these to create a gap in the middle of the load, and wall up the front and the back with short pieces. That way it just looked like an everyday load of logs to be taken to the mill in Enosburg, just a few miles south of the line. This ruse would get them though everyday ports of entry, usually at the smaller crossings, like the Pinnacle, where Ted knew most of the customs guards on a first name basis.

Along with the logs, the smuggled dope was then unloaded and transferred to an American associate that Ted would never see or know in any way. Like any good lumberjack, Ted would take his empty truck back home until next time, complete with a bill of sale from the mill for his logs.

Other drivers would just show up at the farm, climb into a truck without saying a word to anyone, and then make their own trips across the line. Ted seemed to know who they were and when to expect them. Goods went both ways whenever possible, so as not to waste a trip. Usually drugs headed south and booze headed north, plus whatever else was in demand at any given time. That could be anything from TV sets, to car parts from chop shops, to the occasional stripper with a criminal record who needed to get across the border for her next gig.

The drivers often used the unmarked border crossings, although that depended on the weather, what was being moved and how easily it could be concealed. Smaller cargo, like cocaine or handguns, would be concealed in the floor compartments of pickup trucks or cars. Larger items, like television sets or pallets of booze, were hauled onto trucks and usually concealed behind cargo, where an unsuspecting customs officer would never bother to look.

This system's success depended heavily on how motivated the customs officers were. They couldn't check everyone, so the goal was to not give them any motivation to pull you over for a closer look.

Upon their return to Canada, the trucks would be driven to a designated meeting point. Once again, these places always changed, with the driver handing the truck off to someone else for another vehicle filly-loaded with goods heading south. Sometimes it just boiled down to a simple exchange of cargo.

"It's kind of complicated, but it's all about keeping a low profile," Ted explained. "You don't want the same truck running back and forth across the line too often and attracting too much attention. Sometimes we cross during the day at regular border crossings and sometimes we'll do a night run on an unmarked road. We don't speed, or do anything that will get us pulled over or searched. If a cop stops you, you stop. Always be polite, even when you're busted. You'd never be able to outrun them, anyways."

But, for the time being, Frank McConnell Junior was working in the woods, biding his time while Charlie McKiernan straightened out his new driver's licence. Seeing as the police only had a vague description from the armoured truck robbery, Frank got to keep his name. But getting a legitimate licence through illegitimate means took time. For Frank, it was going to be a long, hard winter.

12

Discoveries

Frank Junior ducked his head as he entered through the small door and moved into the kitchen. It was hot, unseasonably so, even for June, and he was sweating profusely. Diane was fussing over the electric stove, putting the finishing touches on lunch. Without a word he went to the sink, stuck his head under the water for a few moments and then straightened up to scrub his hands, which were stained black by engine oil and diesel fuel.

His forearms were filthy to the elbows. No work in the woods today, but there was work to be done in the garage. With the doors open, it was moderately cooler than in the direct sunlight, but since it had been brutally hot for most of the week, the climate inside the garage was still oppressive and miserable. Junior's pale, freckled skin had taken on a distinctly pinkish hue.

"You get that hose replaced on the skidder?" Diane asked, not lifting her head from her work at the stove.

"Not yet. We don't have anything that'll fit. I need to go to C.L. Autoparts in Cowansville and try to find something."

The door latch snapped as Ted came in, followed by Rex. The massive hound promptly made a bee-line for the cool spot behind the dormant wood stove and collapsed onto the worn linoleum. Frank glanced over, wondering if it really was any cooler down there. For a moment he considered giving it a try.

"Sweating like a whore in church out there," Ted said, prompting an immediate dish towel swat from Diane. He feigned offence at the blow, though the towel had barely touched him. He smiled at her, then turned to the sink to wash up.

Before heading to the kitchen table, Ted reached into the fridge, took out a bottle of Molson Export and then opened a can of tomato juice. He emptied the beer into a large glass, poured in the tomato juice and then added some salt.

"Need to get some salt back into me after all that heat," Ted said. Everyone knew that Ted really didn't really mind the hot weather that much, but it was a good enough excuse to help himself to an extra liquid lunch.

This had become Junior's routine over the last four years. At first he chafed at country living, hoping to bide his time for a few months and then head back to the city and his old life with Elwood. He missed the familiarity of the streets, of knowing what he was doing and what needed to be done. But during this passage of time, Ted and Diane had provided a living environment that he'd never experienced before, one which left like a legitimate family. So much so that, when the time came for him to return to the city and resume his former life, he decided to stay in the country instead.

* * *

Getting Frank's truck licence all sorted out without him actually meeting with the authorities proved to be more time consuming than expected. Charlie McKiernan was a careful man, and he didn't want the gaze of authority to fall on this young kid's face, with his distinctive red hair and his Griffintown background. It would create too many loose ends. As it was now, if Junior got caught at the border, it wouldn't raise too many eyebrows, but a Montreal cop familiar with that disastrous armoured truck heist might to have cause to look twice.

Luckily, McKiernan, or more precisely one of his associates, had a contact at the licence bureau. Unluckily, the contact was on holiday in Florida when Junior first arrived in Frelighsburg. Then, when Charlie's boy finally got back, there was a training seminar. By then it was getting into March, which was licence plate renewal month in Quebec. This mean that their guy was now spending most of his time at the wicket serving customers and handing out fresh new white-and-red plates with the Olympic logo emblazoned on it. Lineups were long, and the opportunity to get his hands on the right paperwork were limited.

During that time, Junior adapted to the physical demands of his new life and toughened up. Between the rigours of his hard labour and Diane keeping him well-fed, the boy added considerable bulk to his boxer's physique. He worked five days a week in the woods, doing everything from skidding out logs to cutting firewood. Saturday was a half-day, and in the evening, he would head down to the Quebec House with Ted for a few beers and the chance to watch hockey on a colour TV. Maybe play some pool against the locals.

One day his new driver's licence arrived in the mail, concealed in an official envelope just like anyone else's. When Junior opened it, he was surprised to see that it gave him the authority to drive just about anything on the road, from an everyday automobile to a full-sized tractor-trailer truck.

"That's what we call a 'chauffeur's licence'," Ted said. "Welp, I guess we're going to have to teach you how to drive the damned things."

Frank's first driving experiences were shuttling empty trucks around from one drop-off point to another, to ensure the right drivers were in the right place at the right time. Diane handled much of the phone work, while Ted kept everything fuelled, repaired and organized. The couple were the first on their road to have a private phone line. Turns out, it's pretty tough to organize a smuggling ring with the neighbours listening in on a party line.

The most delicate part of this dance was to ensure that you didn't have the same trucks going back and forth across the border in ways that aroused suspicion, or have the same drivers in different trucks all the time. Some would go over at night via unmarked crossings, while others went through customs in the light of day. Trucks and drivers changed their roles now and then, with smugglers sometimes switching with the drivers to haul both legal goods and contraband back and forth between Montreal and the Townships.

"It gets nerve-wracking hauling our stuff back and forth across the line," Ted explained one day. "At least I can change them out and it gives them a bit of a rest from it."

The bottom line was to avoid drawing too much attention to any point in the process while maintaining a steady flow of cargo. Making the most of every trip was critical, and special orders always required some extra precautions.

As for Ted, he'd been in the game for over twenty years, and during that time he'd done his own fair share of midnight runs and had his own close calls. *But he'd never been caught.* These days he stayed away from regular shipments, sticking instead to sneaking stuff down on his log truck. He knew most of the border guards by name, and the sight of an older local farmer with a load of logs for the mill in Enosburg didn't raise any eyebrows. This also gave him a chance to get a feel for the atmosphere at the border. If he witnessed extra checks and more border patrol cruisers, he'd let the other drivers know about these potential complications. Since Ted was just as particular as he was, McKiernan knew he was in the right place...and he treated him like gold.

Frank became a valued asset during his time in Frelighsburg. He learned the finer points of transport truck driving, mastering two-speed rear differentials and various gearbox configurations. He learned the ins and outs of truck maintenance. He was polite at the border, low-key when crossing in the dead of night and spoke little to the people he met at the drop-off and pick-up points.

During one of the periodic border crackdowns, Frank was sent out with a carry crew. Four men, three haulers and a driver would head down to Vermont in an old Dodge Bell Telephone van. After crossing the line, the haulers would be dropped off at a dead-end near the border. Then the driver would go to pick up booze through a backdoor arrangement with the Enosburg liquor store.

Once the van was back at the dead end, bottles of rum, whiskey and vodka were wrapped in rags and placed into large canvas sacks. Each hauler carried as much as he could handle, setting off through the woods to cross the line. Human pack mules.

Despite his work in the woods and his boxing training, Frank found himself pushed to the limit just to keep up. Carrying over a hundred pounds each, the haulers set off at a brisk pace that was just short of a run.

"Don't just put your head down," admonished one of the haulers, known only by his nickname, Zeke. "You're watching for Mounties, helicopters, border patrols, farmers, dogs... anyone. You get seen, we all get fucked. We get fucked, we drop our bags and split up."

So, through all the stress, sweat and burning pain in his legs and shoulders, Frank kept his eyes and ears open, ready to react at the slightest sound. Black flies and mosquitoes were the haulers' constant companions, sometimes becoming victims of their own insatiable appetites by getting mired in their sweat.

An hour later they emerged into a field just across the line. The van was waiting for them, doors ajar, with the driver calmly sitting behind the wheel, smoking a cigarette. Like the others, Frank loaded the bags into the back before taking a few short seconds to get his breath back.

* * *

In the village of Frelighsburg, Frank was known only as a lumberjack who happened to be a distant nephew of Ted's. Like many of the locals, he'd "come to the area from away to make his living on the local farms," pruning apple trees in the late winter, picking fruit in late summer, or doing any of the dozens of tasks that orchard work required. He even developed a few friendships, including a drinking buddy everyone knew as Hooky Dewclaw. But Frank kept his past to himself, and most people only knew him as "Junior."

By early 1976, things had begun to shift. There were more RCMP patrols, and more questions at the border. Nothing major, but more than the usual easy wave-through from an officer you knew. This quiet friendliness had created, at a local level, an unofficial form of free trade.

It was early spring when things really began to change. It all started when one of the drivers, using a well-known unmarked road, nearly ran into a fence in the middle of the night. There were no warning signs and, as such, he nearly wiped it out. Puzzled, he managed to get his truck turned around and find another crossing point. As soon as he got back, he told Ted about this.

As the weather warmed, more crossings were made impassable. That first fence became a deep ditch, and excavators were soon at work on various little dirt tracks along the border. One of Ted's drivers, who worked for an excavation company in the daytime, found himself digging up one of his preferred crossing points. On a couple of occasions, Ted and Frank would go out for a Sunday drive in Ted's old brown Ford F100 pickup, exploring to see which spots were open and which spots had been closed.

Then, one night, Frank was driving a GMC six-wheeler down, loaded with a dozen bricks of cocaine and a bale of compressed Jamaican weed tucked behind several pallets of industrial felt. He was on Verger Modele, the same road he once lived on, known on the Vermont side as the Boston Post Road. He came around a curve and there, stopped in the road, was an International six-wheeler with its lights off. It pulled ahead slowly, edging to the side to let him by. As he came alongside, he looked over but couldn't make out the face. He assumed the other driver was probably trying to do the same.

But they both knew that no-one would be driving a big truck across the line at 2 a.m. unless they were up to something sketchy. As soon as he returned to the farm, he let Ted know and the very next day his boss drove to the city. Nothing more was said, and Frank knew enough not to ask. Life continued as normal.

There'd been two other incidents since then, with trucks crossing paths at spots where it was obvious that the other guy was up to something. Frank recognized the simple math of it all: fewer crossing points, same number of trucks.

All of this was happening at a time when a fortune could be made bringing cheap booze to Montreal. The Olympics were coming up, and Montreal's downtown bars were expecting the biggest summer since Expo 67. The demand was there, as was the supply, thanks to someone Ted knew through his contacts in Enosburg.

* * *

As Frank finished up his lunch, he glanced across the kitchen table at the most recent issue of the *Granby Liar*, dated June 20, 1976. There was an article about some guy named "Booker" who'd been sent to jail, but recently released on bail pending his appeal. He picked it up and scanned the text, only half-paying-attention at first. One-by-one the details grabbed his attention: former cop missing, people for an English-Speaking Quebec burning a house down, obstruction of justice. Then the paragraph that changed everything:

"Despite a number of run-ins with the law, Booker has remained relatively unscathed over the years. Strangely, the only other time he did serve was over two decades ago, also for obstruction of justice in the disappearance of Quebec Police Force detective Frank McConnell."

13

The talk

Frank stared at the *Granby Liar*, trying to take it all in. He didn't want to believe it, but, at the same time, he *did* want to believe it. Connections. Things were shifting in his understanding, but he hadn't come to any conclusions yet.

"Have you seen this?" he finally said to Ted, tossing the paper down on the table, folded to the Booker story.

Ted suspected what this was all about even before he picked it up, but the last paragraph confirmed it. *Frank had figured out what happened to his dad.*

"I guess you and I need to have a chat," Ted said. He glanced at Diane, silent, both knowing that the secret they'd been bound to keep was a secret no longer. "Let's go out to the woodshed."

They stepped out through the small door, down the narrow passage and into the adjoining woodshed. Ted headed for the far corner, where an old, unused cast iron box stove sat buried under a pile of firewood. He opened the door and pulled out a pack of Export A's, then fished a pack of matches out of his pocket. He lit it up and then tossed the burnt match into an empty tin pail.

Frank didn't know Ted smoked.

"I guess there's no way around it now," Ted began. "Charlie swore me to secrecy, but you figured it out anyways. One of the guys who killed your dad lives in these parts. And it's his trucks you've been seeing on the back roads at night. He's a mean son of a bitch, one of the only ones to stand up to Charlie and live to talk about it. Not that he says a word about it. But you just can't kill the bastard."

Ted paused, his words hanging in the air like the cigarette smoke that now filled the woodshed. He just stood there, staring at his feet as if waiting for the feisty Irish kid to explode.

But the explosion didn't come. Junior was too stunned.

"And you weren't ever going to tell me?" Frank asked.

"Like I said, Charlie swore us to secrecy. And you know what happens with him if you talk out of turn. Not just for us, but for you too. It's a big fucking mess that Charlie wanted to keep secret."

"Well, the cat's out of the goddamned bag now."

"That it is. But you can't do anything about it. Charlie will step on you, and you sure as hell don't want that."

"But if we could just get rid of him...that would also solve our traffic jam problem on the line," Frank pleaded.

Ted could see that the kid was already looking for a reason, a justification to lash out. "It's not so simple," he replied.

"Look, I deserve an explanation, at least!" Frank shouted back. Although he could feel his anger rising, he cared for and respected Ted in a way that he never knew, never expected. As such, he could never raise a hand against the man.

"Back in the day, Stubby Booker and his sidekick, a guy named Rogers, worked for the Irish. They knew the area around here better than anyone, and they'd been sneaking stuff back and forth across the border for years. At first they were just kids. Rogers' family were bootleggers from way back, and they were just looking to make a buck any way they could. Charlie was a young punk back then, full of piss and vinegar. When he took over in Montreal, he had the port, but Rogers and Booker had the border. Deals were made."

"Where were you in all this?"

"I knew Stubby and Dave Rogers from around. I even did some of my first runs for them, bringing stuff over the Boston Post Road, mostly things people didn't want to pay duty on at the border. Smokes, booze, the occasional bit of farm equipment. It was a chance to make a few extra bucks on the side.

"So Stubby and Slippers – everybody called Rogers 'Slippers' –go and meet up with Charlie McKiernan's father, Fred, who ran things back in the day. They just drove to Montreal, walked into the tavern and introduced themselves, bold as brass. Well, naturally, Fred set his boys on them, and they managed to work 'em over, but those two put up a hell of a fight. I think one of Fred's boys lost an eye. By the time Stubby and Slippers left, they had a deal: they'd be handling all the cross-border smuggling for Fred. Not long after, Charlie took the helm, and kept things pretty much as they were.

"It worked pretty well. I was busy and making more money than I'd ever had. Even got enough to buy this farm and start fixing it up. Those were good years. We never saw the cops around here, and Stubby made sure we kept a low profile. If anyone opened their mouth or got too obvious, he was sure to cool their jets."

Ted paused to light another cigarette, stepped out of the shed into the heat, and then strolled over to a pair of lawn chairs under a large maple. There was always a bit of a breeze there. He waved for Frank to sit in the one with the battered green and white webbing, its white plastic arms yellowed and cracking from years left in the sun.

"But Stubby and Rogers got greedy. Worked out a side deal with the Italians. The wops needed smugglers too, and they started doing a bit for them on the side. It didn't take long before Charlie found out.

"That's where your dad came in. Sorry to say it, kid, your dad might have been a cop, but he ended up working for Charlie. Nothing much, just had to pay a little extra attention to people here and there. If a guy wasn't pulling his weight, he'd start getting regular visits from the cops. Needless to say, they'd get the message pretty damned quick. Charlie had a few cops like that. Well, not long before Stubby and Rogers started working for the Italians, Frank got transferred to the Townships."

Junior could feel his face flush. The secrets of his past now stood revealed, and he didn't like what he was hearing. But, after a lifetime spent waiting for a glimpse, Frank Junior couldn't look away.

"So, Charlie decided to send Frank over to Stubby's for a chat. Give him a scare. Hell, I'm not even sure Booker knew Frank was working for Charlie. We don't know what happened next, but we *do* know that Stubby was a hothead and your dad had a temper of his own to spare. Bottom line is: no-one ever saw your father again.

"In the middle of all this, Slippers ends up going to the cops and says he'll tell them everything. When Stubby got arrested, Charlie figured that things would resolve themselves. Stubby'd be put away for life for killing a cop, and Slippers, who'd always followed Stubby's lead, would either end up useless or dead.

"But that's when things really went to hell in a handbasket. First off, the cops couldn't find your father's body. Zero evidence of anything. Frank had just vanished. Then Rogers did something that still doesn't make a lick a sense to me. Instead of fucking off someplace, he went to work in the high steel in the city. They'd charged him as an accessory to murder, probably to make sure he'd testify to get a lighter sentence, and maybe part of his bail conditions was to stick around. Anyway, once it became clear that Stubby was only going to get a slap on the wrist for obstruction, Charlie made sure that Slippers took a tumble.

"Things got really rough there for a bit, but by the time Booker was out, he and Charlie had worked out a truce. Stubby had the eyeties, we handled our own stuff. We each had our roads, and stayed out of each other's way. That is, until they started closing the border roads. Now we're tripping over each other."

Frank glanced over at Ted, who was now staring out into the trees across the field. He looked old, older than he should, probably because he'd dealt with a lifetime of borderlines, doing things on the sly, keeping secrets, telling half-truths and always listening. Always waiting for the other shoe to drop.

Ted looked back at the boy. In a perfect world, he'd be the kid that he and Diane always wished they could have raised. But as he looked at Frank, he knew.

The other shoe had dropped.

14

No fixing feelings

Junior didn't explode into the rage that Ted had expected. Once their conversation was over, he got quiet and drifted off to spend that afternoon in the woods. In the evening he took to the workshed, unleashing all of his hurt and anger on the old sand-filled canvas duffle bag that he'd hung from a rafter to keep his boxing skills sharp. Knowing that you can't fix somebody else's feelings, Ted kept his distance.

Frank skipped supper, instead making a bee-line through the kitchen for the bathroom to get cleaned up before heading off to his room.

"He sure smells like a teenaged boy," Diane said quietly to Ted, an attempt to lighten the mood that fell flat.

Like Ted, Diane never liked their sworn secrecy over Junior's past. They knew, better than most, how a young man can be affected when things fall apart. He was still, in many ways, a growing boy who had a long way to go to understand and embrace his full manhood. In the time spent with him under their roof, they'd grown to love him. Sure, they'd seen flashes of his temper, but he always remained respectful towards them. Perhaps on some level, this was Junior acknowledging that they were giving him the stable, safe home life that he'd always craved.

"He's got a lot to figure out," Ted said. "It's probably going to take some time before he can settle. *If* he can settle."

"I hope he can settle," Diane said. "If he can't, we're going to have our hands full."

* * *

Now towelled off, Junior dropped into his bed. He wasn't tired, nor was he as shocked as he thought he would be. Sometimes, when the force of events is so great, a person goes numb. The grim reality rests before their eyes, and they can only stare. Junior's life had shifted, and it hung from the ceiling, untouched as yet by emotion. Even when he closed his eyes, it was still there. Waiting.

Even before he even felt the anger, he knew that he'd have to get revenge. He knew it the instant Ted pulled back the curtain on his past. Vengeance had been part of his life ever since he'd beaten George senseless in that back alley in Griffintown. Charlie McKiernan had taken that anger, trained it, focused it and honed it. Most importantly, he'd divorced it from hate and made it an everyday part of Junior's life, to the point where the anger no longer shared space with hate.

In the city, Junior's work was all about using anger like an accountant used a pencil on a ledger. A client didn't pay, you brought out your anger to balance the books. Hate didn't enter into the equation. The idea of hate rarely entered his conscious thoughts. Not even when he was knocking the teeth out of a deadbeat shopkeeper or twisting the arm of a backalley junkie late on a loan payment. He was a professional, doing his job. Even when one of his hapless victims landed a lucky punch, he didn't hate them for it.

But now Junior felt hate. Plenty of hate. As he lay on the bed, he could feel it start to bleed from that deep place, boil up in the pit of his stomach and seep out in search of its old companion: anger. When that family reunion happened, it was bound to create the incestuous and ugly beast called vengeance.

After a night where his only sleep had been filled with dreams of dying fathers and shattered lives, Junior put in another solid day fixing machinery. As is often the case, a tired, frustrated mechanic will encounter more than their share of stripped bolts, lost tools and cut fingers. By 4 p.m. he went in to get cleaned up. It was Friday, and he'd had enough.

"I'm going to the Quebec House," he said.

"Be careful out there," Diane replied. She wanted to tell him to be calm, to know that they loved him and that he was a good kid. But she stayed quiet, knowing that the affirmations would fall on deaf ears. Frank Junior was his own person, and he was beyond the control of her maternal worries as he went out into the world.

He took the old Ford LTD, a big boat of a sedan with an oversized engine that could pass anything but a gas station. It rumbled quietly as he coasted down into Frelighsburg. Hell, once he was out of the driveway he could pretty much drop it into neutral and roll the entire trip. In fact, it would have been a fairly easy walk from Ted and Diane's to the Quebec House, but he didn't like the idea of walking back up the hill in the dark with a belly full of twenty-five cent draft.

He was about three beers in when his friend Hooky Dewclaw showed up. After Hooky ordered a small and a large O'Keefe for himself, he settled into his chair. The small beer was emptied quickly, then used as a spittoon. He cut a piece from a plug that was nearly as dark as a hockey puck, tucking it into his lower lip before taking a swig from the quart. The two different-sized bottles helped to ensure that he wouldn't drink from the wrong one as the night progressed. The barmaid hated when he made spittoon bottles, but Hooky either didn't notice or didn't care.

The two men talked about their week, with Junior holding back on the one revelation that now dominated his thoughts. Instead, they exchanged small talk about equipment repairs, rumours around town and the barmaid's ass. Hooky put a quarter on the pool table, won his game and then squared off against Frank. Hooky won the first two games, but Frank rallied to win the third. Then they settled back into their chairs. The Expos were on TV, though neither man paid much attention.

"You look like a man with something on his mind," Hooky Dewclaw said during a quiet moment. "You all right?"

Junior's pale, freckled face reddened a bit. He exhaled hard, staring at his beer glass. He didn't answer right away, deciding instead to call the barmaid over.

"Can I get a pitcher...and a shot of rye?" he asked.

"Sure thing," she answered, her face devoid of emotion. She knew that smiling at the customers would only result in unwanted proposals, or worse. Best to remain cool, distant. "Anything for you, Hooky?"

"I'm good right now," he replied, holding up his half-full quart. "Maybe in a bit."

As she headed for the bar, Frank leaned in. As per Charlie's strict orders, he'd been secretive about his personal life during his time in Frelighsburg. He knew that sharing too much information could spell trouble not only for himself, but for Ted and Diane, and maybe even Charlie. He left a few bits out of his tale, like how his father had been working for Charlie McKiernan. He had wanted to say as little as possible, but between the beer and the sheer burden of what he'd learned, he ended up sharing a bit more than he'd intended.

The barmaid reappeared, pitcher in one hand, rye in the other. Frank handed her a five dollar bill. "Keep the change," he said. It was a big enough tip that she graced him with a smile, revealing one slightly-crooked eye tooth in an otherwise perfect row. To Frank, this charming imperfection only added to her allure.

"Well, Jesus," Hooky said, as she walked away. "That's pretty big stuff. What're you gonna do about that? Can't just leave that lying there."

"Don't know yet. Maybe nothing," he said, though it was clear to both men that he was lying.

"You're gonna have to do something. But I mean, *Stubby Booker*...he's a tough sonofabitch. He's killed more people than just your dad. The cops can't even touch him."

"I gotta figure this guy out. Might take a while, but the

fucker's got to pay for what he did."

"I remember people talking about him killing a cop once," Hooky said, unaware of the connection and anxious to share his limited knowledge of the matter. "Had help from this other guy, who ended up turning on him. But *that* guy ended up dead before he could share his story with the cops."

Hooky was a little drunk, but not drunk enough to miss the look on Junior's face.

"Oh, Jesus!" Hooky said.

The two men were silent for a few minutes, Frank drinking his rye a sip at a time before turning to the pitcher of beer. Hooky cut a fresh plug of tobacco, tucked it under his lower lip.

"Look, I know a guy. Not well, but well enough that we both know what the other is up to," Hooky said. "He's a driver for Stubby. Granted, I didn't hear this from him, but rumour has it that he's getting a little sick of being paid shit to do Booker's dirty work. I could ask him, real quiet-like...just see what's going on with him."

"What's this asshole's name?" Frank said, the rye burning his stomach, letting his hatred drain into his anger.

"I don't know his real name. But people call him Shaky."

* * *

It was just after midnight when Frank climbed into the LTD for the trip home. He felt very drunk and very numb. He rubbed his face and got his bearings before dropping the car into drive and quietly rumbling out of the yard of the Quebec House. The village was quiet, and the gas station across the street was darkened for the night.

He took his time climbing the hill out of town, straining to see the road ahead. Rex was waiting out in the yard for him, having chosen to spend the warm summer night outdoors in a cool spot under the porch by the front door that no-one ever used. He emerged from the shadows, announcing Frank's arrival and coming close to be sure it was really him.

Junior opened the car door, but made no effort to get out. Rex lowered his large head onto his lap, just barely visible in the glow from the yard light that was on over at the barn. He looked down at the dog.

And that's when the pain gushed to the surface, and the tears finally came.

15

Hooky and Shaky

Hooky Dewclaw was as good as his word. The following Tuesday evening he met up with Shaky at the Dunham Hotel, picking out a small table in a corner while the regulars held court up at the bar. Neither man recognized anyone in the room, which was just as good.

Both men were bone thin: Hooky from a life filled with hard work and a bad diet and Shaky from some sort of long-time thyroid problem the doctors couldn't quite sort out. He'd picked up the nickname in high school, right before he dropped out. Once he was old enough, he made a living as a long-haul truck driver until a bad accident out on the Prairies nearly killed him. When it was revealed that he was drunk at the time of the crash, he ended up going back home to Cowansville, just in time for Christmas, 1969. He recovered, but with a tainted driving record, scrawny build and trembling hands, he couldn't land another highway job.

That's when Stubby Booker took him on, first getting him to deliver building materials, pick up parts and run errands. Shaky proved reliable, showing up for work every day on time without a word of complaint. And when Stubby sent him on his first couple of illicit jobs, Shaky proved to be a man who could keep secrets and remain discreet. Far from your typical thug, his thin frame and friendly disposition allowed him to fly under the radar. The only intimidation he needed was the open knowledge of who his boss was.

By 1976, he'd become Booker's right-hand man, as close to the action as it got within the business. Shaky didn't know everything, far from it, but as the main driver on the smuggling operation, he knew more than most. More than the local rumour mill, anyways.

Both men wore jeans and a t-shirt. Hooky's was dirty from the day's work and Shaky's plain black garment was relatively pristine. His workday would only start later; a cross-border run that would keep him up most of the night. He knew something was up with Hooky, since getting a call from him out of the blue like this was unusual. They were more like the kind of friends who might revolve in similar circles or randomly run into each other out in public versus making plans to meet up for a beer. So, after the two men went through the regular settling-in conversation, Shaky sat back with his short bottle of Molson Export, lit up a cigarette and waited.

Sensing that it was time to talk, Hooky Dewclaw gave a heavily-censored version of events around Frank McConnell Junior. He left out Junior's name, and the parts about Booker murdering his dad, and how he wanted Stubby dead. Just that his friend had been wronged by Booker, and he wanted to know more about the man.

"Look, I'm not going to step in this," Shaky said. "I mean, I have my problems with Stubby, but I try to keep that to myself. I show up for work, I drive, I help him out around and I go home. I don't want no trouble."

"Okay, that's fine," Hooky said. "I heard rumours that you were sick of working for him, I figured I'd check in, see what was what."

'All it takes is one beer too many for the seed of something to slip out in conversation with friends,' Shaky thought. 'Somehow, a little nugget like that makes its way through the rumour mill, grinds bullshit flour out the other side, and suddenly you find yourself on the cusp of quitting your job and ratting out your boss. Jesus, these small towns are a pain in the ass sometimes.' He made a note to keep his mouth shut in the future. If his idle words could make their way around the Townships to Hooky Dewclaw, where else could they end up?

"People don't know what the fuck they're talking about," Shaky said, looking to shut things down. "Yeah, I got problems, but it's more about the border these days. They dug up the goddamn border after the Olympics, and now we're tripping over these other assholes bringing stuff in. Stubby doesn't want to do anything about it, but it's a traffic jam out there. Something's gonna go wrong, I know it. And I don't want to be around when the shit hits the fan."

'Shit,' he thought, 'Even *that* was too much information.'

"And that, my friend, is strictly between you and me," he added.

Shaky paused, lit another cigarette and stared at the red-and-white plastic Molson Export clock on the wall. He felt like he was being bled for information and was worried that he'd already shared too much.

"You'd best tell your friend to leave well enough alone," he said. "You don't want to mess with Stubby Booker."

Sensing the tension in Shaky's voice, Hooky realized his overstep and decided to let things lie. He'd known Shaky since elementary school and he really liked the guy. He deliberately shifted the conversation, so that the meeting became less about intrigue and all about two men sharing schoolyard memories in a haze of beer fumes and cigarette smoke.

16
Caught

The "Deer Police" hangover lasted longer than usual. The sheer volume of alcohol was bad, but it was particularly stupid to mixing the hard stuff with the beer. I was a hurtin' unit for pretty much of the rest of the week.

The ride-along was supposed to accomplish two things: give me some insight into the smuggling story *and* show me what the game wardens typically do. Unfortunately, the evening had been anything *but* typical. I hadn't witnessed anything to expose the smuggling story or reflect well on the region's game wardens. And, if I was going to be honest about what those guys did, then I had to be honest about the fact that I was falling-down-drunk at the time.

The very thought of that was ridiculous. Bankroft would never let that into the paper, and I might very well lose my job for turning a work assignment into a bender. So, I busied myself with other tasks, putting it off, pushing the discomfort down into a growing nest of uncomfortable feelings.

* * *

When Fernand Dubois phoned, I was quick to take the call, hopeful for a distraction. A car accident? Maybe a theft or an armed robbery? It was the fall, so marijuana plantation busts were in full swing.

"Fernand the man, where do we stand?" I said, trying to sound chipper. "What's new in the world of crime and punishment?"

"Oh, just police doing good work," he quipped. "Doing our jobs and bringing in the bad guys."

"What have you got for me today?"

"Last night at about midnight we were called to assist the

RCMP down on Dufur Brook Road in Glen Sutton," Dubois said. "The Mounties spotted a suspicious truck and tried to pull it over. The driver tried to get away, but one of our patrol cars was nearby. The driver was stopped and arrested without incident."

"Okay, what did they find?"

"The RCMP suspected the truck had come across the border illegally. It had a closed box on the back, and inside they found several cases of alcohol and about a dozen television sets."

Oh, this is great, I thought. It was the perfect use for the background I'd gathered about smuggling, and I didn't have to get into the "Deer Police" fiasco. *Perfect.* I could feel the stress lift just a little and the lingering psychological hangover lightened a bit.

"What about the chase? Anything there?"

"No, he pulled away from the RCMP, but when he saw our car in front of him, he pulled over and surrendered to the officers on the scene. It was a GMC one-ton, the kind with double wheels in the back. Not something that could get away very easily."

So no grand exciting car chase, but still some solid info. I was already drafting the smuggling story in my head.

"The driver was brought in by the RCMP for questioning and released on a promise to appear in court at a later date to face charges," Dubois said, shaking me out of my reverie.

"Isn't that a little unusual, considering what they found?" I asked.

"It is, but sometimes if there's a lack of space at the local jail, we'll sometime we'll let 'em go on their own recognizance if they aren't violent or a flight risk. Granted, I don't have all the details on this particular case."

"Do we have a name?"

"No. He hasn't been charged yet, so we can't release his name."

Even though I already knew that, I asked anyway, just in case he'd drop a name. If he had, it would have been fair game, with Dubois getting into trouble and not me. It was all part of the dance we did, with me asking questions I already knew the answers to and him giving pat answers. A few years back, some Quebec Police Force functionary gave him the job of handling the media and he turned out to be very, very good at it.

"Have you noticed any increase in the amount of cross-border smuggling recently?" I asked. "Since the closing of the small border roads?"

"Not really," Dubois said. "But since the Olympics finished our patrols along the border, regions have returned to their normal levels. That's left mainly to the RCMP. You should check with them."

By the time the phone call was over, I'd already excavated my notes on smuggling from the pile of papers on my desk. Knowing that this story I'd been snooping around on for awhile was going from a drag to something substantial, I felt better now than I had in days. I went and got myself a cup of coffee from the break room. Nasty, strong stuff, but delightfully so.

Then I called a photographer who lived in the Bedford area. The RCMP had a spot down that way where they parked impounded vehicles, and I figured the smuggler's truck would likely be there. I told him to watch for a one-ton GMC, a little bigger than a regular pickup truck, with a closed box on the back.

Doing my duty, I called the RCMP detachment in Bedford, but the duty officer there only gave me a pat answer about how the Mounties were always on the lookout for illegal activity. After giving me nothing, he told me to call Fernand Dubois. I think I caught him at a bad time, and he just wanted to get off the phone.

And away I went, building the story the same way a sculptor creates a statue from a lump of clay. I started with the facts of the incident: "The Royal Canadian Mounted Police teamed up with the Quebec Police Force Monday night to arrest a man in Glen Sutton who is alleged to have smuggled a significant quantity of liquor and stolen goods across the Canada–US border..."

Then I was able to blend in the details of my research: how cross-border activity was a long-standing tradition in the Townships, since before there even *was* an actual border. Then I led readers through the "Roaring 20s," with Prohibition in the US being a genuine bonanza for Canadian smugglers. Finally, I brought recent history into it by mentioning the authorities closing many of the unmarked border crossings as part of the increased security due to the Olympic Games.

In a moment of pure speculation, I opined that, since smugglers had fewer places to cross, there might be some extra tension along the line as they tried to dodge each other and the police. No hard facts to back up the observation, but I left it hanging there for the readers to think about.

By the time I was wrapping it up a couple of hours later, the photographer had already dropped off the film, and it was being developed by one of our guys in the back. When the wet black-and-white was laid out on the counter to dry, there it was: a rather beat-up looking one-ton truck, with the licence plate on the front reading "N-5545." A four-wheel drive farm truck from the looks of the front hubs, with a shadow underneath betraying the front differential.

I went back to my desk, typed up an extra paragraph with that information and inserted it into my copy using scissors and tape. I might not have had the driver's name, but I figured there'd be at least a couple of people out there who would recognize the truck and have a pretty good idea of who got caught.

I also left out any mention of the deer police.

* * *

Junior was embarrassed for being caught. Nothing fancy, he'd just been at the wrong place at the wrong time. He'd been expressly told not to attempt a getaway from the cops if it was difficult to do so, so there was no spectacular chase, no potential car crash and no risking life and limb. He'd been instructed to pull over, surrender peacefully and be agreeable, but don't tell them anything.

"Is this your truck, sir?"

"No."

"Are you aware of what's in the back?"

"No."

"Why are you out driving so late, sir?"

"Just out for a drive. I like to drive at night."

"Sir, you'll have to come with us."

"Okay."

The questioning continued at the RCMP office in Bedford. Having successfully stayed out of view all these years, Junior had never been grilled by the police before. He surrendered to the situation of the moment, let the questions wash over him, stayed tight-lipped and gave one and two-word answers to the Mounties, which yielding nothing of value.

When they let him make a phone call, he called Ted. Unsure if they would be listening in, he said precious little. Despite having been woken up at 3 a.m., Ted got the message loud and clear. He'd gotten these kinds of calls before, and knew what to do next.

"I'll have to make a call," Ted said. "Sit tight, stay quiet. We'll get you out of there."

'Like I'd be able to go anywhere if I wanted,' Junior thought.

Junior was brought back to the interrogation room, which also served as the detachment holding cell. They didn't bother to put his handcuffs back on. During this time, he reflected on his last few months, learning about his father, about Booker. About how Charlie McKiernan wanted to keep it all a secret. Now this shit.

At least they hadn't caught him on the way down. He had about two-hundred pounds of hashish in the back, most likely bound for New York or Boston, he didn't know which. It wasn't a smuggler's job to ask such questions. You take a load, cross the line with as little fuss as humanly possible, don't get caught and then bring it to the drop spot. Sometimes someone was there to meet you, usually someone you only knew by sight. No names or personal information would be exchanged. Sometimes no-one was there at all, you just dropped it in a shed, behind a building or whatever the receiver wanted. Then you left quietly.

To make the most of the trip, Junior had met up with their liquor supplier and added a few hot TV sets to round out the load. It would make for a profitable trip back. Waste not, want not.

He turned his attention to his surroundings. Across from where he sat was an RCMP poster marking the 1973 centenary of the police force. A tattered copy of *RCMP Quarterly* sat on a chair in the corner. Next to it was a pamphlet entitled "Drug Abuse: the Chemical Cop-Out."

He could hear muffled phone calls and office chatter just outside the steel door, all in French. The combination of the two made it impossible for him to figure out what was going on. Then all he could hear was the occasional word exchanged between the two officers on duty and the white noise of cops busily filling out reports on his arrest in the office pool. He put his head down on the small table and dozed.

At 6 a.m. his arresting officers came back in. Junior rubbed his eyes as one of them put a foam cup of coffee in front of him.

"Look like this is your lucky day, sir. Seems all the holding cells in the area are full and we've got no place to put you, so we're releasing you on what we call a 'promise to appear.' In other words, we're letting you go, but you'll have to agree to appear in court at a later date, at which time you'll be formally charged in connection with your arrest."

"I 'have to agree to appear'? What if I don't agree?"

"Well, sir, then we'll put you in a cell with several others, where you'll stay until you're charged, and then you'll go back to the cell until there's a bail hearing."

"Okay, I promise to appear," Junior said. "That's fine with me."

And with that, Junior was escorted out of the room. He was then made to sign a bunch of papers, which swore to his name, address, and the fact that he wouldn't leave town. He also agreed to come in once a week to check in with them. They gave him copies of each paper he signed and pointed him to the door.

"Here's a dime. There's a pay phone down the street."

A half-hour later, with the sun climbing over Pinnacle Mountain in the east and most of Bedford just beginning to stir, Ted's white LTD rumbled quietly up to the curb.

17

Empty shell

My efforts had yielded a newsworthy article from a little roadside bust story. My editor, Harry Bankroft, liked what I'd done with the smuggling story and ran it on the front page, including a photo of the truck. I picked up a few more beers from the corner store across from the *Granby Liar* offices and rifled three back on the way home, tossing the empties out the window. Let the local kids collect them and take them to the store. At five cents each, they could load up on gum, hockey cards and Popeye candy cigarettes.

Two more beers at home and I fell into a mercifully-dreamless sleep.

The next day I was at work early, noting the after-effects of the beer, but otherwise feeling moderately better about things. I even considered writing my "deer police" story. Make it into a puffy little piece about conservation-minded folks enforcing the rules and stopping illegal hunting. No guns, no bottles of gas, no drunken binges.

Not many jobs force people to regularly make decisions about what's right or wrong, but news reporting is a constant challenge to one's morality. One wrong choice can have a direct impact on the people you're writing about. Twist a few things here or there and you can literally turn someone from a hero into a villain. Twist too far and you'll ruin your reputation, which has its own subtle ways of coming back to bite you.

When it came down to it, I had a lot of respect for what the volunteer game wardens were doing. Yes, there were a few bad apples, like the deer jackers using their position as club wardens to further their own interests. Billy and Steve, while over-armed and alcohol-fuelled, were trying to do the right thing. They even went after a couple of their own when they saw what they were doing. Maybe a follow-up with my hosts would help clear things up on the murky moral front.

I called Billy, but got no answer. Steve was home, and we spoke for a few minutes.

"I can honestly say I've never had a night like that," he said. "Most nights we go out and don't see a damned thing. We end up driving around and shooting the shit for a few hours. But when we see stuff like that, we can't just let it slide."

I could tell that he was nervous about what I was going to write, and how it would reflect poorly on not just himself, but the fish and game club as well.

In the end, I decided to bend the moral code just a bit. Like I said, there was no way to write this thing honestly without admitting that I was loaded at the time. That wouldn't just get the game wardens in trouble, but Bankroft would kick me to the curb for sure.

So, it was settled. I'd lose some of the colourful storytelling, but it certainly beat the alternative. I was reasonably sure that I could use enough background about hunting, hunting laws and conservation-minded volunteers to make it work.

I was about to plunge into my mostly made-up, sanitized version of the deer police story when Linda, the newsroom secretary, informed me that Fernand Dubois was on the phone. No one else was around, so I took the call.

"A body was found on a farm in Brigham this morning," Dubois said. "We suspect some kind of foul play."

"Okay, so what's the situation?"

"There aren't too many details yet. Someone was out for a walk with their dog and they came across the body on a farm on Des Erables. The crime scene investigators are there now. It doesn't seem like there's anyone living at the farm, or at least no one was home."

Dubois gave me the address, and without much further thought, I grabbed a camera and headed for the car. It might have been unfortunate for the dead guy, but in that moment I was relieved to have an interesting story on my hands that would get me out of the office. Even the prospect of possibly seeing a dead body didn't deter me.

It was a crisp, sunny day as I made my way up Cowie Street, hanging a left onto St. Charles at the Woolco. The Vauxhall was running well, and I reached into the glove box for my sunglasses, which were scratched and a bit dirty. With my knee against the wheel, I used the corner of my shirt to wipe them off before putting them on. I was out of town in a few minutes, headed for Adamsville. The once-vibrant green leaves, which were bursting with life just a few short weeks ago, had begun to turn muted and dusty. As I got out into the country, I passed a farm where a combine was harvesting wheat. Grain farms were rare in this part of the world, and the sight of that brilliant golden wheat demanded attention.

Because of my time living in Brigham, the route was a familiar one. Even though it felt like a lifetime ago, it struck me that it had only been a year. I longed for the simplicity of those days, before Stubby Booker and before learning about my father. I missed the peace that comes with ignorance, with not knowing that your entire understanding of the world is, quite simply, wrong.

As I dropped over the big hill just a couple of miles before the village of Brigham, I could see a police cruiser parked on the side of the road up ahead. Beside it was an ancient farmhouse that appeared to be abandoned. The dark grey clapboard, weathered by decades in the elements, had likely never been painted. An ugly khaki, yellow-doored Ford Econoline Sûreté du Québec van was parked in the barnyard. Two officers, one with a camera, were standing next to it, smoking.

Just past the cruiser was a second car, this one a newer, reddish-brown Plymouth Caravelle, with a thin man in a leather jacket standing next to it. He was smoking too. I immediately recognized him as Richard, a colleague at the French language newspaper *La Voix de l'Est.* Because he was always friendly, and probably knew more than the cops in the patrol car, I decided to check with him first. I pulled up behind him and parked.

"Nice day for a murder," he said.

"Nice day for a drive in the country," I responded. "What's happening?"

"Waiting for Dubois," Richard said. "The body's out behind the barn. They've been taking pictures and measuring things, but now they're on their union break."

"Place looks abandoned," I said, stating the obvious. One of the four pane windows upstairs was missing glass, and the porch roof was sagging. A piece of tin on the main roof had begun to curl, waving gently in the cool fall breeze. To the northwest, clouds were blowing in, ragged and grey. No rain in them yet, but a warning of weather to come.

"But there's cattle in the field just over there," Richard observed. "The property line comes close to the barn on this side. Maybe it was the neighbour who called it in. Not sure who else would have seen it over there."

This was the camaraderie I'd grown accustomed to over the last year. Even though we worked for papers that competed for advertising, we each had our own linguistic audiences. While we might occasionally try to scoop one another on a given story, relations were easygoing. And, since the *Granby Leader-Mail* only published twice a week while *La Voix de l'Est* was a daily, the opportunities to scoop the "competition" were limited.

"Think they'd let us go around back and get a better look?" I mused.

"Not likely. They don't want us trampling all over their crime scene," Richard said, stepping forward to crush his cigarette butt under a well-worn cowboy boot.

Every crime scene was a delicate dance. Us reporters always want to get a closer look, but if you overstep your boundaries and got an officer angry, you could get sent to the back of the class pretty quick. Ever in search of gripping visuals, photographers and camera operators pushed the boundaries more than reporters did. But ultimately it was up to the cops, and some of them really didn't like the media all that much. If they accused you of contaminating a crime scene, things could get really sticky.

We stood around and waited, keeping an eye on the scene while visiting. Richard asked about the future of the *Granby Liar.* Yes, rumours were going around that we were circling the drain, but that had been going on since before I'd been hired and I'd gotten used to it.

"Hey, it looks like they're getting back to it," I said, pointing to the investigators as they pulled on their gloves and trudged back behind the barn. In a moment they were out of sight, leaving us with even less to look at.

About twenty minutes later, Dubois pulled up in an unmarked Plymouth Fury, the colour of which was the typical putrid olive drab of the provincial police, but without the bright yellow doors and no flashers on the roof. We couldn't help but notice the pump shotgun holding pride of place up by the dash between the two front seats.

"I thought they took his gun away," Richard said.

"He probably nabbed the car from the motor pool when no one was looking," I said.

Dubois stepped out of the car, set a clipboard on the roof and then hitched his pants up over his pot belly. He walked towards us, his slow saunter learned and perfected from years as a beat cop. Dubois was always friendly when he had news to share and, as per his standard procedure, he asked how we were doing, if we'd been waiting long and various other pleasantries.

"So, the farmer who owns the land next door is the guy who has the cows," Dubois said, pointing. "He came to check on them this morning with his dog and found the body. Well, technically the dog ran under the fence and found it. The farmer called us, and we've been examining the scene for the last couple of hours. The body was found behind the barn next to a drainage ditch."

"What do we know about the body?" Richard asked. Dubois checked his clipboard.

"Male, probably in his thirties. Looks like he'd been there for at least a couple of weeks. Still waiting for the autopsy to confirm, but it looks like he died violently and the death is being treated as 'suspicious.'"

"Can we say he was murdered?" I asked.

"Only the autopsy can determine that, but it doesn't appear to be accidental or a suicide at this point. Granted, we still have a long way to determine exactly what happened."

"Do we have a murder weapon?" I asked, though I pretty much knew the answer already.

"We haven't found anything yet, but we're still examining the scene," Dubois replied. As he said so he turned, and one of the investigators could be seen looking in a patch of tall grass. The other crime scene guy was apparently out of sight around the corner of the barn.

"Can we get a closer look?" Richard asked.

"Just a minute."

Dubois went over to the detective in the grass, trampling his way along until he was signalled to stop. There were a few hand gestures and some conversation we couldn't hear, and then he came back.

"This way."

We were brought around by the roadside fence line, and then stepped over the rusted twin strands of barbed wire into the neighbour's pasture. It didn't give us much, other than a distant view of the other detective leaning over a blanket on the ground. I gathered up my camera, an old Argus that lived at the office for reporters to use when the photographer was busy, and snapped off a half-dozen frames. From this distance, it probably wouldn't amount to much. No zoom lenses for me. I'd get a shot or two of the farmhouse, a cop car and a crime scene guys in their coveralls, I.E. something visual to go along with the story. It also would also prove to Bankroft that I'd actually gone out to the crime scene.

"So, was this person shot or stabbed or what?" I probed.

"Like I said, the autopsy will confirm the cause of death," Dubois said. He paused, staring at his clipboard, considering his next words. "Off the record, his hands were bound and he was shot in the back of the head. But, for the love of God, please don't mention details like that until we have the autopsy. Check with me later and you can have it as soon as we confirm it."

Good old Fernand Dubois. He just couldn't keep that to himself.

"No problem. I'll check in with you later." I had a day before deadline anyway, so I could afford to wait.

"Do we have any idea who owns this place? It looks abandoned," Richard added.

"We're trying to determine that now," Dubois said, double-checking his clip board. "The guy next door said he heard a couple of years back that the place had changed owners, but he's never seen the new owner."

It certainly looked like no one had been there for some time. The pasture grass was nearly waist high in some spots, and raspberry bushes were growing up around the house. The structure itself looked like it had once been a nice place to live, but chronic neglect had led it to little more than a ruin. A ruin with the shell of a human life crumpled in the grass behind the barn. A shell filled with secrets.

18

Shell gets a name

The next day I got double confirmation of the murder. Richard's story in *La Voix de L'Est* cited a source within the police force saying the victim died of a gunshot to the head. A phone call to Fernand Dubois said essentially the same thing.

"We only got that confirmation this morning," Dubois said. "I'm going to have a talk with Richard about that."

As if to reward good behaviour, he provided a bit of fresh information. The victim was Martin Traynor, a single, thirty-five year old truck driver. Originally from the Sherbrooke area, he'd moved to the region a few years ago, hauling a variety of goods for a local trucking company. Next of kin had been informed, and the police were still working on further background to see what they could learn.

"What company was he driving for?" I asked.

"That's one of the things we're investigating. His truck was found at his home in South Bolton, but it belongs to a numbered company. We're still working on who it belongs to."

"And how about the farm? Any information on who owns it?"

"Nothing yet," Dubois said. "The town clerk is off today, so they have to call him in for this. In a small town, not everyone at the town hall works full time."

I made a note to call back later and then got on with the tasks at hand, including drinking coffee and reading the other newspapers that covered southern Quebec and beyond. There was other news to be written, and I still had to figure out what to do with the "Deer Police" story. I'd pretty much settled on how to write it, knowing that, in this case, honesty was not the best policy. If Bankroft actually printed the honest version, Billy and Steve would take one look at it and come kick my arse. And I had seen enough of them to know that they could do that with scarcely any effort. I was constantly flip-flopping on my approach, but, since the pros outweighed the cons, I drifted back to the idea of writing the sanitized version.

I just wanted to bury the "Deer Police" story, but I also knew that Bankroft thought it would make for a solid feel-good piece about local volunteers doing their bit to tackle the poaching problem. Of course, Bankroft's version didn't include Molotov cocktails, massive amounts of alcohol and roadside fistfights. Not to mention me getting fall-down drunk and waking up in my car outside the Abercorn Hotel.

That thought launched me out of my chair. I needed to get out of the office and clear my head before tackling that beast.

I took a stroll down Drummond Street, past the funeral home and headed towards the lake. I struck up a brisk pace, determined to hit the park before anyone from work saw me. It got the blood circulating, and it felt good. I'd seen people jogging before, but these people were still generally regarded as oddballs. Jim Fixx had yet to popularize it as a sport with his bestselling book, so for most people, running was little more than a way to tire yourself out. Unless you were a competitive athlete, what was the point? But like I said, it felt good, so I kept going. Without even thinking, I broke into a run...as well as a full-blown panic.

By the time I reached the park, I'd been sprinting for several hundred yards, and I couldn't get enough air. My pace slowed, but I kept moving, unsteady on my feet, afraid of what might happen if I stopped. I finally dropped to my knees in the grass, retching as the cool fall breeze stung like needles. Things went black.

In that moment I once again found myself clinging to a girder high above the Montreal skyline. I had no idea how I got there and I could only see one way down, and that was to simply let go.

"It's going to be a long, hard fall. Blow you to pieces in the dark."

I felt something cold and wet on the side of my face. I was back in the park and a big yellow dog with a black nose was sniffing at my face. I heard a woman. She was talking, and in that moment I had no idea what she was saying. When I looked up, the woman pulled the dog back and I could see that her eyes were wide like saucers. I finally figured out that she was speaking French, but my head wasn't clear enough to figure out what she was saying.

"Sir, are you okay?" she said, switching to English, a slight tremor in her voice.

Things weren't working properly just yet, so it took me a moment to respond. My arms and legs thrashed uselessly as the world around me kept spinning.

"Yes, I'm okay," I responded.

"Are you drunk?" she asked in French.

"No, I'm not drunk," I answered, suddenly angry at the thought. Not at this time of the day. Of course not!

"Do you need help?"

"I'll be fine," I said in French. "Thank you."

I sat up, the wind and sun stinging my eyes and my skin. She stepped back, and wordlessly walked away, dog at her side. I glanced at my watch. I thought I'd only blacked out for a few seconds, but it must have been longer. It was almost noon.

I got my head back together on the walk back down Drummond to the office. Unsure if I was wiping off dog slobber or my own vomit, I rubbed the side of my face down with the sleeve of my jean jacket and tried to straightened up my clothes and hair. The words kept coming back to me over and over: *It's going to be a long, hard fall. Blow you to pieces in the dark.*

Once inside the *Leader-Mail* building, I headed straight for the bathroom to get cleaned up before anyone noticed. I needed to pull everything back inside that felt like it was out there for everyone to see. 'Don't let them see,' I thought. 'Please God, don't let them see.'

When I got back to my desk there was a note to call Fernand Dubois, but I held off for a bit and busied myself with other things. I lined up some briefs to write, including a boil water notice from Cowansville and the announcement of a special town council meeting over in Brome Lake. Deadline day stuff. By immersing myself in the everyday minutiae, I got myself grounded.

After getting the briefs written up and settling my nerves over half a sandwich, I made the decision to call Dubois back. But I kept putting it off, my dread over the prospects of a simple phone call was overwhelming. Apparently my aversion to so do anything at all had returned with a vengeance. I'd experienced this sort of thing before, after the problems last fall, but somehow I managed to push through it and keep doing my job. But this paralysis was worse. *Far worse.*

It took four rings before Dubois answered. He was in a good mood, as he usually was when he had some big news to share.

"That farm in Brigham," he said. "We found the owner, and he's been brought in for questioning. The victim was one of his truck drivers."

"So what's the owner's name?"

"That farm belongs to Stubby Booker."

19
Bail

The weekend passed more-or-less uneventfully. Not that I would have expected the world to come crashing down after I'd written about Stubby Booker. Booker was in jail, after all, and probably hadn't even seen the paper. Plus, he probably had bigger fish to fry than me. Still, paranoia can wreak havoc on your inner monologue.

And, to be honest, if he was looking for the reporter who made him look bad, he had a lot of choice. While I hadn't freelanced the story to the *Montreal Star* like Harry Bankroft suggested, one of their enterprising reporters picked it up and ran it in the Saturday edition. Sure, it was buried on page A3, but it was still there. The *Montreal Gazette* also had a paragraph, and our local French papers all gave Booker's arrest a lot of space. As for Richard at *La Voix de l'Est*, he really outdid himself, including graphic details and even talking to Martin Traynor's distraught mother.

"Besides, people don't read the *Granby Leader-Mail* like they did, you know that," Jen said, which wasn't nearly as comforting as she intended. "It's like you've been hearing around the office... all of the English people are all leaving."

I could tell from the expression on her face that she felt bad after saying this. Normally I would have stepped into the silence, to ease the discomfort we both felt, but this time I left it hanging there, not unlike the future of my job. Given previous events, part of my approach was to mention Stubby as little as possible, mainly because I didn't want to raise questions that I might not be able to answer truthfully.

It was a quiet weekend overall. Friday night I drank the last three beers while I was out walking King, and that was just enough to calm the dreams to the point where I didn't wake up in a sweat. Saturday we got groceries at the A&P down by the new shopping centre, and that night we went out to the Café Terrace to see some live music. Local boys, belting out cover tunes to a full house. It felt good. Almost normal.

Jen and I even went for a drive to look at the leaves, which were just reaching their peak fall colours. As always, it was stunning. We explored the back roads around Dunham, Frelighsburg and Stanbridge East, stopping to put ten bucks of leaded in along the way, enough to cover our drive and most of my week's running around for work.

It all came crashing back Monday evening, when Harry Bankroft let me know that I'd be covering Stubby Booker's bail hearing Tuesday morning at the courthouse in Cowansville. Knowing that the demons are quieter when they've been fed, this news prompted a trip to the *depanneur* again for more beer.

Tuesday morning I waited until the last minute before heading into the Cowansville courthouse. A stately old building located in what was once known as Sweetsburg before it merged with Cowansville, the structure had the local provincial jail tacked onto the back. This is where Stubby Booker had spent the weekend and where he'd continue to spend time for obstruction. I'd never had any reason to be inside the jailhouse and hoped I never did.

The courtroom was busy when I walked in, and the judge already had the proceedings underway. I quietly slipped into the back row, while Richard and a couple of other reporters were up in the front. I left my notepad in my coat pocket, not wanting to be obvious.

The first hour was roll call, with various people being asked to appear on a wide assortment of charges, most of which were read out through a series of codes. "So-and-so" charged under "section such-and-such" following an "altercation on 'X' date." For most of the accused, the court appearance was a formality, setting a date for a proper hearing later on. Pretty dry stuff, especially if you don't have your copy of the Criminal Code handy. Richard knew the codes of the most interesting crimes, and was taking his notes on a copy of the roll provided by one of the guards. Richard was a regular, and they had an understanding.

As the roll progressed, the audience began to thin out. Most were the accused, who left after their court dates were pushed off or their bail conditions were modified. Some were accompanied by friends or family, all of whom got out of there as soon as possible in order to get on with their lives.

I instinctively hunkered down slightly when I heard Sanford Booker's name called. The audience had thinned out quite a bit, and I was feeling exposed. Then I heard a clinking sound as Stubby was brought to the prisoner's dock. They had him in hand and foot restraints, with his wrists tagged to a chain around his waist.

Moments after he was sworn in by the court clerk, he turned slightly, scanning the room. Our eyes met. 'Oh shit, here we go,' I thought. I looked down, fishing out my notepad as I did so. I glanced back up, and he was still looking at me. That's when he winked at me, just like that, and turned back to the judge.

The hearing lasted all of five minutes. George Carson, Stubby's lawyer, explained that his client was already out on bail pending the appeal of his obstruction case and he was following all of his conditions to the letter. He also noted that Stubby hadn't been charged in connection with the events that led to his arrest and that he didn't present a flight risk.

Crown Prosecutor Andrew Sims, a tall, thin man with greying hair and a drawn, almost sickly-looking face, argued that Stubby's earlier case involved the disappearance, and possible murder, of a former police officer. And, although Booker hadn't yet been formally charged with the murder of Martin Traynor, he was definitely a person of interest. He implied, in carefully-worded legalese, that a murder charge was on its way, pending the conclusion of the investigation.

Justice Paul Fuller stared down at the sheaf of paperwork before him, pausing momentarily to flick a piece of fuzz off his robes. He pushed his wire-rimmed glasses up his nose, scratched his chin and then looked around the room.

And then, just like that, Stubby Booker was out on bail again. The judge simply added another $10,000 to his bail bond and let him go. Booker barely had time to thank the judge before he was led away, and the next name on the docket was called.

I made a point of not wasting time getting the story done. I knew it had to happen, and putting it off wasn't in anyone's interest. Granted, I still had days before the story had to be ready for the Friday edition, but I also knew that it had to be done and Harry Bankroft wasn't going to let me sit this one out. Like taking a bitter pill, I swallowed hard, then washed it down with a couple more beers from the back seat of my car.

The weekend passed more or less peacefully. I was able to put the Stubby story behind me and concern myself with simpler things, like some mild tune-up work on the Vauxhall, taking King out for walks and touring the countryside with Jen and the dog for some more leaf-peeping. Once again, I had to admit that I lived in paradise.

Jen was aware of the bail hearing, but made no mention of it. I was okay with that. We busied ourselves with other topics of conversation, from the coming election campaign to a lovely little sheep farm we'd seen while touring the back roads.

I even managed to get a couple half-decent nights of sleep. No dreams of my dad, or the high steel. No need to be drink myself to sleep, or risk waking up with a hangover.

So, with all of this behind me, I was in a pretty good mood when I walked into the office Monday morning. It was 10 a.m., but I already had a message waiting for me from Fernand Dubois. This was odd, since we rarely heard from him before noon. He answered on the second ring and got right to the point.

"It seems that Sanford Booker has been reported missing."

20
Gone

It took me a second to grasp what he said.

"You mean he skipped bail?"

"No," Fernand Dubois said. "He was reported missing. Mr. Booker was, under the terms of his bail, supposed to report to the Dunham detachment today, but early this morning one of his people showed up and said he was gone."

"So what happened? Are we saying that he was kidnapped, or did he just decide to leave?"

"This is what we're trying to determine," Dubois said. "An investigation has been opened, and we are talking to those close to him. Mainly his employees and the like."

Dubois was quiet for a moment, and I was trying to figure out my next question.

"Off the record, for now, we think he was abducted."

Another silence, as I my mind tried to put together how, or even why, someone would do that. I mean, this was Stubby Booker. You don't just walk up to him and take over the situation. I knew first-hand that he was a tough sonofabitch.

"So what can I say about this, other than he's missing?"

"Look, as soon as I can confirm it, I'll let you know. But for right now our investigators are trying to determine what happened, and then find out where he is. We honestly don't have much to go on."

"So, if you don't have much to go on, how come you think he was abducted?" I pressed.

Another pause. "Okay, but you have to keep this really quiet until I say so," Dubois said. He sure was trusting for someone who dealt with reporters for a living. But, then again, we all knew that if you burned Dubois on a story, he could freeze you out, make sure you and your paper didn't get anything, while giving the good stuff to competing news outlets. Not a good career move to burn him on a scoop. It was all about *quid pro quo*, give and take.

"One of his people showed up for work this morning and didn't see Booker around, so he went over to his house. The front door was smashed in, and there was damage to some parts of the house. It looked like there'd been a fight, but there was no sign of Booker, and his vehicle was still in the yard."

"What about his other farm, the one in Brigham?"

"Our people are checking it out now. They were there just a few days ago, so they know their way around."

"Any idea of when we'll be able to report on this?"

"For now, it's not clear. You can report that he's missing, but as for the other details, we need to wait to get confirmation. The guy who reported him missing isn't much of a talker, and isn't giving us much to work with. So, I'll have to get back to you."

"Remember, we publish tonight, and I really want this before then."

"It's not up to me, but I'll see what I can do," Dubois said. He then hung up without a further word.

So, it looked like I was going to be reporting on Stubby Booker again. I pulled out the bail story from last week. There were a few paragraphs I could still use, like the background stuff. In the context of a man already twice released on bail with a dead truck driver found on his property, things were getting intriguing. I found myself forgetting the stresses of the last year, drawn in by the understanding that there was something bigger going on here. But you can't just say that.

It's a crappy way to write a story, but sometimes it has to be done. There's no flow to a story where you can't share everything, no satisfaction of sitting down at your typewriter, starting with the lead, working through what's known, what isn't known, and then finishing off with some background. We reporters are taught to write in paragraphs that can easily be cut up and moved around. The *New York Times* may have said, "All the news that's fit to print," but often it's more like, "all the news that's printed to fit." When putting a page together, it's better to cut a paragraph off the end of a story, where the less important information is, than to lop off something important.

So I waited around, wrote some briefs (don't drink the water in Cowansville, special town council meeting coming up in Dunham, Roxton Furniture in Waterloo on a hiring spree). After spending some time considering if I should apply to work at the furniture factory, I started putting the Stubby story together.

At 4:30 p.m. I caught myself staring into space, lulled by the hum of activity all around me, so I decided to give Dubois another call. I knew he liked to be done by 5:00 p.m., and I was frankly sick of waiting.

"You can print it. Our investigation so far indicates that Mr. Booker was apparently abducted from his home sometime between Sunday and this morning," Dubois said. "So far, we haven't determined why he was taken, or where he could be."

* * *

Sitting in the office at Booker's place, Shaky didn't know where his boss was, but he had an idea of who might be involved. He replayed the conversation with Hooky Dewclaw over and over, sifting for information. Not much to go on.

Shaky really had no choice but to report Stubby missing. Booker was supposed to check in at the cop shop today anyways, so they were bound to start looking for him once he didn't show. Any excuse to get his bail yanked, especially after getting bail a second time during another murder investigation. So Shaky kept the story to a minimum, telling them that he showed up for work Monday morning and his boss was missing.

Stubby's house, always uncommonly neat and tidy for a bachelor, was trashed. The windows were broken, the furniture was smashed and the kitchen table was flipped over. Must have been a hell of a fight. He guessed that there was more than one person involved; it had to be to take someone like

Stubby down. Seemingly not much blood, so Stubby was likely still alive. That or he was taken somewhere to be disposed of.

Shaky knew that this had something to do with the cross-border trade. He'd been coming across a lot of traffic along the line ever since the government had dug up the roads for the Olympics. Hell, he'd even been chased once. Goddamned government, coming in and fucking everything up. He'd heard rumours that those other trucks were working for the Irish mob in the city, but Booker had always been tight-lipped about it. He suspected that Stubby knew more about the competition than he let on. 'Can't ask him now,' he thought.

Then Martin Traynor ended up dead. Pity, too, he was a good guy: reliable, always showed up for work and didn't ask too many questions. Even though he was paid decently for his trips to the States, he lived modestly, stuck to his own and liked to spend his time off fishing. *Poor bastard.*

Shaky lit a cigarette with a Zippo lighter; the wick pulled up to make the flame flare high. Then he reached into the desk drawer for the Canadian Club bottle that was always there. Not his liquor of choice, and Stubby might not like Shaky drinking his booze, but under the circumstances, he figured he could get away with it. Besides, Shaky needed to clear his head.

Fucking Hooky Dewclaw. Shaky had always liked the guy. He wasn't complicated, just seemed content to work all week and have a few beers out on the weekend. Even though nothing much was said and people bitched about work all the time, the memory of their conversation at the Dunham Hotel stuck with him.

But it was all pretty innocent stuff. Bitching about work was a way of life for pretty much everyone he knew. Shaky had spent many an evening sitting in dimly lit bars listening to people talk about how they'd told their boss off, or were going to. Or were ready to quit. Or were refusing to quit, because they didn't want to give their boss the satisfaction.

In the end, almost all of them would go home, get up the next morning and go back to work. The bluff and bluster was temporarily forgotten, or packed away until it was turned loose again by a few beers with friends.

What Hooky Dewclaw didn't realize was that, while Shaky may have complained about working for Stubby Booker, he wasn't about to knowingly betray his boss. In fact, Shaky was pretty close with his boss, closer than most. He managed the trucks, had a good idea of what went where and even ran the show to some extent while Stubby was in jail. In return for his confidence and discretion, Booker opened the door to his private dealings just a crack, letting him catch a glimpse of the inner workings of the business. And he'd been compensated accordingly.

They were close enough, in fact, that Booker had given him strict instructions if anything should happen: keep the business running as usual, but make sure you settle the score. He'd even given Shaky an update the day he was released on bail.

"I don't know what's gonna happen next, but if they come after me, things are gonna get messy," Booker had said. "And it just might be you that has to clean up the mess. Bring in Merle and Jake, and do what you have to do. But be careful, be smart and take your time. Don't just go off half-cocked and make a bunch more trouble. These things have a way of getting out of control, and that doesn't help anyone. Cover your ass, keep your head down and stay out of the way of the cops."

As instructed, Shaky had already called a Montreal number from a phone booth in the village. Let them know that things were going to be on hold for a few days. The boss was missing... *stay tuned.*

"Okay," came the one-word answer on the other end.

In the garage outside the office, he heard the familiar drag of Merle's combat boots shuffling across the concrete floor. He was light on his feet when he had to be, like when he tossed that Molotov cocktail onto the porch of that separatist's house in Brigham last year. He sure as hell didn't drag his feet up the driveway then. But when it came to just walking about, Merle seemed physically incapable of lifting his feet. Jake always wore running shoes, winter or summer, and Shaky never seemed to hear him coming. Like now, when he soundlessly stepped into the office just ahead of Merle.

The three men had been in "People for an English-Speaking Quebec" together, until Colonel Wright turned himself in and everything kind of fell apart. But even though the PESQ was no more, Shaky, Jake and Merle stuck together, keeping their combat skills sharp and their assault rifles polished and ready. They'd even gone on a few weekend "hunting" trips, bringing along their contraband Belgian-made FN assault rifles.

Jake and Merle already knew what had happened. They'd been summoned, and knew things were about to get deadly serious.

"No driving tonight boys," Shaky said. "Looks like we've got some shit to figure out. I have no fucking idea what's going on, but we've got to figure out what's next. Stubby's out there, but we don't know if he's dead or alive. If he's alive, we gotta find him. If he's dead, we're gonna have to settle the score."

"What about the cops?" Merle asked.

"They're doing their thing. I don't know, maybe they think he skipped bail, trashed his house and took off," Shaky said, reaching for another cigarette with nicotine-stained fingers. "I can tell you, there's no way he'd have done that. And the house is fucking wrecked. There must have been a hell of a fight. I looked around, but there's not much to go on."

As the last of the daylight set fire to the sky in the west, the three men gathered around the Canadian Club altar and drove the fall chill out of Stubby Booker's office by filling it up with cigarette smoke and bad ideas. Eventually the bad ideas got better and, ultimately, the early seed of a plan began to germinate. Regardless of what stage of growth the plan was in, there was always one common thread:

They had to get even.

21

Bound

Stubby Booker didn't move when he first came to, choosing instead to take a moment to glance furtively around the small room, the polished pan of the sugar arch catching glints of sunlight from cracks in the wall. The side of his head ached, and the memory of the baseball bat returned to him. He could feel the pressure of the swelling, and one eye was nearly closed. The room seemed empty, so he sat up. His hands and feet were in chains, similar to the ones he'd worn when he was brought to jail. At least his hands were in front of him, and he could get up and shuffle around.

He shivered in the dim. Luckily, he'd been sleeping with his pants on, a habit he'd picked up from years of always being on guard. His white tee shirt, spattered with blood, didn't provide much warmth, and his bare feet were freezing cold. He reached instinctively for the folding knife he always carried in his front pocket. Gone.

Shit, shit, shit. *This wasn't good.*

If only he hadn't hidden his guns. He'd squirreled them away after he was first released on bail, knowing that nothing got bail conditions revoked like a spot check that turned up firearms. So, when those bastards smashed their way into his house, all he had was a length of pipe at hand. He remembered a handgun in his face at one point, but that wasn't about to stop him. The pipe came up and the gun went down. A seasoned fighter, he gave as good as he got at first. He landed a few solid blows and was pretty sure that he broke someone's knee, but that fucking red-headed bastard moved like a weasel. All of a sudden, the lights were out.

He had a faint memory of being in the trunk of a car bouncing around on rough roads, unable to move. After passing out again there was the vague recall of being dragged out of the trunk. Now fully awake, he realized that he was a prisoner. Whose prisoner exactly, he wasn't quite sure, but he figured it was probably someone connected to the Irish.

Stubby Booker and the Irish had been working the border alongside each other for years now, more or less at peace. Back in the day, when he worked with Slippers, the Irish had leaned on these hayseed country smugglers pretty heavily. But once that dirty cop McConnell was taken care of and Slippers was dead, he'd come to an agreement with Charlie McKiernan: stay out of each other's way, nobody else gets hurt and we all make a living. Career people like Stubby and McKiernan didn't seek out violence. Violence drew attention, and attention was bad for business. Violence was just a tool, to be used as needed.

The removal of McConnell also helped Stubby build ties with the Italians, which really paid off once the initial police investigation died down. Avoiding jail time for killing a cop raised his esteem in the eyes of the mafia, and working for the Italians gave him some backup against the Irish. Stubby kept an eye on Ted, and Ted kept an eye on Stubby, but, by all accounts, Ted just wanted to do his business for the Irish and be left alone. And that's why this was all so baffling. Peaceful coexistence had worked well over the past two decades, and this sort of thing definitely wasn't Ted's style.

"I guess that's all in the shitter now," he mumbled quietly, the sound of his own voice surprising him. He reminded himself to keep quiet, in case someone was outside, waiting for him to wake up so they could come in and dole out another beating. Better to stay quiet and buy some time to figure out what to do next before meeting his captors.

The same feeling of tiredness he had when he was sitting in his jail cell returned to him again. All he wanted these days was to have enough money to retire and not have to worry every time a strange car pulled into the yard. A simple life. And, yet, ever since that Rogers kid showed up, his life had been one complication after another. Not the kid's fault, just shit going off the rails.

That wasn't all quite true, and he knew it. Sure, he was tired of all the BS, but he was also self-aware enough to know that he was addicted to the adrenaline rush of landing deals, moving outside the law and getting away with it. His ability to avoid a criminal conviction all these years was a point of pride and proof that he was smarter than most, despite his fourth-grade education and shotgun-shack upbringing. But he was also smart enough to know that his considerable luck would eventually run out. Hell, maybe it just had.

Truth be told, Stubby wasn't even sure he could handle the quiet life he daydreamed about in those low moments. He hadn't been fishing in years, and while the bucolic life of a beef farmer sounded nice, he also knew that it was a lot of work for not much pay. What would happen if he fell out of love with this idyllic new life? Would he just backslide into his old habits?

Stubby shook off the melancholy, knowing there were more pressing matters at hand. To achieve the dream of retiring, in whatever form he could live with, he had to deal with his current circumstance. He quietly moved around the small sugar shack, listening for movement outside while looking for keys (no such luck), tools or anything that could be used as a weapon or a means of escape. He gently tugged at the big sliding door, knowing full well that it would be locked, then scanned around for any alternate ways out. Anything to give him an inkling on how to puzzle - or fight - his way to freedom.

There was only one source of light in the sugar shack: a small, high, crooked window that looked out onto the maples, which obscured any points of reference on the horizon. He craned his neck to look out the window and couldn't see anyone. Climbing through this thing wasn't an option he wanted to entertain, especially with chained hands and feet. He'd likely get caught up in the frame and would be trapped there until his captors returned.

There was a trap door in a far corner, but it was too small to function as an escape route. Most likely it connected to the holding tank room, where sap would be piped in for boiling. Maple syrup season was a long way off, and people usually didn't set foot in their sugar shacks during the other eleven months of the year. Once the pans and buckets were washed and the woodshed on the side was filled for next year, that was it. This place could belong to anyone. The real owner likely had no idea of what was going on. Hell, his kidnappers could leave him here and he'd starve to death, with no one to find his body until next spring when the sap began to run.

The thought gave him a sharp shot of adrenaline, and the fear that started running through his veins like electrical fire brought him fully awake. He looked away from the window, choosing instead to stare at the darkest corner of the room until his pupils adjusted. In the dim light he spotted his boots and a jacket on the floor, probably pulled from the peg by the door on the way out. In the coat pocket was a single Old Port cigar. Crushed, but salvageable. No lighter, though. *Shit.* He sure could use a smoke right now.

He contemplated his chains. Not police-issue manacles, but rather lengths of dog chain, bound with bolts. Holding his wrists to the window, he could see they were bound tight, the bolt threads mashed to keep them in place. There was no way out of them unless he did some serious damage to his hands. The same shackles were on his feet.

He quietly paced the shack again, memorizing its features, searching for anything that could give him an edge. Counting the paces from corner to corner so he could find his way around in the dark. He knew it was probably futile, but it beat doing nothing.

That's when it struck him: matches! You could usually find

a box of wooden matches in a sugar shack somewhere. *Bingo!* He spied one box of "strike anywhere" kitchen matches, nearly full, resting on a beam near the door. He took most of them out and put a few in his shirt pocket, and then stowed the rest just inside the cast-iron door of the sugar arch. If his captors looked, they'd find the box of matches, but not all of them. They'd have no clue about his secret stash. Any advantage... that's what it was all about.

His aching head suddenly overwhelmed him. Feeling unsteady on his feet, he pitched forward, chains rattling as he dropped down onto a block of wood by the wall. The room began to spin, and a few minutes later he threw up into the wood dust on the floor. Clearing the spit from his mouth, he realized he must have a concussion. The tired feeling returned and he tried to fight it off.

Then he turned to his oldest friend: anger. If anything was going to get him out of this, it would be brutal, controlled anger. When the opportunity came up, and he knew it would, anger would give him all the impetus he needed to fight, to escape and to avenge.

22

Lonely

Jen switched off the black and white Zenith, the screen silently retreating to a single white dot before fading to dark grey. It was 11 p.m. on a Wednesday, and Dave still wasn't home from work. *Again.* It wasn't a deadline night, and he'd assured her that he'd be home at a decent hour. But he still wasn't back. *Again.*

Things always seemed to come up with Dave. Town council meetings ran late, important calls never came, fires took longer than expected to get under control...both figuratively and literally. And whenever he promised that he was "just going for a drink" and "he'd be home soon," time became a vague concept. One hour became three, which translated into who knows how many drinks. He'd come wandering in, looking vaguely sheepish and vaguely drunk. Or, if he was really drunk, he wouldn't look sheepish at all.

She busied herself in the kitchen, wiping down the faux-marble counters and the chrome-trimmed melamine kitchen table and then emptying the wire dish rack by the sink. King nudged her leg, reminding her right on schedule that it was time to go out. She grabbed the leash from the hook by the door, and he began the ritual dance of excitement that preceded every outing.

Over the last year, Jen had become used to Dave being gone at odd hours. That was part of his job, and she expected it, but there was much more to it lately. Ever since his run-in with Stubby Booker, he'd become distant and detached. He went out with his colleagues more often after work and spoke less to her about his job. Something had happened, but her subtle attempts to get him to open up had been met with gentle, but firm, resistance. Whatever he was going through, he was going it alone.

The drinking thing had been building up more and more lately. At first there just seemed to be more beer around than usual, no big deal. But, over time, Dave's beverage of choice seemed to join them for every occasion, evolving from a few on a quiet Saturday night in front of the TV to Wednesday evening with supper. Or Thursday. Then, pretty much every day after work. And this didn't even include his increasingly-frequent stops at the bar on the way home.

And then there was that Saturday a couple of weeks back, when they were having dinner at her mother's place in the city and Dave was drinking wine. He'd always hated wine, but he drank most of the bottle, while Jen and her mom contented themselves with a single glass each. He then rooted through the cabinet next to the stove, finding the last precious few ounces of gin in the house. As Jen's mother looked at her, both women acknowledged the moment without a word.

Yes, Jen had become one of *those* women, the ones who silently looked on while their husbands got drunk, acted badly and slept it off the next day. The ones who quietly cleaned up the messes and apologized for the bad behaviour of their mates. She'd become one of those quietly-suffering women that she'd been so critical of in the past.

Be careful what you look down upon, 'cuz it could very well become you, she thought. Life had a way of imposing a certain humility on you.

Pulling on a sweater against the evening chill, she brought King out for their regular nighttime walk up along Laroque Street, onto Royale and back down Decarie. Every few feet, King stopped to sniff the latest markings of the neighbourhood dogs. Having nothing to get home to, Jen let King take his time.

With Dave being more physically and emotionally distant from her, Jen and King had developed a stronger bond over the last year. This was made stronger still by the attack at the house last fall in Brigham. Jen put up a solid fight, just managing to get the door open to turn King loose on her attacker. She was left with a few bruises, but the man lost an eye and got a serious bite to the crotch. Ever since that fateful night, King was never far away when she was home, and while Jen had largely gotten over the shock of the assault, she found comfort in knowing where he was. And when she answered the door, she always made sure he was nearby. The mere sound of the doorbell would prompt a solid bark from King, and a jolt of fear from Jen. As she continued to try to deal with her own trauma, King had become a major source of emotional support. Dave wasn't opening up, so in response, neither was she.

It had become a lonely life. She'd developed a small network of friends through her work at the library and maintained a connection to her core group of close friends in the city through occasional long-distance phone calls and increasingly-rare visits to Montreal. But money was tight, and long-distance calls expensive, so the conversations were kept short, with little opportunity to open up naturally about the problematic areas of her life. Always guarded by nature, Jen wasn't about to lay out her problems for perusal by people she didn't know well.

There was also the fact that her life had become so different from that of her city friends. Not so much on the surface, but beneath the skin. Changes in pace, in energy, in financial success. In things she couldn't quite put her finger on.

Dave had always been her confidant, especially after their marriage. Shared experiences, values and a life-vision made it easier to open up, and this usually came with an undercurrent of fun-loving compassion. With Dave she could laugh off her problems, the mirth never coming at one or the other's expense, but more at the absurdities of modern living. Of realizing that the miracle of life brought with it an endless array of colours and textures.

Having known and lived in that beauty, she felt the present lack of connection much more keenly.

As Jen turned back onto Decarie, she spotted a parked police cruiser with the lights off sitting in front of her house, the silhouette of the rooftop flashers visible under the streetlight. A closer look revealed that it wasn't a blue and white Cowansville town cop car, but a Sûreté du Québec cruiser, its bright yellow doors standing out in the dim of the night. Approaching closer, she saw two uniformed police officers at her door. That familiar electrical charge snapped through her system before she even understood what she'd seen. She broke into a run, King at her side.

"What's going on?" Jen said to the backs of the two men standing at her door. She choked back fear, hoping against hope that this was nothing serious.

"Mrs. Jennifer Rogers?" one of the men asked as they turned.

"Yes, that's me," she said.

"Ma'am, we're trying to find your husband, Mr. David Rogers."

"He hasn't come home from work yet," she answered, struggling to keep the initial rising sense of panic tamped down. It pulled her core tight and made it a fight to breathe.

The two officers glanced at each other. "Can we come inside please?" said the taller of the two officers.

Jen escorted the two men in, King sniffing intently at their feet, his leash dragging on the floor. She let the dog loose, and he continued his inspection of these two intruders, forcing the tall officer to push him away as he tried to sniff his crotch. Jen first offered them a seat at the kitchen table and then coffee, which they politely declined.

"Ma'am, earlier this evening we found your husband's car on Adamsville Road. Apparently his vehicle went off the road and hit a tree."

"That's the road he takes home from work."

"Well, the problem is, ma'am, that we haven't found your husband. The car was pretty badly damaged, but there was no one inside."

Jen felt the earth shift underfoot. Her bottom lip quivered, and she gripped the edge of the table to steady herself.

"*Where is he?*"

"This is what we're trying to establish," the shorter of the two men said. "We're searching the area around where we found the car. It's possible he got out and wandered off, or maybe someone picked him up. That's why we came here, to see if he'd been brought home."

"No, I haven't seen him. He works at the *Granby Leader-Mail*...he should have been home by now. He should have been home a few hours ago."

Jen had been raised to always maintain a certain dignity, no matter how undignified the circumstances, but she fought to keep it together in this moment. The waves of panic were building exponentially. 'Tamp those feelings down,' she coaxed herself. 'Don't indulge the fear. Deal with the moment. There'll be time to unpack the emotions later.'

The police proceeded to ask a number of questions about Dave, everything from his driving habits to his personal history. Were there any problems in the marriage? Did he have any enemies? Was there a place he might go to if he was in a crisis?

Jen answered their questions as relevant to the situation as possible: I.E. there were no problems with their marriage and Dave had no enemies. She also told the police that they weren't from the area, so there was really no other place where he'd go. After giving the cops a full physical description, she went in search of a photo. The one she found showed a slightly-dirty Dave sitting on the ground next to a car, the wheel off and the drum brakes exposed. He was mugging for the camera with a goofy grin on his face. Jen idly noted that it was summer time in that picture, a simpler, more carefree time before everything went sideways. The sense shock was settling in now, doing its part to keep her feelings at bay.

The taller officer asked to use the phone to call the SQ offices in nearby Dunham. Once connected, he spoke quietly in French, but Jen understood everything he was saying. The gist was that Dave Rogers is missing, they don't know why, they have a description and they need to start searching for him immediately because he may be injured.

* * *

On the Adamsville Road, just north of the intersection of Racine Road, a pair of accident scene specialists and a tow truck operator had been examining the remains of the Vauxhall, which had been badly smashed against a large maple. The car was dragged from its resting place by the tow truck, revealing deep gashes in the bark. Despite this damage, it was pretty clear that the tree had won this battle and the Vauxhall had driven its last mile.

The officers examined the wreck again, surveying the damage to the front end, scanning the ground with flashlights for anything of interest. Nothing but broken glass and bits of chrome.

"He, or she, was lucky that the impact was mostly on the passenger side," one of the officers said, shining his police-issue flashlight around the interior. "Stinks like beer, so either they were drinking, or they were bringing something home. Kinda hard to tell, 'cuz there's broken glass everywhere in here. It's like a bomb went off."

"I think there's a bit of blood here too," the other cop said, training his flashlight on the dash. "So wherever they are, they're probably injured. Maybe the driver caught a ride to the hospital or something."

The driver's door was still open, much as they'd found it. There was also a deep crease down the driver's front fender. The tree hadn't caused it, and there didn't seem to be anything in the surroundings that had hit that side during the crash. He called his colleague over, shining the light on the fender and the two men crouched down to take a closer look.

"Might be a long shot, but unless that was already there, it looks to me like he was run off the road," he said, assuming it was most likely a man at the wheel. "Given the skid marks, we know he didn't hit that tree because he wanted to."

"We'll take another look at it in the morning when we can see better," the other cop said. "Also have another look at the crash site, just to make sure we didn't miss anything."

The officers radioed back to headquarters and asked the dispatcher to run the licence plate to get an idea of who owned the car and where they lived, and also check with the hospitals in Cowansville and Granby to see if an accident victim had turned up. Maybe he just went home, though that seemed unlikely.

As the tow truck pulled away with the Vauxhall winched up behind it, the two police officers played their flashlights over the scene one last time before heading back to the office. It was time to write up the report on what would normally be a simple crash. But this one had one crucial difference:

Where in hell was the driver?

23

Chains

Wednesday at work was very quiet, as Wednesdays usually were, and there was no news from the cops on the still-missing Stubby Booker. I had a couple of days before we put out the weekend paper, so I wasn't too worried. Well, no more than the usual waves of paranoia and panic.

To be honest, I was kind of hoping Stubby would be found dead somewhere. Yeah, I know it's not nice to wish someone dead, but hearing this would put a lot of my personal demons to rest. Thoughts of missing disgraced cops, a certain murder that I was an accessory to and even a few family secrets could all be tucked away for no one else to see. Just me and Jen, getting on with our lives while those memories stayed in a tiny box at the back of a closet somewhere. Maybe, once I got a better job at a bigger paper that wasn't rife with rumours of wrack and ruin, we'd find a nicer home and all of these terrible memories could get left out with the trash during the move.

Who knows, maybe my dad would start talking to me again. Or maybe I'd finally be able to get a decent night's sleep for a change. Sorry, but it would be a delightful change of pace if Booker's body turned up somewhere.

But, having seen the violence that goes along with creating a dead body, the whole idea made me feel kind of guilty, and a little bit sick. Even if he really did deserve it. Yes, for some strange reason I felt a bit of sympathy for the devil.

Tonight, the plan was to get home at a decent hour, with my only stop being the little store across the road from work to pick up a six-pack of 50. I'd drink the one or two I already had in the car on the way home, and have another three or four more at home. That way I'd look like a vaguely-responsible drinker to

Jen, but, on the inside, I'd be numbed out just enough to get a decent night's sleep.

Have a nice supper, watch TV, walk the dog, maybe get laid... the possibilities were endless. A little after 6 p.m. I bid my farewells and headed out the door.

"What are you leaving for?" Harry Bankroft said. "It only just got dark out."

"I figured nine hours was enough for today," I said. "So, I'm just gonna turn things over to your capable hands."

With the newly-acquired six-pack in the back seat and a freshly-opened bottle nestled between my legs, I turned onto St. Charles, heading south. As I passed the old red brick Imperial Tobacco building and headed out of town towards Adamsville, I noticed a car close behind me. Nothing unusual, but the vehicle had the same headlight pattern as a police cruiser and here I was with an open beer in my lap. Must be a Ford LTD. Well, at least my little shitbox Vauxhall wasn't the sort of thing to attract attention. The exhaust was good and the lights all worked, so as long as I stayed within the speed limit, he shouldn't have a reason to pull me over. The last thing I needed now was a fine for drinking and driving.

The car kept following me outside the Granby town limit. 'Probably not a cop,' I reasoned, relaxing a little. It was much more likely that he was just some other random schmuck like me, heading home after a long day at work. As we hit the autoroute overpass, his tailgating was starting to get on my nerves, so I eased off on the gas to give him the chance to pass me on a straight stretch.

But he just stayed there, right up tight. Now out in the country, I considered my options: either speed up and pull away, or pull over to the shoulder and let him by. Then I could enjoy my beers on the drive home in relative peace and quiet.

Before I could decide, he pulled out to pass just as we hit a straight section. *Good, go ahead*, I thought. Pulling alongside, a flashlight appeared in the window of the LTD, glaring right in my face, causing me to lose half of my field of vision. *What the hell?*

The next thing I knew, the driver veered into me and the bumper of the LTD crushed into my front fender, crumpling it. I hit the brakes, saw the tree and then plunged into darkness.

I have a vague recollection of being dragged out of the car, seeing faces swimming before me in confusion. I don't recall feeling anything, but the side of my face was wet, struck cold in the cool night air. This brought me awake, but only for a brief moment. Then nothingness.

When I came to it was total darkness. Was I blind? Where was I? It took me a few seconds to figure it out. I was in the trunk of a car with something over my head.

The first thing I learned about being locked in the trunk of a car is that there's not nearly as much room in there as you'd think, even in a big boat like an LTD. I was on my side, with my shoulder rubbing against the trunk lid. I tried to stretch, to feel out the space in the darkness, but there wasn't much space to feel. I was pretty much stuck in the fetal position and the bag on my head was tied tight. I could still breathe, but every time I swallowed I could feel the rope cutting into my throat. It was old burlap, probably a feed bag, judging from the dust that made me cough and gasp.

I'm not one of those guys who gets short of breath in a small room. I don't like it, but I can usually keep calm and do what I need to do while confined to a small space.

But not this time. This time I flat-out panicked. My nightmares, everything I was afraid of, washed over me in that instant. I thrashed around, screaming for help, but that just made the rope holding the bag dig even further into my neck. Strange how people will scream for help, even when they logically know that all the screaming in the world won't save them. But when logic vanishes and, on some level, screaming beats doing nothing.

"Shut the fuck up back there!" came a voice from up front. "Don't make me pull over and put the boots to you!"

"What's going on?" I replied. "What are you doing?"

"You just wait and see. In the meantime, enjoy the ride."

I could hear two men laughing. One louder than the other, riding the high of an adrenaline rush. The other, quieter, in control.

My nose was messed up, probably bleeding from the wet I could feel on my face. I must have bashed it on the steering wheel in the crash. Lucky, since I'd be spitting out broken teeth right now if the impact was an inch lower. One hand felt like I'd punched a wall, and there was something up with my left knee.

It suddenly struck me that I should be trying to count stops, turns and where we sped up and slowed down in an effort to figure out where we were going. But I lost track almost immediately, and besides, I had no idea how long they'd been driving before I came to. So I focused more on trying to determine what shape I was in, and what these guys wanted to do with me. The feeling that I was pretty much screwed was settling in.

After what felt like hours, the car slowed down and turned sharply to the left. Then things got really rough, like we were driving on farmland. I tried to guess where we might be, but it was pointless. Eventually the LTD pulled to a stop and the engine shut off.

I heard the key, and the trunk popped open. A big flashlight was in my face, its light visible through the fabric of the bag. The rope came off, followed by the bag, but with the light shining in my eyes I couldn't see a thing. One of them reached in, grabbed me by the arm and pulled me out of the trunk with apparent ease. My balance failed, I fell face-first onto the ground and now I could feel the soft dirt sticking to the drying blood on my face.

"You might want to clean that up," joked the other man, a tall, skinny guy holding the flashlight. "Here, let me help you."

That's when he dumped some cold, odd-smelling water onto my head. I screamed, convinced that he'd just dumped something toxic on me and was trying to kill me outright then and there. For a second I thought he'd just poured gas on me and was intending to set me on fire. Even though I was certain that these strangers were on the verge of murdering me and I was close to a total meltdown panic, I just looked up and did my best to appear calm.

Don't give them the satisfaction. Don't let them see you squirm. I was holding on during this internal battle for control, but just barely.

The other man, the one who'd pulled me out of the trunk, was about my height, maybe a bit bigger. I still couldn't see his face for the water in my eyes and the darkness all around, but it was clear from his grip on my arm that he wasn't to be messed with lightly. The handgun he stuck in my face captivated my attention and sealed the deal.

"Here's what's going to happen," he said. "We're going to put you in here for a bit. Don't try to get away, because you won't be able to. You try to leave, we kill you. And then we'll kill your wife. Maybe your dog, too."

"You leave my wife out of this!" I said, trying to sound stronger than I felt.

"I've seen your wife. She's cute. Maybe I'll just move in to comfort the grieving widow," the gunman said. The skinny guy, who walked with a bit of a limp, laughed.

And with that, the skinny guy chained my wrists, snapping a padlock into place. Then, with the other man holding the chain, he bent down and put links around my feet, giving me just enough length so I could take small steps.

"Shuffle your ass over this way," the one with the gun said. "Right, over, *here!*"

And with that, he shoved me head-first into a door, my bloodied nose and face taking the brunt. The door didn't open, and I just stood there, my face smashed up against the splintered hemlock.

"Oh, sorry about that," he laughed. "Guess I'd better open it first."

I heard the click of the lock and felt his hand tense on my back before the shove. I managed to twist slightly, catching the door with my shoulder this time. The effort cost me my balance, and I fell onto the dirt floor.

"Now you girls keep each other company until we get back," the man said. "Then we'll take care of you properly."

With that, the door slammed shut, and I was in complete darkness. There was nothing to be seen in the night, just a voice. A hauntingly familiar voice accompanied by a deep growl.

"Who the fuck is there?"

Stubby Booker.

24

Searching

Harry Bankroft didn't like 6 a.m. phone calls, especially when he'd only gotten to bed a few hours earlier. Woken from a deep sleep, he growled unintelligibly into the receiver as he picked it up.

"Hi, Harry, it's Jen. I'm so sorry to bother you..."

"What's going on?" came his brief reply.

"Did you see Dave last night?"

"Only at work."

"He never came home, and the cops came by late last night to tell me that they'd found his car, but he wasn't around. The car is pretty badly wrecked," Harry could easily detect the palpable anxiety in Jen's voice bleeding through the line. "Harry, Dave's missing, and I don't know what's going on!"

"Oh, Jesus," Harry muttered, the cobwebs clearing from his head. "Did the cops tell you anything?"

"No, only that they found his car on the Adamsville Road, smashed into a tree. They couldn't find the driver, and thought that maybe he'd caught a ride home, or been picked up and taken to the hospital. But, so far... nothing. The cops told me to stay close to the phone, and then they left."

Harry had only met Jen a few times over the last year, but he knew she was typically level-headed and calm by nature. The woman he was talking to now was on the cusp of hysteria, with her breathing coming in uneven rasps. He exhaled deeply and contemplated the floor between his feet.

"Okay, I'll be by in a bit. When I get there, I'll call the cops. The night shift will be done by then and maybe the duty officer can let us know what's going on. In the meantime, stay off the phone just in case they try to call. I'm sure that he's fine and he'll turn up somewhere. People don't just vanish," he said, adding, "The fact he's not there is probably a good thing. He was well enough to leave, so he's probably okay."

Even though he really didn't feel that last bit, it was the only reassuring thing he could think of in the moment.

Pouring himself a cup of instant coffee, Harry considered the situation. As far as he could tell, nothing particularly unusual had happened recently. Sure, Dave had hesitated to write up the story about the body found on Booker's farm, but beyond that, nothing particularly out of the ordinary was going on. At one point he'd been forced to set the boy straight, but he'd gone on to cover the bail hearing and Booker's disappearance without complaint. Harry quickly ran through the stories Dave had recently worked on in his mind. No, nothing too controversial, nothing to piss someone off. Certainly nothing to merit an attempt on his life.

Did the dummy drink too much, crash his car and stagger off into the woods or something? Possibly. Did he spontaneously decide to run away from his wife, his job? Unlikely. Dave seemed every bit the devoted husband and dedicated employee, a guy who showed up every day and had become a solid reporter in the process. He didn't know much about Dave's personal life, except bits and pieces picked up from office banter. No red flags there.

Harry picked up the phone again and called Rachel Porter, who had a phenomenal ability to dig for information. She was, without a doubt, the best reporter he'd ever worked with. Contrary to the common mantra that you "don't hire a woman to do a man's job," he'd ignored that supposed "wisdom," and it had paid off handsomely. Bankroft figured he could get her to work the phones while he went to check in on Jen.

A sharp chill met him as he stepped out his front door and onto Young Street. It had been cold last night, on the edge of the first frost. His Austin Mini, flecked with brown rust, coughed to life. He put the heater on, knowing that it would do little more than keep the windshield clear. He pulled down to the corner, turning right onto Main Street, then left onto St. Charles and then out towards the country. His head was clear now, and he watched the sides of the road carefully, looking for any signs of where the accident would have been.

He needn't have worried. Coming onto a straightaway, he could see a Sûreté du Québec cruiser parked by the side of the road. As he pulled up, he could clearly see a deep gash taken out of the bark of a large maple tree. He stopped his car and got out. Two uniformed officers were off the road in the woods, searching the scene.

"Is this where the accident was last night?" he said in French.

"Yes," one of the cops said. "We're just examining the scene."

Harry explained that he worked for the *Granby Liar*, the driver might have been one of his employees, and he was on his way to console the wife. Did they have any information he could pass on to her?

"We really don't have much right now," one of the cops replied. "It's like the Rapture or something. The car was smashed but the driver just vanished."

"You've got nothing?"

"Believe me, if we had something, I'd tell you. There's really not much of anything here. We're going to the impound lot after to look at the car. Check in with the duty officer later; maybe we'll have something by then."

As Harry Bankroft pulled away, he felt skeptical that the duty officer would have anything for him. Could Dave Rogers have been kidnapped?

Kidnapping was never far from mind these days. The "October Crisis," sparked by the abductions of James Cross and Pierre Laporte, had occurred only a half-dozen years earlier. More recently there'd been a number of high-profile kidnappings, like the spectacular disappearance and reappearance of newspaper heiress Patty Hearst. Popular police television shows all featured kidnappings, typically with the victim tied up in an apartment somewhere while the bad guys waited for a suitcase of cash to be dropped off by a phone booth somewhere.

To Harry it seemed very unlikely. Kidnappings were usually meant to either extract money from people or raise awareness for some political cause. As far as he could tell, there wasn't much money to be found in Dave's family and, given his job at a low-profile newspaper on the verge of bankruptcy, the man was far from influential or wealthy.

No, he told himself, Rogers had most likely been picked up by someone, taken to the hospital and the cops just hadn't figured that out yet.

He was still thinking that as he pulled up outside the Decarie St. duplex in Cowansville. Maybe in the time he'd been on the road, there'd been some news. That thought evaporated as soon as he saw Jen at the door, her expression telling him that nothing had changed.

* * *

Rachel hated being woken up. Like many reporters, one of the things that attracted her to the profession was the fact that news had to happen before you covered it. That usually meant not getting up too early. Fires and other disasters were the exception, but those provided enough excitement to override the feeling of futile frustration that came with the early morning call.

She contemplated the situation while enjoying her morning cigarette and waiting for the percolator to brew up that precious first batch of coffee. Lots of people were drinking instant these days, but she figured coffee was important enough to wait a bit longer and get something decent.

Admittedly, Dave was a little bit off lately. Nothing he specifically said or did, he just seemed agitated. And then there was that day recently when he practically ran out of the office and came back an hour later with his hair all messed up and looking like he had the flu or something.

Come to think of it, he hadn't been looking very well for awhile now. His colour was off, and he looked like he'd lost even more weight, despite always leaning on the skinny side.

The overhead fluorescent lighting of the office did him no favours, further accentuating the dark circles under his eyes.

Even though she'd noticed these things, she stopped short of talking to him about it or asking if something was going on. Rachel was great at spotting devils hiding in the details, a skill that served her well as a reporter. She noticed things that her colleagues would overlook, giving her stories a depth that others lacked.

She brought herself back to the moment, looking over to see the coffee burbling in the percolator's glass carafe. A quick cup, a piece of toast and then off to work. She'd be the first one in the office this morning. It was going to be a long day.

* * *

Shaky didn't have much to go on. His boss was missing, and it probably had something to do with all of this current business around the border. Discussions with Merle and Jake had gone on for hours, with every thread of conversation veering into the weeds regarding what they'd do once they "got their hands on the bastards." But the fact that they had no clue who they were dealing with, or where Stubby's kidnappers were, inevitably brought them to a dead end. By the time the bottle of rye was laying on its side, Shaky sent them home to await further instructions.

Shaky already owned a pair of attack dogs, but what he really needed now were bloodhounds. That, it seemed, was up to him.

The one snippet he had to go on was his conversation with Hooky Dewclaw. The chat felt strange at the time, by Shaky reasoned that the beer must have dulled his concerns. Looking back on it, he knew now that Hooky had been grilling him for information. That was too much of a coincidence and it didn't smell right.

He didn't know where Hooky lived, but a couple of calls to some old school buddies put him on track. Turns out, Hooky Dewclaw lived in an apartment over a bar near Bruck Mills in Cowansville.

He didn't bring a gun. There was no way he was going to shoot this guy and make a big scene; it wasn't that kind of a relationship. He'd start with a sit-down conversation, then back it up with something more serious if he didn't get some answers. As such, he decided to bring a blackjack along with him, silently hoping that it wouldn't be necessary.

Sitting in his car outside the building, Shaky tested the weight of the blackjack, shuffling the lead shot in the leather tip under his fingers and feeling the spring in the grip. He hated having to dole out violence, especially on someone like Hooky. He was harmless enough, or so it seemed. Shaky smoked one final cigarette before getting out of the car and making his way across the street to the building. As far as he could tell, there was no formal entrance, except through the bar, which wasn't open yet. But, after poking around for a bit, he discovered a welded steel fire escape bolted to the side of the building which led up to the second floor.

Hooky came to the door on the second knock. From the looks of things, his visitors mainly came up this way. He was dressed in jeans and a t-shirt, with no shoes or socks. Rubbing the sleep from his eyes, he welcomed Shaky in with a smile.

"What are you doing here? How did you know where I lived?" Hooky said.

"I made a few calls," Shaky returned. "Todd let me know where you hang your hat."

"Todd? Man, I haven't seen him in ages," Hooky said. He was on edge now, fully awake and realizing that this wasn't a normal pop-in visit.

"I've got some questions I need answers to. About that friend of yours who was asking about Stubby."

Hooky's face blanched. He reached for his chewing tobacco.

"Look, I don't want no trouble," Hooky said, sitting down at the kitchen table and using a butter knife to carve off a hunk of plug. "He just wanted to know some stuff, and I thought I'd introduce you two. Figured you wanted to quit working for Stubby, and he was looking for someone to haul logs. Maybe if you two got along you could help each other out, is all."

Smelling bullshit from a mile off, Shaky left the conversation hanging for a few moments as he considered his next move. Hooky had lied to him, so whatever came next was his fault. Might as well get to the point.

"So this friend of yours," Shaky began, doing his best to stay calm and keep things quiet. "You think he would have wanted to do something to Stubby?"

"Junior? Naw, I thought it was all just talk," Hooky replied, immediately realizing that he'd just slipped up. He paused and quickly reasoned that his best course of action was to keep going, but try and soften the information as much as he could. "He told me he found out Stubby had something to do with his dad's death. I told him Stubby Booker isn't someone you want to be messing with."

Shaky shot up from his chair, grabbed Hooky's shirt and pinned him against the wall. Neither man was very big, but Shaky had the edge and the adrenaline was making him even more intimidating. Now virtually nose-to-nose with one of Stubby's top people, the typically- passive Hooky was far too scared to put up a fight.

"Now, you look," Shaky said, struggling to keep a quiet, calm voice. "Stubby's missing, and I think your buddy had something to do with it."

He pushed the business end of the blackjack into Hooky Dewclaw's face, which was now a mask of sheer terror. He could smell the chewing tobacco on his breath and see the juice dribbling from the corner of his mouth.

"Missing? Oh Jesus, did he really go and do something? I thought he was just pissed off. I mean, people say stuff like 'I'm going to kill that guy,' or 'that son of a bitch is going to pay' all the time, but they never actually go and do something. I mean, I was pretty loaded when he asked me about Stubby. I figured he was just lettin' off some steam."

"Well, looks like he did a helluva lot more than just let off some steam," Shaky said, letting Hooky go. Clearly he didn't need to put the fear of God into this guy any more than he already had. And besides, his heart wasn't into doling out a beating. At least not yet.

"Your buddy is in big trouble," Shaky continued. "He's gonna wind up dead. Jesus Christ, you don't just go and kidnap Stubby Booker. He's some special kind of stupid if he thinks that's just gonna blow over."

"Look, I don't know much about where this guy is. He's just someone I met at the Quebec House in Frelighsburg a few months back. He's there pretty much every Friday night. We play pool, drink some beers together or watch hockey on Saturdays on the big colour TV. He lives somewhere around there. Drives an old white Ford LTD. I saw him get in a fight once with some guy who was hitting on the barmaid. Demolished the guy in a few seconds."

"Well, I think it's time you introduced us," Shaky said.

"*No, no, no,*" Hooky said, slowly sinking back into his chair. "Shit, *this is not good.*" He was completely oblivious to the fact that he'd swallowed the plug of tobacco.

"Oh, it's gonna happen. The sooner the better. *Make it happen.*"

With that, Shaky grabbed a pencil from his jacket pocket, tore open an empty pack of cigarettes on the table, scribbled a phone number on the inside and then threw it back on the table.

"If I don't hear from you by tonight, I'll be coming back... with some company," he said. "I know we've been friends since we were little kids, Hooky, but this is some serious shit. If you make this happen, you don't have to get hurt."

With that he stormed out of the apartment, the nerves making his legs shake as he walked down the stairs of the fire escape. Between that and his breaths coming in ragged gasps, Shaky was thankful for the steel handrail. As soon as he unlocked the car, he collapsed into the seat, rested his head against the steering wheel and then reached for his cigarettes with shaking, yellowed fingers.

He really wasn't cut out for this.

25

Planning is key

It had been a busy summer for Frank McConnell Junior. When he wasn't occupied on Ted's farm or running the border, he'd been making plans. And really, with the exception of getting caught out by Glen Sutton, things had gone reasonably well.

Once Frank McConnell Junior got his rage under control and the cool settled in, he managed to put a plan together. Learning from the botched armoured car robbery a couple of years ago, he knew that planning would be key. He needed to learn more about Booker, and he also wanted to keep Ted and Diane out of it. So he decided to head for Montreal, to see the man who held the secrets: Charlie McKiernan.

In part, the trip was to confront his boss for concealing the details of his father's life, the organization's connection to him and the circumstances surrounding his death. He daydreamed of grabbing the old man by the shirt collar and screaming at him, but he knew that wouldn't happen. He'd likely have a bullet in him before he even got a good grip on McKiernan. No, there would be time for that another day.

Instead, he went on bended knee, asking for a few minutes to talk privately. Charlie already knew why, having talked to Ted days earlier.

It was grey and overcast when Junior arrived at the nameless tavern, the wind blowing leaves around his feet on the sidewalk. He hitched up his canvas coat to block out the cool air that bore the dampness from the nearby St. Lawrence River. The river, and the concrete of roads and buildings, conspired to make Montreal stiflingly hot and humid in the summer, but cold and damp in the fall and winter.

This part of the world had been his entire universe for most of his life, but now it felt oddly unfamiliar. He made a mental note to go see his mother, but keep what was happening away from her. With everything he'd learned, he knew that if he brought it up, tempers could flare and things would escalate into an argument. She'd want him to leave well enough alone. Besides, other than whatever secrets she carried, it really had nothing to do with her.

The grey overcast outside was palpable in the tavern. It was quiet, with McKiernan standing behind the bar and Ellwood astride a stool with a beer mug sitting in front of him. At the far end of the bar sat another man Junior didn't recognize, probably Ellwood's newest protégé.

The greetings were friendly, with Ellwood stepping off the stool to give his former partner a warm hug, which also included a subtle check for weapons. McKiernan turned on the charm as well.

"Glad to see you, young man," he said. "You're looking good. I guess Diane's been feeding you well. Good cook, that woman."

Charlie went on to tell a short story of how he first met Ted and Diane, winning them over from the competition and becoming friends along the way. How he took them up north fishing a few years back and helped Ted get set up on the farm. There were a few good laughs, which Junior found himself joining in on.

After the informal conversation wrapped up, Ellwood moved over to join the other man, giving Charlie and Junior an opportunity to talk quietly. Charlie lit his pipe, then leaned over, putting his elbows on the bar as he smoked.

"So, I understand you've unearthed the family secret?" McKiernan said. "You have a right to be pissed."

"With all due respect, sir, but what the fuck?" Junior replied. "Here I am working for you all this time, living out in the sticks, and the guy who killed my father was right there. And you guys knew about it all along."

"Look, it wouldn't have done you any good to know that your cop dad worked for us, or that he ended up dead doing business for our organization. I could see that you had a temper, and if that truth came out, I knew that it would ruin you. If you'd found out a few years back, you would have gone off half-cocked and gotten yourself killed. Hell, you still might."

"But why didn't you do anything? Why did you let that bastard Booker get away with murdering my father?"

"Believe me, we tried. Had ourselves a bit of a war once we figured out what happened. Hell, we even took out his right-hand man, this guy named Rogers. But Stubby's a tough sonofabitch, and things got messy. We even tried to blow him up in his truck, and he walked away from it."

"In the end, we came to a truce," McKiernan said, pausing to relight his pipe. "He does his thing, we do ours and that's worked out for most of the last twenty years. Plus, he has the Italians on his side, and we do a lot of business with them. We're not in this so we can run around shooting anyone we don't like. We keep things quiet, and we try to make a living. Hell, you know how things work around here. You might want to get even, but sometimes that's the dumbest possible thing you can do ."

"Well, we have to do something," Junior said, changing tactics in an effort to appeal to McKiernan's business side. "Look, we're already tripping over his guys at the border. There's no place to get across without seeing them, or them seeing us. If we take him out, we can have the whole border down there to ourselves."

"Look, there's only so much we can risk for you to get even. We can't just go down there, guns a-blazing," McKiernan said. "But you're right, things are a little crowded down on the border and I've been talking to Ted about that. Unfortunately, we've got to make do until we get an opportunity. Don't underestimate Stubby; he's a slippery bastard who always seems to be one step ahead."

McKiernan puffed on his pipe, choosing his words carefully.

"I know you don't want to hear it, but we can't be starting a war down there. Not now, there's too much at stake. Most of the cops just want to go to work, hand out a few traffic tickets and go home. They know who the players are, and they leave us alone for the most part. If you stir up trouble, you're likely to land us all on their shit list."

"So we do nothing."

"Sorry, Junior, but that's just the way it has to be."

"C'mon, you gotta let me take this guy out. We'd have the whole border to ourselves!"

"Sounds like a good idea in theory, but trust me, if you try to take him out, we'll have a war on our hands. Booker has lot of friends, connected friends... and more than just the *eyeties*. He knows more about what's going on out there than you can even imagine. Hell, he taught Ted the ropes."

"I can't. I just can't."

"Leave it alone. Sure, you might know a thing or two about leaning on people, but it's a whole other thing to take a life. It changes you. Saves you a special place in hell right here on earth. Some people can handle it, but most can't. Just look at all those old war vets you see drinking themselves to death. They aren't doing it for fun. They're feeding their demons, hoping one day to forget what they've done. Stubby Booker isn't worth doing that to yourself. You won't get the satisfaction you're looking for."

And so, stymied by his boss, Junior began to make his own plans. *Fuck Charlie*, he thought. *Old man's getting soft.* If he took out Booker, then he'd be in line to run the show on the border. Hell, this might even set him up to inherit Charlie's job when the time came.

He needed help, but he also knew that his barroom buddy, Hooky Dewclaw, wasn't the man for the job. He was too gentle, too much of a yokel.

By sheer coincidence, an old acquaintance in the city mentioned that Andy O'Brien was recently released on parole. Junior then spent the next couple of days touring his old haunts, searching for his old armoured car robbery buddy. Junior knew and trusted him, remembering how Andy had kept up his end of the bargain during the robbery and also kept his mouth shut when he was arrested. In fact, O'Brien had spent most of the last three years in prison for his silence. If he helped out, Junior would make sure to reward him well for his loyalty.

Junior knocked on a few doors and managed to track him down. With no job and no money, O'Brien was quick to agree to Junior's plan, which conveniently omitted McKiernan's opposition to the idea. As such, O'Brien saw it as an opportunity to get back into McKiernan's good graces and out of the rut that he was currently in. Before leaving Montreal, O'Brien managed to source a pair of revolvers and a sawed-off shotgun, courtesy of a taxi driver he knew who "found them in the trunk of his car one night."

Junior's anger continued to simmer over the summer. He started by harassing Stubby's drivers whenever the opportunity presented itself. All the while he kept digging, learning about the local legend that was Stubby Booker. Most of the rumours and gossip he encountered turned out to be false or impossible to verify. Whatever information he came across, it all served to justify his vision of Booker as a man who needed to be eliminated. In his mind, Frank was the hero who would rid the world of this evil human being, all while exacting the revenge he so desperately craved.

Frank did a little more digging, snagging some extra tidbits from Hooky, who liked to talk and seemed to know everybody's business. There was a constant stream of rumours, innuendo and bullshit to sift through; all folk tales about the notorious local criminal and his legendary feats of theft, robbery and smuggling.

And then there was some interesting trivia about his former partner, Dave "Slippers" Rogers, whose son now worked as a reporter for the *Granby Liar*. *I bet he knows more than he's letting on,* Junior thought. *I bet that little prick is no better than his dad.*

It doesn't take much to plant the seed of hate. All it takes is a little bit of attention and, in a matter of moments, it will germinate, grow, bloom and ultimately consume like a rampant weed.

* * *

One hot August afternoon, Junior took a trip to the Cowansville Library. A pleasant, attractive blond woman in a floral sundress helped him locate some old *Granby Liars* from around the time when his dad disappeared. He gave her some dates and she came back with a decent stack of time-weathered newsprint.

"Sorry for the dust. These old papers will choke you if you're not careful," she explained before leaving him to it and going on with her day.

Even though the coverage was spotty and incomplete, it didn't take long to glean some information on Sanford Booker and Dave Rogers. There was an article about their arrest and Rogers flipping as a witness against Booker. A few months later, Junior came across a death notice for Dave Rogers, formerly of Dunham, who died accidentally in Montreal, where he'd been working on a construction site.

Then he found a final clipping about Booker being convicted for obstruction of justice. Along with his "business associate," Dave Rogers, he'd been accused of murdering police officer Frank McConnell. But, since there was no body or hard evidence, and Rogers was now dead, the case against Booker fell apart. After all that, Stubby only got two years in a provincial jail. Two measly years for killing a cop... *for killing his father.*

He was hit with a wave of anger and sorrow. Anger at Booker for getting away with murder, and sorrow over never having known his father, the man who should have been his mentor, his role model. The man his mother tried not to talk about, if only to avoid perpetuating a lie that his dad had been a good and honourable man. How do you live up to the image of a man who you'll never really know, never really understand?

"Sir, are you okay?" It was the librarian again. He realized he was shaking in an effort to keep himself wired tight. Like many ginger Irish, the skin between the freckles on his face was glowing red with the effort.

"Yes, I'm fine, ma'am," he replied, collecting himself. "Just dealing with the dust from these newspapers."

"Let me know if there's anything more I can help you with," she said, putting a hand on his shoulder. Pretty smile, he thought, bringing himself back to the present moment. It had been a long time since he'd felt the touch of a woman. One more thing to be longing for. One more thing that would have to wait awhile longer.

But he sure would like to get her name.

* * *

Frank learned about Booker's farm in Brigham by accident one night when he was at the bar under Hooky Dewclaw's place on Leopold Street in Cowansville. The day shift at Bruck Mills had let out, and a bunch of them were getting primed for the weekend by having a few beers after work. Hooky was talking with a guy whose wife worked at the Brigham town hall, and she told her husband about the day she saw a property tax cheque with Booker's name on it. For fifty bucks and a case of smuggled rye, Junior had an address within the week, no questions asked.

His first thought had been to burn the place down. By all accounts, Booker had a flair for torching the competition, so it seemed only fitting. But when he drove by to look at the place, he knew that wouldn't amount to much. The house was a tumbledown affair, with a slew of broken windows and the verandah roof hanging off. The barn wasn't much better. The entire property was little more than a fancy burn pile, and it looked as if no one had lived there for years. He'd probably be doing Booker a favour by setting a match to it.

Then there was the Martin Traynor incident. After learning about this guy and looking him up in the phone book, Frank planned to go to South Bolton, haul him out someplace quiet and then lay a beating on him to send a message to Stubby and maybe draw him out.

But Traynor, suspecting that he was about to be murdered and acting like he had nothing to lose, managed to get his hands on a tire iron while he was locked in the trunk of the LTD. When the trunk opened he came out swinging, caught Junior in the ribs and winded him. He then went for O'Brien, who shot him.

"Aw, you stupid fucker!" O'Brien yelled as he watched Traynor die. "Now look at what you made me do!"

O'Brien turned away, overcome by the immensity of his own actions. He seemed unaware of the finality, the brutality, of taking a life until it was too late.

Frank got to his feet, standing over Traynor, transfixed by the vision of a man's life leaving its body. He heard the death rattle, as the being before him changed from living human being to empty husk. To his surprise, not only did the whole process fascinated him, it also failed to horrify him. He imagined standing over Stubby Booker, witnessing his essence evaporating. It thrilled him to know that the last thing Booker would see is the face of his vengeance.

He decided to dump the body on Stubby's farm to try and stir up some shit and maybe even get him dragged in by the cops. If Booker thought that someone out there knew the secret about his farm, and maybe more, this might rattle his cage a bit. Especially if that someone clearly wasn't afraid to take things to extremes.

Slowly, Frank McConnell Junior focused his anger, assembled the pieces of his plan and then prepared to set it into motion. During this time he kept his eyes open, picking up little scraps of information wherever he could find them. He'd bide his time, and by the end, Stubby Booker would know just who wanted him dead, and why.

Then, when Stubby got arrested, who should make a big deal out of it but Dave Rogers? Front page news. His article even threw in a bunch of stuff about the border problems. All of this made Frank despise Dave Rogers sight unseen. In time, this anger grew his hate exponentially into a blackened, bitter beast, ready to consume all who stood in its way.

Now he had Stubby Booker and the newspaper reporter chained up in a sugar shack. Soon he'd eliminate not just Booker from the face of the earth, but also Dave Rogers, the seed of that father-killing turncoat bastard.

And then, when the moment was right, he'd also exact a little revenge on Charlie McKiernan.

26

Shacked up

"Where am I?" I asked the darkness.
"How the fuck should I know?" came Stubby Booker's reply. "And who the fuck are you?"
Oh no, it is him. No mistaking it.
"You don't recognize my voice?" I said.
"Oh, shit. It's little Dave."
"What's going on?"
"Same answer. I don't know why we're here, or who brought us here. At this moment, I don't know a damned thing more than you."

I heard steps, felt fingers fishing around my neck. *Oh, please, don't let him strangle me.* I recoiled from his touch.
"Calm down, I'm just taking the bag off your head."
The bag came off, and I inhaled deeply. It was the middle of the night, so I still couldn't see a damned thing. Despite the fact that my nose was mangled and my face was likely caked with dried blood, I could still smell the cool, damp air and the rich smell of earth around me.

A match lit up. In the sulphur flare I could see the facial features of Stubby Booker. He looked like he'd been beaten, with the side of his face swollen and one eye nearly shut. Though I'd only ever spoken to him once before, I knew the timbre of his voice. It would be hard to forget.

"So, I wonder why they brought you here," Booker said. "Seems like someone's mad at us."

I sat up, trying to take stock of the situation. The match went out, and the utter darkness didn't help. My arms and legs still worked, although one arm was getting a little stiff. My nose was clearly messed up, my hands and feet were in chains and my mouth tasted like blood and stale beer. I struggled to my feet, feeling dizzy, and tried again to make out my surroundings. Something. Anything. *Nope.* Total darkness.

"Come over here, there's a place you can sit down." An arm fished around and grabbed mine, slowly leading me. "There's a bench here. Have a seat."

"What is this place?"

"It's a sugar shack somewhere, but I don't know where. You can see a bit in the daytime. Just woods outside. I've been here for two days and they haven't brought me anything to eat or drink. I found a pail with some water over in the corner. It's not too bad if you don't stir up the dirt on the bottom."

"Any idea who they are?"

"No idea, kid. I haven't seen or heard anyone since I was left here, except when they came to toss you in. Two guys came and grabbed me from the house. Same ones that nabbed you, I guess. One's a red-headed kid. He looked like someone I'd seen before, but I'm not sure where. The other's a tall, skinny guy. I think he walks with a limp now. He had a gun, but pistols don't work as well in close quarters as people think. Just as likely to shoot yourself as anyone else. You rush a guy at close quarters and it's anybody's guess which one gets the bullet."

"Didn't you have guns? I mean, when they broke into your house."

"No, not this time. Bail conditions, so I was trying to be a good boy. *A fat lotta good that did me.*"

This was my new reality: talk of guns and kidnappings, of cars being run off the road and body parts being smashed. The fact was that my life was genuinely in danger came crashing down on me. I felt sick, like I needed to lie down. In fact, I wanted to lie down and wait for everything to go away, even if that meant never getting up again.

I fumbled with my hands and feet, feeling the chains and the padlocks. I shuffled my feet on the dirt floor.

"Your hands, they chained together with bolts?"

"No, padlocks. Hands and feet."

"Huh, they got fancy with you. They used bolts with the threads mashed over for me. Too cheap for padlocks."

"Lucky me."

I spent the next little while trying to get comfortable; no easy feat when you've just been in a car accident, you're tied up and you can't see a damned thing. The various aches and pains that come with being in a car crash and taking a beating all begin to surface.

"The boiling pan is flipped over, so I tried sleeping on it last night. A stainless-steel mattress is none too comfortable," came Stubby's voice in the dark. "You're better off on that bench or on the floor. Do what you can to keep warm, just don't ask me for a cuddle."

Now that things were calming down, I could feel the night's chill settling in. I was wearing a jean jacket and jeans, but the temperature wasn't much above freezing. I backed myself up against the wall and curled up into a ball. I was exhausted, but sleep refused to come.

I must have eventually drifted off, because the next thing I knew I could see the first signs of daylight coming through the window. Not much, but after awhile the features of the sugar shack began to take shape. It seemed colder now than when I first fell asleep. I was clenched up and didn't dare move, for fear of losing heat. And I really had to take a leak.

A few feet away was Stubby Booker, lying on the floor on an empty feed bag. He was also curled in an unconscious effort to conserve heat. His breathing was ragged, even stopping at times. At one point I wondered if he was still alive. Then came a sudden snort, as the apnea broke and the rhythmic breathing continued.

I felt a sudden wave of self-pity wash over me. Sorrow for coming to work at the *Granby Liar*, for not having a father, for *having* a father, for misleading my wife and for crossing paths with Stubby Booker. Literally everything. I even felt sorry for things that weren't really all that bad, but when you drop into the gully of despair, everything can feel like too much. I could feel the tears welling up. For far too long I was paralyzed by my own misery.

"You'd better get up and move around, or you're gonna freeze there," Stubby said. He'd woken up while I was mired in self-reflection. I quickly choked back my tears, not willing to let him see.

"You stop moving, you die."

He rolled over onto his knees, got to his feet and stretched, pulling his chains taut. He took a couple of steps towards me, looking at my face as I sat up, his dark, bushy eyebrows knitted together.

"Shit, kid, it's hard to recognize you. Your face is covered in blood. You look like something out of *The Exorcist*, or the ghost of your dad come back to haunt me."

"He's too busy haunting me, so you'll have to wait your turn," I said. "You said we had some water?"

"We can't be using that to clean you up, because there's not much there. Not like we're going anywhere fancy. Flake off the dry stuff as best you can, then I'll take a look and see if there's any damage."

I brushed my face tenderly with my hands, feeling scabbed blood sloughing off. Then I probed carefully around my nose. Definitely broken. *Shit.* No other cuts or broken bits, though, and thankfully all my teeth were where I'd left them.

"What in the hell is going on?" I mumbled, mostly to myself.

"Like I said, I have no idea. More importantly, I have no idea how we're going to get out of here. I've been here for almost three days now, and I've gone over every inch of this place and can't figure a way out. Especially not tied up like this or without food or decent water."

"So, the great Stubby Booker gets kidnapped, brought to a cabin in the woods to be starved and I've got a front row seat to watch. Tabernac. Just fucking lovely. Maybe I'll get lucky and freeze to death first."

I was startled by the sound of Stubby snorting with involuntary laughter. I looked over and he seemed to be in the throes of a memory.

"Your father and I nearly froze to death once. Believe it or not, but it was actually worse than this. It was springtime, and we were running some booze across the border. This was a few years before you were born. We had this old broken-down Ford that we'd bought out behind an auction barn. I think the owners had chickens living in it. Didn't have any registration or anything. We stole a licence plate from Honest Homer's scrapyard to put on it for show."

"So Slippers is driving, and we've got empty cases of booze in the back, because glass was in short supply at the time, and we're coming up from Richford. It had been pouring rain by that point for several days and there was lots of snow melt. Anyway, we swing around a curve and suddenly there's no bridge; it's completely washed out. We didn't even see it, we just went nose first into the water and all the bottles in the back seat flew out onto us. Couldn't tell which way was up for a bit and I thought I was going to drown. Then your dad grabbed me and pulled me out of the car. So there we were, south side of the border, soaked in river water, bits of glass in our hair and clothes.

"'*Tabernac.* Just fucking lovely,' your dad said. Sounded just like you did a moment ago." Stubby laughed quietly at the memory.

"We just left the car, waded across the river and started heading north in the middle of the night. It's not like we could call a tow truck or a taxi, not unless we wanted to make a side trip to the local lockup. And, trust me, you don't want to end up in the slam in Vermont. We damned near froze to death on the walk back. By the time we made it up to Butler's farm, the sun was coming up, and I didn't feel cold anymore. I felt nice and warm. Almost laid down to sleep it off, but your dad kept me going. Probably saved my life."

"Butler's? You mean Wilson Butler?"

"Well, it was his dad back then. He didn't take too kindly to having a couple of yahoos showing up at the crack of dawn. He let us warm up for a bit, then had Wilson drive us up to the Rogers' place. Your grandmother was not amused."

He sat back, the recollection fueling a genuine smile. With his two black eyes and swollen face, he looked distorted. The left eye might have been nearly closed, but the right burned with blue-green fire. Guessing from my dad, I estimated that Stubby was around sixty years old, but he looked much older than that. He looked down, strained at his chains, the futility of the act only adding to his aged appearance.

"Your dad taught me to never give up. When his mind was made up, nothing could stop him."

We quietly considering our current circumstances for awhile. I needed to take a leak, so Booker directed me to the pissing corner.

"We don't know how long we're gonna be here, so I don't need you pissing all over the place," he growled. He growled a lot, I noticed.

"Maybe I should piss by the door, so whoever comes in will step in it," I said. There was no response, so I opted for the far corner.

Call of nature answered, I began my own tour of the sugar shack. I knew the basics behind making maple syrup, but this was the first time I'd been in an actual sugar cabin. I wasn't looking at how everything worked, though. More for a way out, or weapons or anything vaguely useful.

"Not much to work with," Stubby said, rising to his feet. "They really cleaned this place out. Usually there's something in these places, tools or whatever. We got sweet fuck-all."

I spotted a large spike on the wall, just above head level. Thinking I could pull it down, I hooked the chains on my wrists over it and lifted myself off the floor. It didn't budge, and the links bit painfully into the back of my hands. Stubby just sat and watched.

"I tried that. I can almost free up a hand, but I'd probably fuck it up pretty bad."

I sat back down, rubbing my sore wrists. I had so many aches and pains now that my body felt like one big uniform mess and this reality settled back into my profound sense of generalized misery. I had to shake this off; as miserable as I'd been in recent months, and as miserable as my current circumstances were, I wasn't done yet. This couldn't be it.

I needed to take my mind off things for a bit. So I did what I do best: I started asking questions.

"So you and my dad were pretty close, eh?"

"Oh, yeah, we got into all kinds of trouble together."

"I hardly even remember him. I wasn't very old when he died."

"Well, at least you have some positive shit to remember about your dad. This is all I have from mine…" He held up the stubs of his thumbs. "He gave me these right before he killed himself, the bastard."

I grimaced a response. "I think I heard about that," I said.

"I didn't have much of a home life. At least not until I started living with my grandmother around age six or seven. Little shack on Russell, just off Dymond in Dunham. Old lady was pretty tough, but if anyone else laid a hand on me there'd be hell to pay. So I spent a lot of time at the Rogers' farm down on Dymond Road. Your grandmother didn't seem to mind having me around, at least as long as I stayed out of trouble."

"I lived there when I was little," I said. "I barely remember her."

"Quite the old bird, that one. She was an old-fashioned farm wife, about three axe handles wide. Worked hard and expected everyone else to do the same. She couldn't stomach nonsense, and she had no problem pointing it out whenever it made an appearance."

Stubby seemed to relax a bit, softened by the memories. I decided to push on, figuring a few stories would at least make for a break from our situation.

"So, your grandmother was pretty tough, eh?"

"Oh, she had that Irish temper. Probably kept my grandfather out in the fields and away from the house. People used to joke that she was too mean to die, and they might have been right since she made it to ninety-five. One time, when I was around ten, she beat me black and blue. I forget what it was for, but I never forgot that beating. So I decided to run away. They found me the next day, sleeping out at the old Hazard cemetery down the road. I think it was your grandfather that found me. Brought me home, saw all the bruises. He went and saw my grandmother, and put the word on her. She must have listened, because I didn't get beat again for quite awhile."

"The Hazard cemetery... that's the one out in the field, right?"

"Yep. I think we're related to them somewhere. No more Hazards around these days. Not many of my people left that I know of."

There was a lull in the conversation, each of us emerging from the past to contemplate the present moment.

"I think after that beating, your grandparents tolerated me a bit more. Your dad and I did everything together. Fishing, hunting, raising hell."

"Folks don't seem to want to tell me too many stories about my dad," I said. "They just look at me and smile."

Stubby grinned at me, the swollen side of his face making for a lopsided leer.

"Kid, you have no idea. Your dad's point of pride was that he got the strap at least once a day at school. One day he dropped a shotgun shell into the potbelly stove and just about blew the thing apart. Scared the shit out of everybody and filled the schoolhouse with smoke. We all had to run outside. There he was with a big grin on his face, right up until the teacher brought that strap down on his hand in front of all of us.

"I think he got a beating when he got home, too," he said after a brief pause. "We got beat for all kinds of things.

"And climb... Jesus, he loved to climb. I never liked heights, but your dad would climb up anywhere. He'd stand up on the peak of the barn roof with zero fear. He was barely a teenager when they got him to climb up and fix the bell in the steeple of the church over at Farnam's Corners. He didn't even have a rope, just him and his old, worn moccasins. That's why they called him Slippers. *Crazy bastard."*

I knew my dad was a bit of a live wire, but it was comforting to hear the old stories.

"Quite the outlaws, you two," I mumbled.

"I'll blame your family for that," Stubby said. "It was pretty much an open secret in Dunham that the Rogers boys brewed their own hooch. And when their crops didn't work out, or milk prices dropped, which was pretty much all the time, they'd try and make some money by sneaking their booze into the States. When Prohibition hit in the Twenties, they did a lot more. Even though grandmother didn't like it, it kept food on the table, so she kept her peace.

"The first time your dad and I went down, we almost got caught. Loaded this poor pony down with a giant pile of booze and walked it through the woods in the middle of the night. Of course we got turned around in the dark and got lost. When we came out, we didn't know where we were. Wandered into some farmer's cornfield and got chased by a big dog. Finally got to the Enosburg speakeasy and unloaded everything just as it was getting light. Not three minutes after we left, a cop driving a Model T stops us and starts asking all kinds of questions about where we're from, why we're out so early and what's up with the pony. We'd never thought of a cover story, so we just made it up on the spot. I forget what we told him, but he eventually let us go."

With that he got up and circled the sugar arch, his leg chains rattling as his eyes kept scanning for a way out. I decided to give the conversation a break and got up to join in the search. There we were, two men in chains, slowly circling the sugar shack like ghostly spectres, trapped by forces we didn't understand.

27

Game on

Shaky spent the next couple of days cruising around Frelighsburg, looking for a white Ford LTD. But, since the car usually only went to Cowansville once a week for supplies and spent most of the time parked out behind Ted and Diane's house, he didn't have much luck. Other than Hooky Dewclaw, he didn't really know a lot of people who hung out in Frelighsburg. The place was an insular collection of everyday farmers, wealthy weekenders and orchard workers, many of whom would put aside social status in the evening to gather together at the Quebec House. The few connections that Shaky did know weren't exactly the kind of people he could easily ask questions of. He wasn't about to phone his grade four English teacher and ask if she knew of a guy with a white car who might have kidnapped Stubby Booker.

Thursday night he went back to Hooky's apartment. He went alone, unwilling to lay a real beating on his old friend, despite the feeling that he deserved it. When he got there, the apartment was dark and deserted. He checked the bar downstairs, but no one had seen him. No luck at the Dunham Hotel either.

By Friday evening, he had a plan coming together. He met up with Merle and Jake at the garage, and they headed for Frelighsburg. Along the way they stopped for a beer at DuChene's in East Farnham, then another at the Dunham Hotel. Everyone was tense, knowing that they didn't have much to go on and that Stubby's life might well be hanging in the balance.

"We're gonna have to teach that guy a good lesson," Merle said. "You can't just go and kidnap Stubby Booker. Man's gotta pay."

"You bet," Jake said. "Fucker's gonna end up dead."

"Hey! We can't go killing the guy, not in front of a bunch of people," said Shaky, wanting to keep control of the situation but also not wanting to shoot down their beer-fuelled bravado. "We just need to find Stubby and let him deal with that once he's back. He's got his own people for that sort of thing."

Shaky may have been Stubby Booker's right-hand man, but when it came to the darker side of things, the only thing he was privy to were the same whispers everyone else in the world heard. Whispers about how Stubby had killed people, that he had people who killed for him and that he was capable of anything. Idle talk about his connections to the mafia and the influence he held over certain politicians. It was typical rumour mill stuff and Shaky had no clue how much of it was true. He wasn't even sure if Stubby had hired killers on the payroll, all he knew was that he personally didn't want to murder anyone or be an accessory to murder. Best to keep the boys reined in until they knew where Stubby was.

He found himself wishing, not for the first time, that Junior would never turn up. So long as the kid stayed in hiding, Shaky wouldn't have to do any of the drastic things they were contemplating now. So, when he pulled into the parking lot of the Quebec House and spotted the white Ford LTD, his heart sank and his stomach tightened uncomfortably.

"Leave the guns in the car," Shaky said. Of all the ways this could go wrong, he didn't want to be shooting up a bar. Just go in, find the guy, drag him out and beat him until he talked. It wasn't much of a plan, but it was something. Just like lies, it was best to keep such things simple. Get to the point and keep the mess to a minimum.

"This Junior guy is supposed to be one hell of a scrapper," he cautioned. "So let's just grab him, drag him out and take him someplace quiet. Then we beat him until he sings."

By the time the three men stepped inside the bar, they were primed and ready for anything. Merle was wearing a leather jacket, unzipped to allow freedom of movement. Like Shaky, he had a blackjack up his right sleeve. Jake had brass knuckles firmly in his grip.

"Hey, who owns the Ford LTD? Looks like someone's trying to break into it!" Shaky yelled. Several heads swivelled, and a redheaded man turned towards them and rose to his feet. *Bingo.*

They rushed him, but Junior was ready. Merle got there first, his arm raised with the baton. Junior easily sidestepped the man, grabbing at his coat and sending him head-first into the wall. He then kicked a chair in front of Shaky, who crashed into a man who had been watching TV. The two fell to the floor in a tangle of arms, legs and curses.

Bigger and faster than his two compatriots, Jake closed in on Junior's right. He knew that this angle would give his wily opponent less room to swing his dominant fist, while increasing his own odds of landing a decent shot with the brass knuckles. He put his shoulder into the uppercut, which glanced off the side of Junior's head and opened up his cheek. Spinning around, Jake grabbed a pool cue, but Junior wasn't quite where Jake thought he was. The swing missed.

Junior's boxing coach always said that he was an instinctive fighter, and this time his instincts served him well. He didn't even need to see Merle rising behind him, he just snapped his arm back and nailed him square in the side of the head with the point of his elbow. In the same movement he grabbed a table and raised it, legs first, as a shield against Jake. Jake tried to skewer any exposed fingers or shins with a few stabbing shots with the pool cue, but nothing landed.

Junior turned the table edgewise and charged, driving it into Jake's chest and then swinging it upward. This connected right under Jake's jaw and folded him backwards over the table. For good measure, Junior brought the table down on him again, shattering the stained-glass light above the pool table and showering Jake in a downpour of coloured broken glass.

With that, Junior turned just as Shaky was ready to deliver a sneaky blow. Shaky's blackjack bounced harmlessly off Junior's shoulder, and he soon went down under a hail of fists and then feet.

The whole thing lasted less than a minute. Andy O'Brien stepped out of the bathroom and limped towards Junior as he surveyed the damage. Things were perfectly tranquil when he'd stepped out to take a leak mere moments ago. Sure, he'd heard the ruckus, but he also had important and immediate business to attend to. Now the barroom looked like it had been hit by a hurricane. As soon as he reached Junior's side, the kid cocked his head towards the door. Yep, it was definitely time to go.

"Sorry about the light," Junior said to the barmaid, collecting his jacket and walking towards the door. Blood was running down the side of his face, but he didn't feel it. "Get them to pay for it."

As he caught his breath outside, Junior knew he'd gotten the attention of Stubby's people.

The game was very much on.

28

No control

Jen didn't get any news. Even Harry, who knew quite a few cops in the region, wasn't able to turn up much, either on or off the record. The following day, a formal search was underway, complete with tracking dogs at the crash scene.

Brought in from Montreal, the dogs didn't get very far. They just circled the scene where Dave's scent was easily picked up and kept coming back to the road. Investigators did a grid search of the woods on both sides of the road, but found nothing. The surrounding swamp made this difficult, but also revealed that there were no tracks or signs that he'd wandered off and gotten lost.

"We're really not sure of this, but it seems like he was picked up. Since there's no sign of him anywhere, we're starting to think that he might have been abducted," said a detective that Bankroft had first met years earlier on a drug raid. "But we've got no motive for it. I mean, no offence Harry, by why would anyone kidnap one of you poor English bastards?"

He had a point. It wasn't like Dave was some controversial columnist for the *New York Times* or something. So the police continued searching, hoping for a clue, but also waited for the shoe to drop in the form of a ransom note or some other sign. Something to work with.

Other than broken beer bottles, blood and some notepads filled with writing that no one could make out, the car revealed nothing. Dave's desk at the *Granby Liar* was pretty much the same thing, minus the glass and blood. After the police left the office, Harry carried out his own search of Dave's desk.

"Jesus, this kid's handwriting is awful," he said as he looked over the stack of old notepads. "Can't make out a goddamned thing." Dave's version of shorthand stymied him, merging at moments with doodles that obscured everything. He could barely make out phone numbers.

Meanwhile, Jen waited by the phone, hour after hour, barely taking time to walk the dog or leave the apartment. Work would have to wait. She called her mother and Dave's mother to let them know what was going before they heard it anywhere else. She knew that it would only be a matter of time before it was all over the Montreal news. Dave might be a reporter for a small-town newspaper, but the apparent abduction of a journalist was a newsworthy event.

Jen kept the calls short, fearful that every second she spent on the phone was tying up the line for the police to call with news. Little detonations of fear and anxiety were going off in the city, with women living out their worst parental nightmares. Beyond exchanging mere words and platitudes, they couldn't even really comfort one another.

The hours passed, but the phone stayed silent. Jen found herself scouring her memories for something, anything of significance, but the effort forced her to admit that they'd hardly talked over the past few months. Sure they'd talked, but not about anything other than day-to-day minutiae. They'd been skating around a few things, dating back to last year when their house had been burned down and then there was the ensuing mess with the now-defunct People for an English-Speaking Quebec. He'd also had that run-in with Stubby Booker, which supposedly had been ironed out.

Even though Booker himself was now reported missing, Jen couldn't help but wonder if there was some sort of connection between that and Dave's disappearance. But why would Booker nab Dave and then be so careless as to skip bail? Even in her desperation to make connections, it didn't ring true to her. Despite her rising sense of paranoia, she couldn't connect the two together.

Jen also had to admit that Dave's behaviour had been different lately, particularly with all the drinking. Nearly every night he'd come home with the smell of beer on his breath. On nights when he didn't drink, his dreams would turn into nightmares about his father, and he'd toss and turn and thrash around in the bed. The next morning she'd often find him exhausted and sprawled out on the couch, staring at the ceiling. After talking to him about the dreams, she reluctantly let the drinking issue slide because at least he could get some rest on those nights, even if it didn't seem particularly restful.

She'd noticed a physical decline in him as well. He looked pale, drawn. Jen admitted to herself that she'd been willfully blind to much of it, chalking up what she did see to the drinking and the dreams.

And then there was that night with the game wardens, which he'd told her about, for the most part. A simple ride-along story that turned into an epic drunken bender. Jen choose to say little, letting her silence reproach him for his sins.

Would he ever write another story? She quickly pushed that thought aside, unable to bear the weight of it.

* * *

Ted wasn't too happy with things, but there wasn't a whole lot he could do about it. He'd tried to talk the kid down, tried to reason with him and get him to see the logic of "live and let live." At the time, Frank Junior said all the right things to placate him, but it was obvious now that it was just lip service, a feeble attempt to set Ted's mind at ease.

The day after Junior went to the city, Ted got a phone call from McKiernan. Yes, the kid wanted to get even. Yes, Charlie told him to cool his jets. 'Just give him some time,' the boss had said. 'Don't worry, I don't think he has it in him to kill anyone. He's just a kid who's justifiably angry. Business first. Keep an eye on him.'

When Junior came home from the city a few days later, he

was dragging that O'Brien kid with him. They didn't like him one bit; he was too slick, too much of a city person. He treated the farm like a summer camp, did as little work as possible and spent most of his time waiting for Junior to finish up so they could go play, which was most nights. Ted wasn't going to let that guy anywhere near the border.

And then Traynor, Stubby's driver, turned up dead. Junior acted like he didn't know a thing about it, but neither Ted nor Diane believed that little fairy tale. Every quiet moment that Junior wasn't down at the bar or off doing who-knows-what, he was out in the shed, knuckles beaten raw in his boxing gloves as he stoked his rage. Even O'Brien didn't stick around for that, usually choosing to walk down to the Quebec House alone.

In the spring, Ted and Diane started to plan for a future that didn't involve the border. They wanted to get out of the business, maybe raise a few sheep and get Junior to gradually take over things while they lived out their golden years without fear of police raids and arrests. They'd profited from hard work and guile, and the fortunate circumstance of a porous border. They'd managed to avoid most scrapes with the law or violence with the competition. Booker had been true to his word and left them alone, even pushing out new opportunity-seeking competitors who would crop up occasionally.

The time had come to reap the benefits of their hard work and to grow old in peace. With a maturing Junior running things, they could hand over the reins, and McKiernan would know his business was in good, loyal hands.

But that feeling had evaporated recently, and the couple, who were first and foremost partners in all things, were unsure of what to do next.

"We have to keep things as open as we can with Charlie," Diane said. "With that temper of his, Junior's going to get out of hand. We can't risk everything just because he's on the verge of flying off half-cocked."

Ted was sitting at the small kitchen table, looking over the latest *Granby Leader-Mail*. Stubby Booker's disappearance was front page news, and they'd both read the story. Then there was the report they'd heard on CJAD about that reporter, Rogers, who was also missing. Both Ted and Diane dismissed the idea that Junior would do something as bold as taking Stubby out of the picture. They knew he was a rough kid, but held out hope that he was incapable of doing something that outrageous.

"No, you're right," Ted declared. "But let's just see where things go. Maybe he'll calm down." This was their unspoken agreement to collectively watch him like a hawk and look for signs of trouble.

This was also Ted's way of putting off making a decision. Caution had played a major part of the couple's success over the years, and sometimes not reacting too quickly or taking unnecessary risks proved to be very prudent. When border patrols were stepped up, they ran fewer trucks. If a crossing was too busy, they found another option. They'd even managed to steer clear of most of the violence between Booker and the Irish years ago. When the dust settled, Ted and Diane went back to doing their thing, and Stubby Booker did his. McKiernan never pushed, respected their judgment, and everyone prospered.

Ted and Diane's conversation was interrupted when Junior came in through the small side door and into the kitchen, ducking his head as he did so. He'd been up early, even earlier than Diane, which was unusual for Junior after a night at the bar. O'Brien was still upstairs, sound asleep.

"What happened to you?" Diane asked, stopping Junior to survey the cut on his face. She reached for his chin, turning his cheek to the light. "Looks like you got into a fight."

"Just a little scrap. Guy hitting on the barmaid again," Junior responded.

"Looks like he clipped you pretty good," Ted said, pushing the paper aside, front page down. "Got a decent-sized lump there."

"Nah, he just got lucky. Sucker punched me and I didn't see it coming."

"You got a cut out of the deal too. Are you sure that was just a punch?"

"He might have had something in his hands. Brass knuckles or something. Don't worry, he won't be coming back around anytime soon."

This seemed implausible. The kid was too alert, too observant and too fast. Ted had seen Junior get into a fight at the bar once. The guy didn't even get close, and Junior wasn't even out of breath afterwards. It was over in a scant few seconds, with the smart-ass lying on the floor, holding his bloodied face. No, Junior was lying about his injuries for some reason.

"You'll probably get a bit of a shiner out of it," Diane said. "Put some Bag Balm on that cut, make sure it doesn't get infected."

"I'll be fine, really," Junior said. "I've had worse."

He walked over to the shelf behind the wood stove, where the work gloves were kept, and grabbed his favourite pair. Stained with grease and oil, they'd moulded to the shape of his hands through days of hard work. He put them on and went back out.

"That was more than just a simple clip from some townie dirtball," Diane said.

"I know. Something's up." Ted glanced back at the newspaper again. He pushed it aside, picked up his plate and brought it to the sink. Time to get on with the day.

Usually, things worried about never come to pass. Over the years, all the worst-case scenarios had danced tantalizingly before Ted's eyes, keeping him up at night. But come the stark light of day, things would resolve, and a clear path forward would emerge.

But now they felt chained into a course of events that they had no control over. That young man, still a boy in many ways, whom they loved and thought of as a son, was not going to be stopped. He was taking them all along for the ride and the road ahead was anything but clear.

* * *

When these bullshit situations crop up, things never go as planned, Shaky thought to himself as he sat in Stubby's office the following morning. His eyes, already surrounded by darkened flesh at the best of times, were now hooded in black. His ribs hurt, and he felt like he'd been hit by a truck.

At least he was doing better than Jake, who was at the hospital with several broken ribs and possibly a concussion. It was amazing that he'd managed to leave the bar under his own steam. Not that they had much choice in the matter, since they were three strangers who showed up at the Quebec House and tried to beat up a respected regular. God knows what would have happened to Jake if they'd left him there. If he hadn't limped out under his own power, they would have had been forced to drag him out.

He heard Merle's dragging gait across the floor of the garage. *Not the best fighter, that one, despite all the brave talk,* Shaky thought. But then the memory of his own mediocre performance came back. Really, Jake was the only one who made any progress in taking Junior down, and now he was in the hospital. He looked up from the aluminum Molson Export ashtray on the desk to see Merle standing in the doorway, the side of his head swollen and obviously delicate to the touch. Merle wasn't wearing his usual baseball cap, it being too tight a fit right now.

"And I thought I felt bad," Shaky said. "You look like you've been dragged through a knothole backwards."

"You'd scare a hound off a gut wagon with that face of yours," Merle said.

After receiving numerous threats from the Frelighsburg locals at the bar, Merle and Shaky fled, dropped Jake off at the hospital and then headed back to Stubby's place in Roxton Pond. There'd been much animated conversation in the car after the fight, except for Jake who lay in the back seat, moaning.

"I've never seen someone move so fast," Merle said. "He's had training or something."

"It's like he didn't even feel it when I clocked him with my blackjack," Shaky said.

"Guys, you seen my brass knuckles?" came from the back seat. "Oh, fuck, it hurts just to talk."

They knew they'd been soundly beaten, both physically and in terms of their plans. *Man, that guy was fast.* The men had all been in fights before, but most bar scuffles involve everyday people who are scared and, as such, are usually terrible fighters. They'd never gone up against someone like Junior before. The kid had no fear and felt as his fists were made of concrete.

Now it was the morning after, and their sense of failure ran deeper than their injuries. Shaky and Merle were questioning aspects of themselves and what it meant to be a man. In that moment, their inability to carry out their plan against Junior was pushing up against their sense of manhood. And, in their world, manhood counted for everything.

"I knew we should have brought guns," Merle said. "Masks... guns, we could have walked him out of there."

"That would have gone wrong and you know it," Shaky said, in part to cover up the inadequacy they were both feeling. He reached into the desk drawer, pulled out a pack of Stubby's Old Port cigars and threw one to Merle.

"I can't. I took a drag off a cigarette this morning and the pressure on my head was so bad I almost blacked out. I puked twice already, and I haven't even had breakfast."

For a while the two men sat in silence, unsure of what to say or do next. Out in the yard they heard a car pull in. It was one of the regular drivers, arriving for a day of delivering construction materials. He stuck his head in the office door, then recoiled in surprise.

"Holy shit, what the hell happened to you guys?" he said.

"None of your business," Shaky growled, getting up to shove a stack of delivery invoices at him. "Here's your day."

"No problem. Let me know if you need anything, like an ice pack or something," the driver said as he beat a hasty retreat. Just like everyone else, this guy knew that Stubby was missing and that something major was going on. In fact, the tension in the entire place was palpable. Shaky recognized the driver as a notorious smart ass who, at the very least, knew his place and had the good sense to keep his nose out of things and just do his job.

For Shaky, it was time to take a breath and consider his options. This was further complicated by the sad fact that he really had almost nothing to go on. Except the knowledge that if he ever faced Junior again, he'd need more than a blackjack.

29

Interview room

For Hooky Dewclaw, things had gotten way out of hand. What started as beers and bullshit about the local thugs had turned into multiple kidnappings and possibly a murder.

He remembered the night he met Junior at the Quebec House. They got to talking about the Montreal Canadiens, and before long they were sitting at a table together with a couple of the other regulars, shooting the shit. Nothing unusual for Hooky, really. He liked the bar scene and was friendly with almost everyone, so he could usually find someone to visit with even if he went out solo. It sure beat sitting at home alone.

Friday nights in Frelighsburg became a bit of a habit, and he knew Junior would be there. Junior was always friendly, with a sense of self-confidence and a sureness of action that attracted people to him. He was charismatic, usually pleasant and quick to crack a joke. Ted, who Hooky knew only as a local lumberjack, had been with him a couple of times, and it seemed as if they worked together. Junior didn't talk much about his personal life, but that wasn't unusual on the bar scene. Work, politics, and dirty or racist jokes were the common fare. If you didn't like what someone was saying, you just shifted away to talk with someone else.

Then came the night when Junior came in and changed everything. Hooky was already about four beers deep when he arrived, and by the time he learned about the Stubby Booker connection, he had a pretty good edge on. That's when Hooky Dewclaw told Junior every rumour on Stubby that he'd heard percolating through town, many of which had been twisted beyond recognition from the original facts. To hear it as he told it, Stubby Booker had killed numerous people and was universally regarded as a notorious outlaw who'd never *really* been caught.

Junior asked Hooky if he knew a guy who worked for him. Yes, in fact, he'd overheard Shaky bitching about his boss not that long ago. Sure, he'd invite his old school buddy out for beers and see what he could find out. Hooky was only too glad to help out his new friend! Sure, it felt a little odd in the sober light of the next day, but he figured he'd do it anyway. Besides, it would be good to see Shaky, catch up on old times and maybe pick up a little more gossip. As it turned out, there wasn't much information to work with after all, just everyday complaining about work. And it quickly became obvious that this guy wasn't about to take part in a plan to oust his boss.

Things died down after that, and Hooky pretty much put it out of his mind. That is until Stubby Booker got arrested in connection with a body on his farm and then promptly disappeared. That set off alarm bells, and Hooky decided it was time to lay low. Stick to home for a bit and maybe not go out quite so often.

But his version of "low profile" wasn't quite low enough. Within a couple of days of Stubby going missing, he had Shaky all up in his socks. Started with a few questions but ended up with a blackjack being waved in his face by a guy who wasn't known for the rough stuff. It was out of character, like being given the finger by Santa Claus. Hooky was nowhere near Quebec House when Shaky and his boys busted the place up, but he heard about it. Third hand, but in precise, dramatic detail.

Unsure if Junior would be out looking for him, or if Shaky was due for a return visit, Hooky Dewclaw decided to go into hiding until he could figure out what to do next. He slept at a buddy's house, then spent the next day at work feeling jumpy and tired. Every time there was a loud noise, he was looking over his shoulder. Smoking in the lumber yard was forbidden, but he went through a half-pack of MarkTens over the workday anyways.

At the end of the day, when his coworkers were going home to their wives and families, Hooky Dewclaw found himself sitting in his car, staring at his yellowed fingers, reluctant to leave. He knew where he had to go. He dropped his dark green Mercury Comet into drive, pulled out of the yard and headed for the Dunham detachment of the Sûreté du Québec. Time to spill his guts.

* * *

The pair of detectives stood outside the interview room, one of them glancing periodically through the door's narrow-slit window at the man fidgeting inside.

"Do you think this guy is telling us the truth?" the first one said.

"He seems pretty nervous. But, if what he says is true, I'd be nervous too."

It was now close to 7 p.m. The pair had been working on the Booker case, which had yielded precious little so far. They were getting ready to call it a day and head home when this guy walked in, claiming he knew who the kidnapper was, but not his full name. He also believed that the same guy probably abducted that missing newspaper reporter, and it all had something to do with a decades-old vendetta involving an unsolved murder of one of their own police officers.

"It's pretty fantastical stuff," said the taller of the two detectives. "Look, you go in and keep him talking. I'll see if I can dig up some dirt on our visitor, see who we're dealing with."

The shorter detective opened the door, stepping into a cloud of cigarette smoke. Other people's smoke always bothered him, so he decided to light one up himself. Hey, when in Rome…

"Monsieur Howard Duclos, my name is Detective Rodrigue," he said, dusting off his English for the occasion. "I've been talking to my colleague about you and your friends."

"Well, I thought they were friends, but now I'm not so sure," Hooky said. "I mean, I'm just hanging out, playing pool with the guys. Next thing I know, there are people getting kidnapped and beat up. And then I get one of Stubby's guys threatening me and God knows what's gonna happen next.

"I just wanted to have a few beers and shoot the shit and now I've got Booker's guys after me for something I had nothing to do with," he continued." And when Junior connects the dots after they tried to beat him up at the bar the other night, he's gonna come looking for me."

Realizing he was babbling, he paused, stubbed out his Mark Ten, pulled the pack out of his shirt pocket and fished out another. Rodrigue lit him with a Cricket disposable lighter.

"And now I'm here, and maybe I should have just shut up. Because if either of them finds out I talked to you guys, I'm pretty much fucked."

"Well, Mr. Duclos, you're here now. And the best way forward is to tell us everything you know."

"Everybody calls me Hooky," he replied, relaxing a bit.

"Why is that?"

"Because when I was a kid I played hooky from school a lot. Then, with my French family name, it just turned into 'Hooky Dewclaw.'"

"What is that, a dewclaw?"

"It's the extra claw on a dog's leg. It hangs there and doesn't do much. Like me, I guess."

Rodrigue laughed in spite of himself and then steered the conversation back when he realized that they were getting off track.

"So, this Junior. Who is he exactly?"

"He's some guy who works in the woods. I don't know his full name, but everybody calls him Junior. His dad was that cop Stubby Booker killed."

Rodrigue's eyebrows raised. His partner, who'd handled the first round of questioning, had already told him about this, but getting it directly from Hooky still surprised him. He'd heard the story of Stubby Booker killing a police officer and then walking away with little more than a short jail stay for obstruction. "Obstruction of justice" was one of those crimes, like "conspiracy," that prosecutors tagged on people that they couldn't nail for anything else. Essentially a "better than nothing" conviction.

A gentle knock at the door brought the questioning to a halt. Rodrigue got up and stepped out of the small room to confer with his colleague.

"He checks out. Young guy, no criminal record to speak of. Got fined for drunk driving once after he sideswiped a car in a parking lot, but that's it."

"What about his cop-killing story?"

"If what he says is true, then Junior's dad was Frank McConnell. He wasn't here very long. Got transferred in from Montreal and disappeared shortly after. Everybody said Booker did it, but there was never any evidence. Not a sign of him, he just vanished, and the only witness fell off a high rise in Montreal."

"Okay, let's go with what we have. Let the patrollers know to be on the lookout for a white Ford LTD. We should call the Sutton and Dunham town cops too, maybe even Bedford and the RCs. The Mounties are always up and down the border... maybe they'll see something. Granted, it's a long shot, what with all the white LTDs around."

"And we'll see is there's a Frank McConnell Junior out there," the taller detective said, glancing at the wall clock. "I guess we'll have to wait until the morning now to check on that. Everyone in Quebec City's gone home for the night."

"We should look back on that old McConnell case, see if there's anything there. I don't know if the file's still here or if it was sent to the archives," Rodrigue said. "And there's gotta be something in Booker's obstruction case file. Maybe call the Crown Prosecutor, see what he has. Probably not much to help us here, but you never know."

"I'll send this guy home for the night. I don't think he's involved beyond what he told us," the taller detective said.

"Besides, we really need to air that room out. Between the stress, the sweat and cigarettes, it's pretty thick in there."

* * *

After pouring his heart out to the cops, Hooky Dewclaw was set free. He left them his father's phone number, assuring them that his dad would know where he was. After all, there was no way in hell he was going to stay at his own place! Besides, he didn't even have a phone, other than the pay phone in the bar downstairs.

Hooky spent the next couple of hours driving around, thinking about the surrounding drama that threatened to drown him. He stopped in at the little store in Farnham Centre for gas and another pack of MarkTens, tearing greedily at the cellophane wrapper as he pulled out of the yard with the window down. Between drags, he found himself sticking his head out the window, desperate for the cool night air.

He consoled himself with the knowledge that he'd done the right thing. He didn't want anyone to end up dead. All he'd done was pass around a little gossip over beers. There wasn't supposed to be any harm in that. Yes, he'd definitely done the right thing.

But, if that was the case, why did he feel so hollow inside?

30
Vigil

Jen felt trapped. She couldn't go to work. She also couldn't stray far from the phone, hoping that it would ring at any moment and Dave would be on the other end of the line, telling her that everything was fine. Picking up on her obvious energy, King paced the floors and whined occasionally, acutely aware that something was wrong.

In this moment, everything was *very* wrong. The world around her felt dark, foreboding, overwhelming. Her husband, her anchor, the man she loved, was out there somewhere. She knew he'd been struggling with things, things he didn't, or couldn't, talk about. At least not yet.

The moments where she wasn't paying full attention were the worst. Slowly, imperceptibly, her thoughts would veer off into darker and darker places, culminating in a sudden instant of sheer dread. Of unbidden visions of the worst possible outcomes. Then she would pull herself back from the brink, only to have the whole cycle repeat itself once again.

At moments, she would catch herself daydreaming about more normal, pleasant things. But then the reality of her current situation would come roaring back, and she would reproach herself for daring to think of anything other than the crisis before her.

Overwrought, Jen hadn't slept much last night. When she did it was dreamless, as if that carefree part of her mind had been powered down. Like a cornered deer that lies down to let the wolf pack have its way with it.

Harry Bankroft had been helpful. Somewhat shy by nature, Jen hadn't yet developed close personal ties with many people in the area. She had friends, but they weren't people she felt she could turn to in times like this. For those, she needed someone from the core...*sister friends*. But they were all in the city, busy with their jobs, boyfriends, husbands and children in a world that bore scant similarity to her current reality.

She heard a knock at the door. *God, please let it be Dave*, she thought. King rushed alongside her to the entrance and watched anxiously as she pulled the door open.

And there, on her front step, stood her mother and Dave's mother, each carrying a small suitcase. It wasn't what Jen had hoped for, but it brought some relief nonetheless. Someone to share the burden and the darkness with.

"We weren't going to sit in the city waiting for news while you're here and nobody knows what's going on," Jen's mom explained as they stepped inside. "And we couldn't leave you here all alone."

The mothers didn't typically have much contact. They knew and liked each other, but had their own separate lives in different neighbourhoods. However, when Dave went missing, Jen's mother reached out, and the two women quickly agreed that sitting in their separate homes just didn't make sense. They would go to Jen, and provide one another with the support they needed in a time like this.

Jen filled them in with the details, going beyond what she'd given them in the brief long-distance phone calls she'd made. Not that there was much to add, but she gave them what she knew, and laid her fears bare on the table between coffee cups and the ashtray that held her mother's smouldering cigarettes.

"David's father told me once that he didn't want his son to grow up here," Mrs. Rogers said. "He kept saying that he had to get us out of here."

"What did he mean?" Jen asked.

"I'm not really certain. I think it's because he knew some of the rougher sorts around here he was afraid that his son would fall in with the wrong crowd. Slippers always seemed to have some sort of trouble to deal with. He tried to keep it from me, but it didn't always work, even when he thought it did."

She reached for Jen's mother's cigarettes. Never a regular smoker, the stress of the present moment was clearly taking command. She lit it with a match, sat back and stared at the melamine table top. There was so much she could say about Slippers. There was the night her husband came home, shaking, almost incoherent and far removed from his typically-relaxed demeanor. She recalled quickly leaving the homestead the next day to go to the police and how their escape from that life lasted barely more than a few weeks. She'd remained silent all these years in order to protect her son, and didn't mind staying silent a little while longer.

"For some people, they need to leave where they grew up to get away from trouble," she continued. "Some people need to come home to get away from the trouble they find. And for some people, trouble finds them wherever they go. I think David's father would have found trouble wherever he went. I tried to ignore it, but it was just in him."

A trait seemingly passed on to her son, she thought. Of all the qualities of his father that he could have picked up, why this? Her fun-loving husband had been a bit of an outlaw, she had to admit, but the younger Dave had never been a troublemaker. No more so than any other typical kid running around the streets of their NDG neighbourhood.

Lost in her own thoughts, she reached over and stubbed out the barely-touched cigarette. She reached over and swiped her hand across the table, drawing the string of ashes into her palm before dropping them in the ashtray.

Jen's mother found herself lost in thought, revisiting her initial misgivings about Dave. At first, she'd been wary of the skinny kid working his way through university, the man who would go on to marry her daughter and then promptly drag her out to the country. But he'd always been respectful to Jen, and while he hadn't exactly been a breadwinner, the couple seemed happy enough. In the end, a child's happiness is all a parent can really hope for.

But what had he done and gotten himself into? Was there some nefarious part of him that she'd failed to detect? Some dark quality that she'd sensed, but chosen to overlook? Or was his disappearance really as random as it seemed?

Each of the women yearned for Dave's safe return in their own way, deliberately keeping their darkest thoughts to themselves. They didn't want to acknowledge their existence or risk any unkindness or offence. Evoking dark words now might cast long shadows later.

And so they held vigil, at times getting up to busy themselves around the apartment, or take King for his long-awaited walk. Powerless to do anything but wait, hope, and pray in moments of solitude. But always, after a time, they were collectively drawn back to the kitchen table, to talk about everything and nothing as they passed the time.

Two widows and a wife.

Two widows, hoping to not make three.

31

Vague on details

Detective Rodrigue was not having an easy time of things. It had been two days now, and there was still no sign of the missing reporter or Stubby Booker. It was as if these two, seemingly unconnected people had just upped and vanished. And now he was working on the weekend in an effort to get a grip on things.

He sat at his desk reading over the latest reports. His own cops had stopped three white Ford LTDs over the last day. The Sutton police also stopped a guy in a white LTD, but this turned out to be the same driver the provincial boys pulled over an hour earlier.

None of them turned out to be the car that Howard Duclos, aka Hooky Dewclaw, was talking about. No sign of a young, redheaded kid. They even asked about him at the Quebec House in Frelighsburg, but the bar owner there wasn't very cooperative. Yes, he'd seen someone matching that description, but he had no idea who he was, just some quiet guy that came in for a beer now and then. Never really spoke to him, didn't know anything about him. No recollection of the barroom brawl. Rodrigue suspected the owner knew more than he was letting on, but let the matter drop, at least for now.

Rodrigue wished there was a system, like a computer of some sort, that could bring up car registration listings based on description. He'd read about such a thing in a science magazine recently, but finding car registrations in this province meant calling Quebec City and getting the automobile licensing people to go digging through aisles and aisles of paper files. It was the sort of task that could take a person days to do, especially with no plate numbers to work with.

He also had to admit that there were a lot of white Ford LTDs around, as well as cars that closely resembled LTDs. The really frustrating thing is that he couldn't entirely rule out the possibility that the car they were looking might just be something similar-looking.

He'd driven out to Roxton Pond to see if he could find anyone connected to Stubby Booker. Fellow cops had already taken statements from a couple of the employees, but it wouldn't hurt to ask again. They might give up a name, an address or some kernel of information they could work with. But no, the guy there, who looked like he'd been in a fight, didn't have anything new. Claimed that he had no idea what was going on, except that he was 'deeply concerned.' Rodrigue figured that he knew something, judging by the bruises on his face.

Rodrigue toured Stubby's house, looking for something like the steel pipe they'd found earlier. That alleged weapon had already been bagged, tagged and analyzed. As for the blood on the wall, they only thing the lab could determine was that it was type "O."

Curiously, there were no sign of firearms in the house. He knew Stubby had guns, but probably moved them elsewhere when he was released on bail. *All these thugs had guns*, he thought.

A visit by a fellow detective from the Sherbrooke detachment to Martin Traynor's family had also come up empty. Traynor's parents had been open and helpful, but it quickly became obvious that the elderly couple weren't capable of abducting their son's boss. Soft-spoken and gentle in manner, the murder of their son had left them shattered and diminished.

He shifted uncomfortably in his office chair and reached over to turn on his transistor radio. It was the top of the hour and it was time for the news. The dial was already pre-tuned to CHEF, the AM station from Granby. The top local story of the hour was the disappearance of the reporter and Booker. The US election race between Gerald Ford and Jimmy Carter was heating up, rumours of an election call in Quebec were circulating and a Montreal with suspected ties to organized crime was found dead and another was recovering in hospital following an apparent settling of accounts. The usual stuff.

The media was clearly starting to pay more attention to the case he was working on. More than he'd like, but it was understandable. Car accidents and bar fights were pretty typical fare in the region, a part of everyday life, but disappearances were rare. Usually when someone went missing, they'd stumble out of the woods within a day or two, or be found hanging in a some shed somewhere after ending their own life. Tragically mundane in the grander scheme of things.

Now he was fielding calls from reporters, likely because this was happening to one of their own and not just some everyday schmuck. Yesterday, Fernand Dubois shunted off a call to him from a Montreal TV station. The police would be dealing with a lot more reporters if there wasn't some progress...*and soon*.

There was a chance that Booker had simply skipped bail and left town, but he figured that was unlikely. Though the body of one of his employees, Martin Traynor, had shown up on a property he owned, they didn't have any evidence connecting him to the murder. It was more likely that someone, had done this as a message to Booker, maybe a rival. And besides, Booker was known for beating the rap. No, the idea of Booker leaving behind a sizeable business and multiple properties to go on the lam for a murder he probably didn't commit was a bit of a stretch.

More likely, those responsible for killing Traynor were responsible for whatever was going on with Booker. According to the report on his death, Traynor was a truck driver who mostly hauled construction materials. Occasional border crossings, so maybe smuggling? Truth was, they had no evidence of that. Legally speaking, Traynor was clean as a whistle.

Then there was Rogers. Given the circumstances surrounding his car crash, that was looking more and more like an abduction. Rodrigue had collected a small pile of the guy's recent articles from the "Granby Liar," but it was mostly community news. There was town council stuff, some Olympics coverage and a story about smuggling that was pretty vague on details. He figured that there was not much of note to provoke a kidnapping; Rogers' boss pretty much said as much when he spoke to them.

That's when he checked with the Mounties to see who they'd arrested in that smuggling story. The lone officer at the Bedford detachment had little to share, and the officers who arrested the guy in the one-ton were off until Monday's night shift. He gave Rodrigue a half-hearted promise to look around and see if he could find the file. As he hung up, Rodrigue knew that he would never hear from the guy again.

He thought of Rogers' wife. She'd kept it together when he spoke to her, but he could tell she was drawing deep to do so. Rodrigue hoped that the next time he saw her he could give her some good news. The thought brought him back to the moment, and the growing pile of paperwork in front of him. Paperwork generated from two missing people and zero leads to indicate that they were dead or alive.

It was going to be a long weekend.

32

Between me and him

I was too stressed to be hungry, but, as the sun was setting, Stubby Booker was heading into day three with no food. Just a bit of stagnant water from the bucket in the corner. Putting it mildly, things were looking a little grim. We were both thirsty and we could feel our tongues thickening.

We'd passed a good chunk of the day prowling the cabin, looking for something, anything we could make use of. A loose board, hinges that could be forced, you name it. You'd think escaping from a sugar shack would be easy, since people don't even lock the damned things. But this place was practically Fort Knox.

"I think this fucker means to starve us to death," Stubby said. He was sitting on a plank on the floor, barely visible in the gloom. Soon it would be pitch black. "Before you can't see a damned thing, look around and find yourself a pebble. It'll help keep your mouth moist."

"I guess," I said. "Don't know how long we need to make that water last."

"The rest of your life at this rate, kid."

We both got up and began to rummage around. Some parts of the floor were concrete, others were dirt. Fine dirt. Even finding a small rock was not as easy as you'd think.

"Not over there, that's just old cement. You don't want that," Booker said.

I finally found a smooth rock that was just slightly smaller than a marble. I wiped it on my pants and popped it into my mouth. The saliva came back, and I relaxed. Not a lot, but a little, and, at that stage, I'd take what I could get. By now the dark was nearly complete.

"So, my dad was quite the outlaw," I said to the darkness, hoping to pass the time, and maybe learn something in the process.

"Oh, he was quite the man," Stubby said. "Just hooked on the excitement of it all. Me, I never had money, so I was always looking for ways to make an extra dime or two. But your dad never seemed to care about money; he just liked the thrill of it all. He once said to me that getting away with it was the best reward."

"But he was calming down by the time he met my mom, right?" I asked, in part because I was hoping he'd confirm it.

"Oh, he quieted down for a little while when he met your mother," Stubby said. "But not for long. The things he pulled off without her knowing..."

"What kinds of things?"

"Oh, you know. *Things*."

My curiosity was officially piqued. Time to start prying the old guy open.

"Look, I've been trying my whole life to learn things out about my dad. And right now it looks like the rest of my life is right in front of me. Can you please tell me about my dad?"

I was pleading now, but I honestly didn't have anything to lose.

"You keep this to yourself. Not to your wife, your mother, and sure as hell don't put anything in that damned paper.""I probably won't get the chance at this rate," I replied sullenly. "I think my days at the *Granby Liar* are just about over."

Just my obituary, I thought, but didn't dare say out loud.

I heard him rustling around. A match flared up, and I could see him lighting a slightly- crooked cigar. He threw the match on the floor, letting it burn out on its own. Then all I could see was the glowing tip of the cigar, flaring slightly now and then.

"Okay, let's start by saying that your father adored your mother. Hell, a lot of people did...she was quite the looker in her day. Nice person, too. She came from a more proper family and ended up marrying the local bad boy. Maybe it was exciting, or maybe she figured she could settle him down, I don't know. Women seem to have all kinds of reasons to marry a man. Some good, some bad.

"And, to his credit, your dad really did try and settle down for a bit, by his standards, at least. He didn't run the border quite so often, or he'd be the one to drive the empty car down and meet the guys who walked across the line through the woods with bags of booze on their backs. That way he could say to her, 'No dear, I didn't run the line today.' He called it his 'borderline truth.'

"But that didn't seem to be enough to satisfy him. He went through money like water, mostly trying to prop up the farm. Your dad might have been good at quite a few things, but farming wasn't one of them. The land was poor, and most of the machinery looked like it dated back to the Fenian raids. Bunch of old junk, all wired up. Your grandparents were good folks, but stingy as all hell. They never owned a nail that hadn't been used a couple of times already. They'd just straighten it out and use it again."

He paused, the cigar tip flaring in the dark. "He really had no head for money. By the time you were born, he couldn't stop. He loved that farm, felt like it was his family responsibility to keep it going, but the place was bleeding him dry. The outbuildings were falling down and that house was like something out of the Ark. Your mother didn't think much of raising a child in a pioneer cabin, so he was under the gun to bring it into this century.

"Every time he made some extra cash, he sunk it right back into the farm. Once, we got our hands on some lumber from a fella out Stanstead way, so he rebuilt the east wall of the barn. Then the west wall started to bow in. He no sooner had that fixed and a windstorm peeled a bunch of tin off the roof. I think that was just before the well collapsed, and you guys had no water, so he and I dug a new well. If you ever want an awful, dangerous job, try digging a well with a pick and shovel.

"When he wasn't working the border or on the farm, he started working for other people. Climbing jobs no one else would do. Barn roofs. Silos. People would pay him what they could, but no one was particularly prosperous around that part of the world. They were frugal folks without much to spare, and, more often than not, he wouldn't even charge them. But the best place to make extra money was the border. You can always make money on the border."

"But my mom, she must have known."

"Oh, I'm sure she knew some stuff, or at least suspected. She was too smart to be fooled for long, but when a woman gets married and figures out that life isn't going quite like she planned, she learns to put on a brave face and put up with things. Oh, she'd crack the whip all right, and he'd be at church in the family pew every Sunday, like a good little Anglican. And the cows were always milked on time. She even got him involved in the Odd Fellows lodge and she was in the Rebekas. I think she figured if she kept him busy enough, he wouldn't have time to be an outlaw."

He laughed at the thought. For a man who I knew wasn't especially fond of me or my dad, he was opening up. And, as much as I wanted to ask about the events that drove him and my dad apart, I didn't feel like asking. I mean, this guy had killed people before, and I didn't want him doing the same to me out here in the middle of nowhere.

"But he did find the time. By then, we'd given up on the still and making our own hooch. The Americans wanted name brand stuff, and it was less work for us once we got a few connections in the city. By then I was out in Roxton Pond. I rented the place at first and then finally bought it. By then, things were changing, and we were bringing all kinds of stuff back and forth."

"But why Roxton? You're way out in the sticks over there."

"Exactly. Nobody knew us! That was my idea. Trucks come and do the drop-off, our guys meet there and then drive stuff over the line or into the city. And your dad liked it because it kept things away from your mom. I liked it because no one would ever think to look for a smuggler so far from the border."

"But the cops seemed to know where to look. I mean, you've been arrested a bunch of times. You built yourself a reputation as the guy who can get away with murder."

Oh shit, I just called him a murderer. Not good. He's going to be pissed.

"Look, I know I've got this reputation as a murderer and maybe I deserve it. If you believe the gossip, I've killed lots of people...and that isn't quite true. But sometimes it's good to have people think you're this big bad guy. If people are afraid of you, they'll probably leave you alone or do as you ask."

There was another pause as the cigar flared once again. He was getting down to the butt, and I could see his weathered face in the glow and the lines around his mouth. My imagination told me he looked tired, old beyond his years and maybe even a little scared. Hell, imagination had nothing to do with it. I knew for a fact that we were both tired, scared and feeling old beyond our years.

The wind was blowing, seeping in through the many cracks in the walls. This place definitely wasn't built to keep the cold out. I pulled myself into a corner, sat on a splitting block and leaned against the wall. Even with the collar up, my jean jacket felt very small. I think I dozed off at one point.

When I next looked up, the room was utterly dark. I had to check because I couldn't tell if my eyes were open. Then, at the far end of the room, I could hear Stubby. He was shifting about, mumbling words I couldn't make out.

"Jesusfuck!" Stubby screamed. He thrashed out, his feet scuffing the dirt of the floor.

"Did you see that?" Stubby said to the darkness, his breath ragged.

"See what?"

"It was him, wasn't it?"

"I don't know what you're talking about."

"Giving me shit. He's always giving me shit."

"Who's always giving you shit?"

"Your father. He comes around in my sleep sometimes. Usually just sits there and doesn't say anything, but I know. I know he's giving me shit for stuff I did. Or didn't do. Or need to do."

"What's he giving you shit for now?" I asked, coming to the realization that I'd been sharing my dad with Stubby Booker for all these years.

"That, kid, is between me and him."

33

Tavern talk

Diane went out to the dooryard to call for Junior.

"Charlie called. He said you need to come into the city right away," she told him. "He made it clear the sooner the better."

It wasn't unexpected, though the speed of McKiernan's summons surprised him. It had only been a few days since he'd nabbed Booker from his home in Roxton Pond, and then picked up that asshole Rogers. He knew Charlie wouldn't like to be kept waiting, so he tucked the note into his pocket and went back to his work. There were a few things he needed to finish up before he went anywhere.

Junior was so deep in his own thoughts that he didn't notice the anxious look on Diane's face. At that moment he was just making adjustments and figuring out how to get everything just right. Without a word, he went across the yard to the garage, dogs in tow.

After popping the truck's hood, he fit the pry bar between the engine block and the power steering pump, forced it outwards, and then pulled the belt tight. Top bolt tight, bottom bolt tight. After double-checking everything, he concluded that things were now good as new. The belt had come off last night and his driver had a hell of a time steering on the way home. Backroad breakdowns are stressful at the best of times, even more so when you have a load of US booze heading north and you're still within spitting distance of the border at 3 a.m.

He was washing up at the sink when Andy came downstairs. Junior liked Andy, but the man seemed singularly unmotivated. A good follower who always did what was asked of him, but definitely not one to take the initiative.

"We're going to the city," Junior said.

"What's up?" O'Brien said, yawning as he did so.

"Charlie wants to see me. We need to talk about a few things, I guess."

"Oh, I see."

"Pack your stuff. Might be good for you to stay in town for awhile."

Junior figured that, at the very least, getting O'Brien out of the house would be good for Ted and Diane. They hadn't said much, but he knew that they didn't really like Andy. Doing this would also help lower their suspicions. Maybe with O'Brien gone, they'd be a little less concerned about what he was up to. He knew they loved him, but he also knew that they wouldn't love what he was doing. Hopefully, despite it all, that love would endure.

* * *

The drive into Montreal was uneventful. It was a sunny fall day and the leaves, now past their golden prime, were being pulled loose one-by-one to swirl in the wind. Taking the back roads to avoid the tolls on the Eastern Townships autoroute, Junior navigated the white LTD as it rumbled quietly along up Bunker towards Stanbridge East.

At one point, they passed a parked Bedford police car, but the pair of cops in it were both looking down, intent on paperwork.

Junior felt a sense of anxiety rising as he crossed the Champlain Bridge. He dropped Andy off outside the Montreal Forum and handed him a five-dollar bill to cover bus fare to his sister's place on a dead-end street behind St. Laurent Boulevard. It was more than enough, but O'Brien never seemed to have any money on him. Once Junior had things settled, he'd give Andy a job and keep him buttoned up.

Off to Griffintown. For a moment, he thought about stopping off to visit his mother. He hadn't seen her in a few months, though they had spoken on the phone once. She'd adapted well to life without George, and seemed happier than he ever remembered. There was a new man who came by to visit from time to time. He was a quiet, gentle soul who doted on her, yet afforded her a level of independence that suited them both. He had his own place and chose to keep it that way.

No, if he had the time, and things went well, he'd see her after he was done meeting with Charlie McKiernan.

Junior parked the white Ford LTD down the street from the tavern, pulling on his canvas coat as he got out. The revolver was in his pocket, where he usually kept it these days. He felt for it and the sensation of holding the polished wood grip in his palm provided some comfort. He had no plans to use it, but it was a bit like bringing a very big friend along for backup. A little extra confidence.

As Junior stepped into the tavern, it took a few seconds for his eyes to adjust to the darkened room. It seemed like any other day at McKiernan's nameless tavern, where business was conducted quietly in the shadows. He blinked several times in an attempt to see better.

The next thing he saw were sparks as a fist hit him square in the temple. Stunned by the blow, he instinctively lashed out into nothing. A second shot caught him at the base of his rib cage just as another fist came from the opposite side, reopening the cut on his face from Jake's brass knuckles. He swiped his left back, just managing to clip the second attacker. Standing right behind him, Ellwood caught his left arm as it came back and then snagged the right arm before Junior could turn. Ellwood's partner grabbed a barred arm and together they shoved him across the room, jamming his torso into the bar and winding him.

He was now laying face down in a puddle of spilled beer, struggling in vain to draw air into his lungs. Junior might have been outgunned, but it was all the two men could do to keep him restrained. Ellwood let one hand go for the customary weapons check, but Junior wrenched his body around like the trapped wild animal he was. The free hand quickly went back to Junior's shoulder where it was needed, tightening his grip to regain control.

"You stupid little bastard," Charlie McKiernan said from behind the bar. "Why did you have to go and fuck things up?"

"What are you talking about?" Junior said, gasping for air that wouldn't come.

"Don't play cute with me. You know damned well what I'm talking about."

"Let me up...I can explain!"

At McKiernan's signal, Ellwood and the second man eased their grip, but didn't let go. Ellwood knew Junior's temper and his talents, and wasn't about to give him too much room to move. Junior looked to his left at the second man: young, big shoulders, and a scowl on his black-bearded face that sent a clear message: *don't fuck with me. I can take you.*

McKiernan didn't respond. He just looked at Junior, waiting for an answer.

"Look, I'm just taking care of some problems out there. There's too much traffic on the border and that bastard Booker won't back down. Someone has to go; might as well be him."

"So what did you do?"

"Nothing...yet. I've got them locked away. Going to give it a little time before they get disposed of."

"And, in the process, you get your revenge, is that it?"

"Well, yeah."

"And the newspaper reporter, what's up with that?"

"You know his dad was involved. Now he's writing stories, drawing all kinds of attention to things."

"So?"

"I'm not letting him go on with his life as if he's innocent. He's his father's son, so he can go join him."

Charlie paused, picking up his pipe in his left hand. As he did this, his right hand shot out, delivering a square jab into Junior's face. The kid's head snapped back, and he could feel the blood running from his nose. McKiernan might not be young, but he was still fast.

"Let me make this clear: this isn't about who gets to get even, or who gets to be 'king shit.' It's about business. We're looking at a war with the Italians over this. We do a lot of business with them, and their man out in the country is Booker."

"But, if we get rid of Booker, then they can deal directly with us. We'll have the whole border to ourselves. They get over it…we get rich. *Everybody wins.*"

"And you get your revenge, is that it?"

"It's more than that! I don't have to be tripping over that asshole and his drivers every time I turn around. I see one of his trucks I just get so pissed off. He took my father from me… him and that Rogers bastard."

"Well, in case you hadn't figured it out yet, here's a little history lesson for you: Dave Rogers Senior was there when your father died. We don't know much more, only that whatever he witnessed left him with a guilty conscience, and he went to the cops. He wanted out, but they wouldn't let him. Instead, they charged him as an accessory and wouldn't let him leave Quebec. Told him if he played ball he'd get a light sentence.

"He wanted to move his wife and kid away and get them all set up before he went to the slam, so he moved here and took a job in the high steel. We didn't take too kindly to the whole thing, so we went after him first. I was one of the ones chasing after him that day. I'd never seen a man climb like that… just like a fucking monkey. But eventually we got him cornered.

"Unlike you, we were smart about it. We gave him a choice: he could jump, which would look like an accident or a suicide, or we could shoot him. But we told him that if it looked like a murder, then we'd go after his wife and kid. He did the right thing to save his family.

"We went after Booker a couple of times," McKiernan continued. "But it never worked. We blew him up in his truck once, but he got out and even managed to wing one of our guys. It all raised hell with business, so in the end, we worked out a truce. He does his thing and we do ours. *Live and let live.* He was already in with the eyeties by then, and we couldn't risk it."

McKiernan calmly lit his pipe, shaking out the match and dropping it into the ashtray.

"Then you went and fucked it all up."

Junior strained against his captors, unwilling to be dominated. He felt the betrayal, the injustice. His father worked for McKiernan, and Charlie should have avenged his murder. But Ellwood and his partner were too strong, too experienced at holding people who didn't want to be held. He relaxed, and his shoulders sagged under the futile weight of the situation.

"This isn't about me, or you. Our people do a lot for this neighbourhood," McKiernan said. "We keep things under control, keep the crime down so people like your mother can walk home safely at night. Ever notice that you and your mom always had a turkey on the table at Christmas? That was us. Same for a lot of people."

Junior looked Charlie in the eye, and felt nothing but hate. Hate at the thought that justice for his father was less important than providing the locals with a Christmas turkey. Junior put his head down, waiting.

"Now you're going to go back out there and fix this. What's done is done," Charlie said. "Okay boys, let him go."

Without a word, Junior turned towards the tavern door. One step, two steps and then a third to give himself some space. He wheeled around, pulled the revolver from his pocket, and squeezed off a shot in a single, swift motion. Charlie staggered back, falling behind the bar. Then Junior swung to his left and placed the second shot into the neck of Ellwood's partner. Finally he pointed the gun at Ellwood, but didn't fire.

"Don't," was all he said. He could see Ellwood with his hands up in front of him. He was talking, but Junior couldn't hear him above the ringing in his ears. Turning, Junior ran from the tavern, convinced that Ellwood would be after him or even try to put a bullet in his back. But he knew he couldn't shoot Ellwood. Not now. Not ever.

He ran down the street to the LTD, glancing back to see that no one was following him. He collapsed onto the driver's seat, the revolver still in his hand. He looked at it, then dropped it on the floor, repulsed by the sight of it.

"Oh Jesus, I just shot Charlie! I just shot Charlie!" he said aloud, barely hearing his own words above the ringing and the pounding of blood in his ears. He started the car, dropped it into drive, headed up William Street to Guy and crossed St. Antoine and St. Jacques before hanging a hard left onto Dorchester.

By the time he got across Champlain Bridge, his mind was already settling and he was starting to plan. It was a long shot, but the only option now was to get rid of Stubby Booker and that Rogers guy. He'd get justice for his father and then go back on bended knee to whoever stepped into Charlie's shoes. He'd beg for forgiveness and offer them complete and total access to all of the cross-border smuggling. Maybe it would be enough.

"But fuck, I killed Charlie," he moaned out loud, the sound of his own voice surprising him. "They're gonna want me dead for that."

Maybe someone's been waiting for this, he thought. *Maybe it won't be so bad.* If he couldn't regain their trust by giving them the entire border, then maybe he could just disappear somewhere down into the States. Head south...or west. Just vanish. It wasn't much, but maybe he could work his way out of it.

* * *

Back at the tavern, Ellwood gave no thought to going after Junior. There would be time for that later.

"Fuck me!" Charlie said, sitting up. "That burns like a sonofabitch!"

"Keep your hand on this," Ellwood said, grabbing Charlie's left arm, and placing his hand on the bar rag. He'd been hit in the right shoulder, up near the collarbone.

Ellwood disappeared the shotgun from behind the bar, stowing his own pistol along with it in a compartment recessed in the office floor. He picked up the office phone, called an ambulance and told them that two men had been shot and the robber had fled. He had a hard time hearing on the phone; his ears were still ringing from the gunshots.

"There's a tavern there?" the dispatcher said. He'd never heard of the place.

"It's small."

After he hung up, he came out of the office to check on his partner, whom he'd momentarily forgotten about in all the mayhem. But there was nothing there, just the mortal remains of a young man who, like Junior, he'd worked with and come to care for. A bullet through his throat.

Ellwood thought back to the look he'd gotten from Junior. For all his rage, the kid couldn't bring himself to shoot him. He appreciated the thought, but he knew that if he ever saw his former partner again, he'd have to kill him.

34

The visit

Junior kept the LTD just below sixty miles - or a hundred kilometres - an hour. One always had to calculate, since the metric system had just replaced the old Imperial system last year. The weather was clear on the Eastern Townships autoroute, and he didn't want to attract attention. He got behind an old AMC Javelin going the same speed and stayed a few car lengths back. The Javelin's driver would see the cops first, slow down accordingly and Junior would have plenty of time to react.

He glanced up into the mirror at his own face and saw dried blood flaking off, both from the reopened cut and his bashed nose. *Damn, Charlie was quick*, he thought. *Never saw that punch coming.*

Then he remembered that he'd killed his boss, a man he'd always looked up to. A man that had plucked him off the streets and allowed him to make something of himself. A wave of remorse washed over him. He didn't have to do that; he could have worked something out. He could have gotten his revenge and kept his life as he knew it, maybe even made things a bit better for himself.

But that ship had sailed.

His heart was pounding harder than he could ever remember. As a boxer, he often started off too fast, spending too much energy too soon. To stay in the fight, he'd become accustomed to pushing beyond his limits. His head would be fighting for clarity while his body fought to stay on its feet. But this felt much, much worse.

He forced his way out of the muddied waters of regret and looked ahead. His plan was far from perfect, and the chances of things working out in his favour were quite remote. But, for Frank McConnell Junior, the only way he could see ahead, survive and live with himself, was to follow through on exacting his revenge and then go from there. After what he'd done, patching things up with whoever took over the Irish mob was impossible. So he decided to make a run for it instead, maybe move west or south and change his name. Send for his mom once the coast was clear.

He mourned the loss of his life, such as it was. Tears streamed down his face, stinging his cuts and burning his eyes. This plan meant leaving his mother behind and likely never seeing Ted and Diane again.

Slowly but surely, ideas began to sharpen. Junior had always planned for a rainy day, putting aside a few dollars here and there. Some of it was his pay; Ted always made sure he was paid fairly for the risks of running the border. And, now and then, he made some extra cash brokering deals between drivers or selling a bag of weed or a cheap bottle of booze for someone here or there. He was careful, but not picky. He kept it in a five-gallon pail under a rock in the woods down off the East Richford Slide Road. It was probably a couple grand in Canadian and American money by now. It was plenty enough to get away, and the border was *right there*. He'd be in California before anyone even knew to look for him.

He'd keep tabs on the situation in Montreal through Andy. If things looked promising, maybe he could get a part of his old life back someday. It was a desperate long shot, but he wasn't willing to close that door just yet. An old life, even a shattered one, can still hold its attractions long after it ceases to be practical or even feasible.

Next was dealing with Stubby and Rogers. He considered fleeing the country, leaving them to starve to death out in the middle of nowhere. No one would find them for months, and by then he'd be long gone. Not only would that be easy, it would serve the bastards right.

But he couldn't bring himself to do that. With everything else falling away, at least he could enjoy the experience of revenge. Sadly, going back to Ted and Diane's wasn't an option. They'd already know what happened by the time he got there, and God knows what they'd do when they saw him. He knew he couldn't raise a hand against them, so it was better to just stay away.

He got off the autoroute at Ange-Gardien and headed south through Farnham towards Bedford. From there, he'd take the back roads through to Frelighsburg and out to the sugar shack.

* * *

I'd pretty much given up. We hadn't seen hide nor hair of the people who'd put us in this God-forsaken place out in the middle of nowhere. Even worse, all we'd had to drink was that nasty bucket water, which was now reduced to a layer of muddy silt at the bottom. I'd spent the past three days shivering in the cold. Even though we had matches, there wasn't a stick of wood anywhere to start a fire with. "Probably in the woodshed outside," Stubby said at one point. Might as well be a thousand miles away, considering how we were locked in.

"You dreamt about him last night."

"Yeah ," Stubby replied after a pause.

"What did he say?" I asked.

"Between him and me."

"Not like I'm going to be able to tell anyone."

I let the silence hang, hoping it would pry him open. I waited.

"He's done that to me a few times," Stubby said. "Dreams. All serious. Not like he used to be at all. Just fucking dreams."

"I dream about him too, but he hasn't spoken to me in them for quite awhile. Doesn't want me digging into his business, I guess."

"He just wants to protect you."

"How would you know that?"

He paused, staring at the concrete floor beneath his feet. "Because last night he said so. Put it on me to get us out of here, like I can do fuck-all."

He went quiet and didn't move for several minutes. Then I heard a rattle and looked up to see Stubby working on his chains as if trying to tear himself free of them using sheer force of will. He was like one of those coyotes that chew off their own foot to escape a trap.

"What the hell are you doing over there?" I asked.

"Trying is better than dying," he answered. "I ain't no Houdini, but if we don't get ourselves out of here, no one will. And I'll be damned if I'm going to starve to death in this dump."

"Well, you'd better hurry," I answered glumly. "I don't think we're that far off..."

"Make your miserable life happy, get over here and give me a hand."

I went over, he got up and together we walked over to the sugar arch. He put one of the chain links under the hinge of the arch door and pulled upwards, trying to make his hands small enough to slip through the manacles. He strained, and, for a second, it looked like one hand might pull through. If only he had smaller hands, not the mitts of a man who did hard manual labour for his entire life.

"Grab my hand... I don't have the strength."

I latched onto Stubby's right arm and started to pull. On one side I could see the base of his thumb come into view just above the chain.

"Stop! Fuck! *Owww!*"

We withdrew, and Stubby was left holding his hand. "Judas Priest!" he said.

We went back to our corners. Feeling more defeated than ever, I glanced over at Stubby and was terrified to see the look of sheer rage on his face.

"No one will ever dominate me," he growled, almost inaudible. "This will not dominate me."

We fell into silence, each immersed in our own thoughts. Stubby didn't move, he just stared at his hands. He was shaking, either from exhaustion, anger or stress. Then, like a caged animal, he got up and started pacing, constantly on the prowl looking for a way out.

We didn't hear the car pull in until it was almost outside the cabin. Our ears immediately perked up at the low rumble sound of a V-8 engine, but since it was on the opposite side of the shack's lone window, we couldn't see anything other than the sun lowering in the sky. I saw Stubby head back over to the sugar arch and fumble with the door. I didn't pay him much attention, choosing instead to fret over who was coming in.

We heard the rattle of chains, and the door opened just as Stubby sat back down.

"*Knock, knock...* Avon calling!" came the voice from the silhouette in the doorway.

"Jesus, it's Frank McConnell!" Stubby said, visibly shaken at the sight of our visitor.

I quickly took stock of our captor. He had blazing blue eyes, a shock of bright red hair and a pronounced cut across the side of his face. He was a little taller than me, probably close to six feet. He was dressed in jeans and a canvas coat. He quickly sized up the situation, looked at Stubby, then over at me and then back to Stubby.

"You must be losing it, old man," he said. "You're off by a generation."

"I've heard about you," Booker said, the gravel in his voice deepening. "Pity no-one else is ever gonna hear about you after today."

Great, threaten the guy who has the keys, I thought. I decided to keep quiet on this.

"I don't think you're in any shape to say that," said Junior. He went over and snapped a quick punch to Booker's face.

Stubby shook it off and looked at him, his expression one of fearless, seething anger.

Junior dismissively turned away and directed his focus onto me.

"So why am I here?" I asked.

"You and I have something in common. Too bad that's not going to end well for you," he answered.

Even though I was on the verge of total panic, I did my best to look calm. I'm not sure if it worked but, then again, he didn't seem to care.

"Back in the day, when we were both little, your father and that other piece of shit over there murdered my father and ruined my life. So now it's time to get even."

"But what do I have to do with that?" I said. "My dad didn't do anything to your father. He was just a witness who was going to testify against Stubby."

"So, you haven't talked about it?" he asked, turning to Stubby. "I wanted to leave you two alone so you get everything out in the open. That way there are no more secrets and everyone knows what they're dying for."

I turned to Stubby. "What is he talking about?"

"Nothing, kid. He's just some asshole whose crooked cop of a father wanted us out of the way."

"Oh, it's a bit more than that," Junior answered. "My dad put the lean on you, and instead of taking the hint and going away, you and Rogers murdered him for it."

Murder? My dad wasn't a witness, but a perpetrator? I could feel the colour drain from my face. I blinked, hoping to get this new information to compute, but it didn't. *It couldn't.* So I just sat there and said nothing.

"Time to make some things clear," he said, turning to me again. "My name is Frank McConnell *Junior*. My father was a cop who also worked for the Irish in Montreal. He was sent out here to deal with the country bumpkins who were getting in the way. You know, border stuff... like what you've been writing about lately.

"After dear old dad and Booker here killed my father, ol' Dave started to feel bad," Junior continued. "He went to the cops, said he'd testify against *this* cocksucker and they worked out a plea deal. They arrested your dad, but he managed to swing bail for being a witness. He wanted to run away, but the cops wouldn't let him leave the province, so he moved you and your mom to Montreal and then went to work in the girders. My guess is that he was hoping to get them all set up before he went to jail, but you'd have to ask your momma about that. Sad that you won't get a chance to do that now. Anyways, that turned out to be a bad move."

"So he fell," I said. "And Stubby got away with murder."

"Not quite. I got a little bit more info from my ex-boss. Newsflash, Mr. Reporter: *your old man jumped.*"

There was a silence. I was too stunned to react.

"What? Cat got your tongue? My boss was one of the ones who chased him up into the scaffolding and cornered him out on a beam over the city. They cut him a deal: jump and the Irish would leave his family alone. But if your dad forced them to shoot him, you and your momma would join him in the afterlife."

Despite their weight, the words hung in the air.

"To his credit, he did the right thing. In the end, at least."

I glanced towards the corner of the room and saw Stubby sitting there motionless with his head bowed.

"Then, because *asshole* over here was already in with the *eyetie* crowd, Charlie's boss and him reached a truce. Everyone agreed to do their own thing and leave everybody else alone. When Charlie took over, he decided that the truce was good business and, let me tell ya, there's nothing Charlie likes more than good business. Well, there's no more room for truces anymore...*just payback.*"

"McKiernan's a shrewd businessman and not one to back out of a deal," Booker said. "There's no way he's signed off on this."

"Well, ol' Charlie got a lead injection earlier today, so he's not going to be running the show anymore."

"Oh, God," Booker sighed. "Please tell me it wasn't you."

"As a matter of fact, it was. But don't worry, I'm sure there are plenty of folks in the organization who wanted him out of the way. This'll be good news for them. You don't run a show like his and not make a few enemies. Hell, maybe *I'll* take things over."

Booker laughed out loud. "What, you? You're just a snot-nosed brat. Don't kid yourself; nobody's gonna follow you!"

"That's really none of your business," Junior said. Both men fell silent, staring at each other. Despite his disadvantage, Stubby didn't break his gaze.

"I still don't understand why I'm here. I'm not a part of any of this," I said.

"You got a part in it when you went out there and dug up shit on people who don't like the attention," Junior continued. "Just proves that you're no better than that turncoat father of yours."

"I'm only doing my job," I said. "What's that to you?"

"Well, your 'job' draws too much attention to us. Now everyone's gonna be watching us like a hawk."

"Look, if you were doing your job properly, I wouldn't have been writing about your precious border," I said, feeling my anger rise and bubble over the lip of fear.

"To be honest, if you were just some go-hunk writing the news, I probably wouldn't have done anything about it. When I learned who your dad was, I was ready to hate you, but I left you be. That is until you started writing about my business. You didn't mention my name, but you did put my truck right on the fucking front page, licence plate and all. Let's just say I didn't appreciate the attention. So, I decided that you were one more loose end that needed to be tied up. Your family doesn't get to go on its merry way like it has nothing to apologize for. In fact, your family line ends *here*."

Those last five words hung there in complete silence. I didn't know what to say but, then again, what could I say? This stranger meant to kill me and even the most clever pleas from me were unlikely to sway him.

"And then, when it's all done, I can sit back and run the show. Hell, maybe I'll get together with that cute little librarian

I met awhile back, make her toes curl," he said. "She can share in my good fortune."

"Your what?" I said. Did he just say what I thought he said? "What the fuck?"

He looked over at me, and a little grin emerged.

"What, you know her?" He continued to look at me. "Oh, shit. You *do* know her. This is going to be sweet. Yeah, I'm definitely going to have to look *her* up."

No, he can't. *I won't let it.*

I saw Stubby rise to his feet. He turned towards the sugar arch, leaning his hands on the overturned pan. It was hard to see, the only light coming from the numerous cracks and knot holes in the weathered hemlock of the walls and that frustratingly-small window. He had his back to Junior, staring at the floor.

"Hey, don't you turn your back on me when I'm talking to you!" Junior said, stepping towards him.

Just as Junior was about to grab Stubby, the old man turned. As he did so, he dragged his hands across the top of the boiling pan and a handful of wooden matches sparked to life. He then jabbed this fistful of flaring matches into Junior's face.

"Get him! Get him now!" Booker yelled at me.

Frank Junior howled in pain as the sulphur flare singed his skin and filled his vision with a bright flash. He lashed out, his fist missing Booker but catching the edge of the pan. He roared in pain and futile anger.

This was no time to sit back and consider my options. I sprang at him, my rage engaged. I came up behind him, hooked my chained wrists around his neck and pulled him backwards. He thrashed about, furious at the world.

Jesus, he was strong. But I knew that if I let go, we'd be done for. I felt the chains biting into my wrists and forced myself to hang on despite the pain. He pushed back, running us backwards into the cabin wall. I felt a sharp pain as a rib cracked. Even though I couldn't breathe, I wasn't about to let go. No fucking way. If I did that, I knew it would be all over.

Meanwhile, I glanced across the room and saw that Booker had turned back to the arch again.

"Help me, for fuck's sake!" I yelled, beyond scared.

I could see Stubby hooked his chained wrists on the arch again, this time on the door. He forced his bonds, turning as he did so, and a painful scream sliced the air like hot razors. I was so engrossed in the melee with Junior that I didn't hear the sound of the cast iron arch door breaking free as the aged masonry crumbled from the force of his effort.

Stubby Booker came at Junior, the heavy door of the arch in his chained hands. He came in low, catching Junior in the abdomen with the edge, doubling him over. The second blow was an upward shot, which battered his freckled face and broke some teeth. Junior fell to the floor with me on his back, and my wrist chains dug into the flesh of his neck. I felt a crunch, which I thought was his Adam's apple. He gurgled, arms flailing.

Despite this, he rose to his feet, hoisting me on his back. Booker raised the arch door edgewise once again, catching the back of Junior's knee. He dropped, but stayed upright. Then I felt the sheer strength of Stubby Booker first-hand as he pushed Junior and I into the corner of the arch.

Junior's face caught the corner, and he fell to the floor. As he collapsed, I could feel my right wrist contort, giving way under our combined weight.

"Lift his fucking head!" Booker said. I forced myself to move against my broken bones, but I could only manage to lift his head a few inches from the ground. Booker's foot flashed by my face, mashing Junior's forehead into the floor.

Junior's body continued to twitch, his arms and legs seeking, but failing, to find their purpose. I felt the air escape his lungs and the coiled strength of his body ebb away. After a few moments, Frank McConnell Junior, a boy who lived his life in the shadow of his dead father, just like I had, was no more.

And that's when I was left with the stark realization that I'd just killed a man.

35
Perpetual darkness

My breath came in ragged gasps, adrenaline pumping. I couldn't feel my broken wrist, which was probably a good thing. Time for that later.

Stubby wasted no time rifling through Junior's pockets to find a revolver.

"Jesus, good thing he never got the chance to pull that out," Booker mumbled. He set the pistol aside and kept looking, his chained hands slowing the search. He rolled Junior onto his back and found the lock keys in the front pocket of his jeans. Due to a combination of chained hands and broken fingers, Booker fumbled with them. One hand in particular looked like a complete mess, but he paid scant attention to it.

As Stubby tried to spring the padlock holding my chain, I finally looked down at my right hand and saw that it was skewed off at an odd angle. I didn't feel any pain, but the sight of it made me dizzy, and I fell to the floor.

"No time for drama. Get up... *now.*"

For some reason I listened. I got up, my legs vibrating but responding. I had to help Stubby open the bolts on his chains, which held hands covered in a dark, nameless gore of blood and burned flesh. I could smell it.

"Let's get to the car and see if we can find something to get me out of these chains," he said, shaking his good wrist.

In the trunk of the car we found a length of rope and a cloth bag with some basic tools in it. Including, thank God, the wrenches Junior and his buddy had used to bolt Stubby into his chains. My hands slipped on the wrench a couple of times, sending bolts of pain through my shattered wrist and prompting curses from Stubby. But finally, for the first time in over three days, his hands were free.

"We just killed a man," I said, half to myself, the impact of it crashing like waves on a rocky shoreline. "I'm a murderer now."

"We did what we had to do," Booker said, presenting it as a matter of fact. "But now we've got work to do or we're gonna be in deep shit."

Gonna be? I pretty much figured we were already in the deep end of the outhouse, with no way out.

"Look, we have to get outta here, and we don't know where we are or if he has friends nearby," Booker said. "And also gotta make this cocksucker disappear, get rid of this car and come up with some kind of a story... what your dad would have called a 'borderline truth.'"

My dad. *Damn.* If he wasn't talking to me before, he was going to be downright pissed at me now. As if I didn't have enough trouble sleeping already. Then I thought of Jen, my mother and everyone who knew me. I dropped to my knees and retched, but nothing came out. There was nothing in there.

"Get up, *fuck!*"

Hearing this was rough at the time, but looking back, I get it. There was no time to indulge all those feelings boiling around inside. There'd be a lifetime to do that, and now I had more potential in front of me than I did just a few minutes ago.

If you've never moved a human body, I can tell you that they're heavy as hell. Junior was a special case because he was good-sized man who probably weighed about two-hundred pounds. And, even though I've moved that kind of weight before, Stubby and I had a hard time shifting him. We were both hungry, dehydrated and had one pair of working hands between the two of us. After hooking a length of rope around his chest and under his arms and, we managed to drag him to the car with great effort. We stopped to catch our breath and then heaved him into the trunk.

"You drive. We gotta figure our way outta here, and I need some time to think," Stubby said.

That's when I realized that we each had our left hands. While I was barely okay to drive, I had to reach over the wheel to drop it into gear. I backed the car around, following the tracks back out to civilization.

"I think we're close to the border," Booker said, as he looked out into the growing darkness. "Hell, we might even be in the States. Hard to tell."

We came to a standard steel farm gate, the rusting wire showing its age. Booker got out, removed the chain, and, with great effort, dragged it open wide enough to let the big car through. He didn't bother closing it.

We drove on in silence, each scanning for a sign of where we were or how we were going to get back home. We were particularly watchful for lights, still unsure if Junior was alone or if he had friends waiting nearby. We crested a hill, and before we could give it any thought, we were in the middle of a barnyard. Time to just keep driving quietly and pray for no reaction from man or beast. *Good God, these LTDs were quiet when you were light on the gas.*

"Looks like we're still in Quebec," Booker said, pointing to the rear bumper of a pickup. "That's something."

I don't remember the various turns we made. I felt disconnected, delirious...like I was driving drunk, but Stubby seemed to figure it out. Within a few minutes, we got on the Richford Road, headed towards the line and took a left at the last second onto Claybank, heading towards Abercorn. The memory of waking up in the Abercorn Hotel parking lot came back to me. Not that long ago, but already in a different era.

"Okay, here's what we're gonna do," Stubby growled. "Drive nice and easy. Once we get to Brome, there's a phone booth outside the store. I'm gonna call someone. Then we'll keep going and head out past Bolton Centre towards Eastman."

"That's a long drive with a body in the trunk," I said, trying to sound calm, but failing miserably.

"That's how we're gonna make him disappear."

"Hey, look, this is my first time. But I guess you've done this before."

"Not as often as people like to believe."

"What do you mean?"

"You think I haven't heard the rumours? Hell, even if you believed half of it, you'd think I spent all my spare time killing people. *Bunch of bullshit.*"

"But you have killed people before," I said. "Like Frank McConnell."

"Yes, I killed him. And I killed our friend out on the Sand Road in Brigham last year. *That's it.* But gossip flies all 'round, makes things bigger than they are."

"And my father helped you kill McConnell," I said.

"He was there, but the two of us were the only ones who know who did what. And even that's a little confused. Let's just say it was a situation that got out of hand. Your old man was no killer, boy. I only ever saw him in a couple of fights, and he could handle himself, but nothing more than that. He might have been a bit of an outlaw, but he never wanted to hurt anyone."

We drove in silence for a bit, our eyes peeled as we cruised through the village of Sutton. On the way out of town, Stubby pointed out a spot where water gushed from a pipe at the side of the road. We pulled over.

"People with bad water come here to fill their jugs up," Booker explained. We gulped the cool, clear water from the end of the pipe. I've never enjoyed water that much before or since. Now feeling slightly re-hydrated, we wasted little time. Sutton had their own town cops, and being stopped would be problematic to say the least. We headed north towards Sutton Junction. I'd never been this way before, but Stubby was calm now, sure of himself. Back in control.

The village of Brome was quiet. Owen's Store was closed for the evening, and there wasn't a soul to be seen. Far different from Brome Fair weekend, when the village was an absolute beehive of activity. This was Brome much as it was for most of the year, before the cattle and the carnies arrived for Labour Day.

Booker fished a dime from his pocket, and I watched from the car as he got out and walked to the phone booth under the streetlight. He seemed a little unsteady on his feet. He turned towards me as he talked on the phone, and I could barely recognize him. His features were drawn and his clothes were dirty and ripped in tatters. He kept his right arm resting on his belly and there was a dark stain down one leg. The thought briefly crossed my mind that maybe he wanted to make a clean slate of things and eliminate me too, but it was barely a ripple in my consciousness.

"Okay, drive, before someone sees us," he said as he got back into the car. He smelled awful, a combination of sweat and stress and blood and gore. With my broken nose, it was the first thing I really got a whiff of in days. I probably didn't smell much better, I figured.

We drove in silence for another few minutes, taking Stagecoach Road past the fairgrounds. Stubby kept us on it, winding our way out and around Knowlton, which also had cops of its own.

"So my dad, he was going to testify against you, but you said he was involved when McConnell was killed," I left it hanging there.

"To be honest, I think he panicked. Some people can live with killing, but not your dad. It was the only time I ever saw him lose his cool. He ran to the cops before he had time to think, told them it was me, and then they arrested him on the spot. Next thing he knows, we're both facing charges. His only way out was to hope they'd pin it all on me and make himself look like a bystander.

"In my head I've killed your father a thousand times," he continued. "But I don't think his last days were happy ones. He was trying to save you and your mom from the humiliation of having a murderer in the family, and things went wrong. My guess is that he was so busy worrying about me that he never saw the Irish coming. Why else would he have moved to Montreal? Made no sense for him to walk right into their backyard."

"But you guys killed a cop. The police must have been pissed."

"Oh, they laid a pretty good beating on me," Stubby said. "On your dad too, I think. But somewhere in there they found out how dirty McConnell was, and when he came to see us, it wasn't on police business. He was there for the Irish. The more they dug, the more dirt they found on one of their own. In the end, I think they didn't chase us too hard because he made them look bad. At a certain point, they just let things peter out. *Fuckers*," he said, punctuated with a quiet laugh. "They still fucking hate me, but they knew it would make a mess. And when it comes down to it, most people just want messy things to go away."

More silence as we entered South Bolton and turned left towards Bolton Centre. Few features were visible in the dark, just more miles of road.

"You mind me asking where in the hell we're going?"

"Okay. Up ahead there's a road to your right that leads to the old Quebec copper mine. It closed in the late Fifties. We'll take care of him there."

When we turned onto the road, we saw the shoulders reflect a deep orange in the glare of the headlights. Now and then, bright orange rock faces loomed into view. We came to a stop in front of a large pile of soil, as well as the remains of the mine's headframe and hoist room piled to one side. The bullwheel tumbled to a sharp angle, still wrapped in cables that disappeared into the earth.

"How in hell did you find this place?"

"I had an uncle who worked here. Spent a good chunk of his life underground. They say that, as time went on, the shaft slowly got smaller and smaller, until the elevator was having a hard time making it back up. My uncle was in the car that day when it got caught on a rock and let go. He broke both his legs. My grandmother sent me to live with him for a bit and help out while he recovered. Mean bastard. The mine closed not long after, and he was out of a job."

I glanced over and Stubby was staring straight ahead, lost in thought, his features barely visible in the gloom. "I think that's when I decided there was a better way to make a living than to grind yourself to the bone," he added. "A life like that uses you all up, and when you can't do it anymore, they toss you aside and find some other young buck to take your place. No way to live."

I left the headlights on so we could see, and Stubby walked up to the pile. On the side was an opening with a thick piece of concrete leaned over a boulder. Stubby picked up a stone, and threw it into the shadow. We listened to the rock clatter off the shaft wall and then heard a final clack several seconds later.

"It's a good three-hundred to four-hundred feet down there," Stubby said. "Good place to make things disappear."

We grabbed the rope and pulled the mortal remains of Frank McConnell Junior out of the trunk. When the body hit the ground, Junior groaned and kicked his feet out.

"Oh, Jesus, he's still alive!" I called out into the night. "Oh fuck!"

But before I could have a total meltdown, Stubby fished the pistol out of his pocket with his left hand. The shot rang in my ears, echoing off the surrounding hillsides and the muzzle flash spotted my vision.

"Oh fuck!" I said again, barely able to hear my own voice through the ringing. "Judas Priest!"

Stubby fixed me with a gaze that shut me up. Junior had finally stopped moving.

"If you do like your father and go to the cops, you'll be joining him down there. Now shut up and help me."

Together we dragged the body over to the hole and stuffed it in headfirst. The shoulders were a bit of a squeeze through the narrow opening.

"It's going to be a long, hard fall," Stubby said under his breath. *"Blow you to pieces in the dark."*

And with a final heave, Frank McConnell Junior's feet vanished from view, disappearing into perpetual darkness and deafening silence.

36

Drop off

Shaky was just getting ready to go home for the night when the call came in. It was late, and he couldn't think of anything else to do but wait things out. Might as well go home, try to get a decent night's sleep and then come back early. Do as he'd been told to keep things running "business as usual."

He turned, grabbed at the phone and very nearly dropped the receiver. It was Stubby on the line. He didn't sound too good, like he'd been having a tough time of things.

"No time for questions now," Booker said. "Meet me in an hour out at the old marble mine in South Stukely. Bring some tools and come alone."

Just over an hour later, Shaky was sitting in his pickup truck, lights off, smoking nervously as he saw the car come into view. With the abandoned marble quarry just around the next bend, he figured that they needed to dispose of something. He didn't like that feeling.

Oh shit, he's got someone with him, Shaky thought as the headlights panned onto his truck and then turned. He put the pickup in gear, eased the clutch out and followed, flicking his lights on as he did so. A white Ford LTD. He'd seen it before. *Shit.* It was the car Junior drove. Feeling confused, Shaky grabbed the .22 Smith & Wesson automatic handgun out from under the seat and put it in the deep inner pocket of his coat. Blood thundered in his ears.

Before the descent to the bottom of the hole, the car veered right, coming to a halt above the cliff face. Sixty feet below was the lake that had formed in the years after the marble mine closed. A popular swimming spot for locals looking to escape the summer's heat, the small lake was deep enough that it stayed cool late into the season. It was also deep enough to hide things not meant to be found.

Stubby emerged from the passenger side, while a stranger climbed out of the driver's door. Both men were dirty and quite obviously injured. As soon as he saw that it wasn't Junior driving, he relaxed.

"Get over here and give us a hand. Bring the flashlight and the screwdriver," Booker said, clearly in charge of the situation.

With barely a word, Shaky went to work. He popped the serial numbers out from the dash with the screwdriver, then opened the hood. It was hard to see in the glow of a flashlight, but, with a little searching, he found the serial number on the engine block. He went back to the truck and returned with a hammer and chisel. In a few minutes, the identifying numbers were disfigured and unreadable. He finished by removing the licence plate.

"Look it over, make sure we didn't leave anything behind," Booker said. "You, Dave. Drop it in neutral."

After placing a tire between the front bumper of the pickup and the rear bumper of the car, Shaky pushed the LTD forward, stopping only as it dropped over the edge. The splash was loud, followed by the silence of a calm fall night.

* * *

Once we got to the quarry, things happened with surprising efficiency. It was pretty obvious to me that this Shaky guy had done this kind of thing before. He knew right where to go for the serial numbers, so if anyone found the car they'd have a hell of a time figuring out who it belonged to. The blood and fingerprints would dissolve into the water. If the cops ever did find it years from now, all they'd know is that someone had dumped a white car there. Not traceable and probably stolen. Stubby surveyed Shaky's work, clearly back in command of the situation. *My God,* I thought, *even after all we've been through, he's back in charge like nothing happened.*

"Okay, now you," Stubby said, turning to me. "If you get any funny ideas about going to the cops like your dad did, you'll be dead before I'm even arrested. If you keep your mouth shut and stick to the story, I'll make sure you're taken care of. Legal representation, the works. All you need to do is shut the fuck up."

"Deal," I said, as if I had any choice in the matter.

"And what is the story?" he said, his form a silhouette in the darkness.

"*Uh,* okay," I said, feeling like it was test time. We hadn't discussed it, so I made it up my own "borderline truth."

"We were both kidnapped by Frank McConnell Junior and brought to a sugar cabin near the border. We don't know why, because he never said. He made it clear he intended to kill us. We fought with him, and he escaped and drove away. He said something about going to the States, but we don't know where he is."

"Good. Now how did we get out of there?"

"*Uh,* we wandered out of the sugar camp through the woods and followed the road. We found a place and made a phone call to have your friend here pick us up and bring us to the hospital. We *are* going to the hospital, aren't we?"

"Not bad storytelling, for a newspaper reporter," Stubby said. He turned just as Shaky came up behind him, handing him a pack of cigars. "Now where did you go wrong?"

I was puzzled. He handed me a cigar and Shaky snapped a Zippo open. I was immediately distracted by the sight of the tall flame and the sharp aroma of lighter fluid.

"We wandered out to a road and a passerby picked us up and dropped us off at a pay phone in Frelighsburg." Stubby said. "You see what I did there? No one saw us that they can talk to. We don't know the name of the guy who picked us up, he was just some old fella. Let's say he was in a pickup and it was dark. That way the cops don't have anyone to check our story with. And where was the sugar cabin?"

"I honestly couldn't say," I replied, feeling like I was going through some kind of oral exam.

"That's because you're exhausted, dehydrated, starving and you don't know the area very well," Stubby said. "That's okay. I pretty much know the general area where it was. If the cops find the place, there should be enough blood and mess to help with our story."

As we smoked in silence together, I was hit by a wave of *Holy shit, I'm still alive!* It felt good. The cigar was sweet and the nicotine hit me like a brick wall, to the point where I had to sit down on the front bumper of the pickup. Slowly, the adrenaline was starting to fade.

"That's the best kind of borderline truth," Stubby said. "Never stray too far from the facts. Just far enough to keep yourself out of trouble."

37

Win enough

I only remember bits and pieces as we drove the pickup to the hospital. Granby was closer, but we decided to go to Cowansville. "We came from Frelighsburg, so it only makes sense that we went to the nearest hospital," Stubby said. Shaky drove while I passed in and out of consciousness and Stubby smoked in silence.

Even though I wasn't fully with it, I felt every single crack, stop and turn in the road. I seemed to slosh around on the bench seat between the two men. Stubby could have pulled over and shot me in the head and I wouldn't have cared.

I helped kill a man. Who in hell am I?

In my half-waking state I saw the hospital loom into view. I looked quiet in the night, just a big slab of institutional beige brick in front of me, bathed in light. I had no idea what time it was and I wasn't even sure of the day of the week.

"Get up, and walk in there like a man," Stubby said, cigar still clenched in his teeth. I did as I was told, somehow managing to keep my balance. I was short of breath, coughing against a cracked rib. A nurse approached at a run, a few blank moments followed and then I was being helped onto a gurney.

"He's in shock!" I heard a voice say. Then everything went dark.

* * *

"I never wanted any of this for you."

It was my dad.

"So, you're speaking to me now?"

"I tried to protect you. From me, from the mess I got us into. I thought my 'borderline truths' might keep you and your mother safe."

He looked different than in my earlier dreams, the ones where he was trying to lure me away from the life I was attempting to build. He looked defeated, disappointed and sad.

"Are you happy now that I'm tangled up in all of this?" I asked. "Now that I've killed a man and I have to lie about it or set a match to what's left of my life? I'm looking at jail, divorce and even a nice trip to hell at the end of it all. How about some straight truth for once?"

He looked at me, and all I could see was that pain-stricken face.

"Despite everything you've been told, or haven't been told, I'm pretty sure you already know the truth."

I realized it without him saying another word.

"So, you killed Frank McConnell."

His silence acknowledged the guilt.

"And you panicked and went to the police and pinned it on Stubby."

More silence. I could see all of him now. He put a hand to his face and rubbed his eyes with his thumb and finger.

"I poured my life into that damned farm and I was still losing it. It was a legacy that I desperately wanted to give to you someday. So, I pushed things too far and took some stupid risks. Then that dirty cop showed up and started threatening Stubby and me. It was 'police stuff' at first, but then he threatened you and your mom.

"To be a man is to be frustrated" he continued. "To learn your limits and realize that you could have been more if only you'd tried harder or gotten that lucky break. And you can see things slipping away, no matter how hard you grab at them. You spend so much time fighting that you lose sight of things. It becomes all about winning, even when you realize that you can't. No one wins without help, but sometimes there's no one who can step in and save the day for you. In the end, every man lives alone with his failures…and then dies with them."

"So when they went after you, you decided it was easier to jump."

"My life was already over before they got to me. It was the closest thing to a win that I could figure out. If I could save you and your mother, that was win enough."

* * *

When I came to, the first thing I saw was the splint on my right wrist. I turned my head slowly to see an IV hooked up to my left. I closed my eyes again. It hurt to breathe. Then I coughed and it hurt a whole lot more. I wanted my dad back. In spite of it all, in spite of the lies and the loss, I desperately wanted him back.

I opened my eyes again. This time, standing around the bed like angels in the afterlife, were my mom, Jen's mom and Jen. In that moment I felt so alone in what I knew.

They stood in silence, waiting for me to speak. I only managed a faint "Hey there…"

Then came a rush of words as they all spoke over each other, statements to each other, questions to me. Maybe it was the morphine, but I couldn't make much of it. I tried to shake my head, but that just made things feel worse. Scraps of phrases made it through the haze. Words like "collapsed lung," "broken rib," "went into shock" and "severe dehydration."

I blinked at the ceiling, then glanced towards the doorway, where a cop was standing guard, looking in. *Oh, sweet Jesus. Just like my father, I'd killed a man.* I glanced at the bed on my right, and saw Stubby Booker sleeping peacefully, in spite of the chorus of excited voices coming from the women in my life which filled the room to capacity.

At that time, I remembered everything. *It was time to begin weaving my own borderline truths.*

38
Sealing the ends

I delayed talking to the cops for as long as I could, but when the doctor mentioned that they were sending me home on the third day, I knew that I couldn't put it off any longer. They wheeled me down the hall to an unused examination room, where two cops asked me a series of questions that took me from being forced off the road to stumbling out of the woods.

By now I had my story cleaned up. Stubby and I had spoken in hushed whispers during the night, keeping our voices lowered so the cop asleep in his chair in the hallway couldn't hear. This allowed us to seal the ends of our tale with the wax of half-truths. We kept it simple: 'No officer, I don't know where he went. No officer, I couldn't tell you who picked us up. Stubby called his hired man, and he brought us straight to the nearest hospital. No sir, no idea why this person kidnapped us. Never seen him before.'

I'd like to say that was the end of it, but it wasn't. In my head, this never really ends. The cops called me back in twice for questioning; clearly they suspected that there was more happening than I was letting on. They asked me the same questions every time, as if hoping that I'd drop some new, previously-forgotten detail. It was a blatantly obvious ploy to trip me up, but, once again, I kept it simple.

I stuck to the same story with Jen and the mothers. That was a door I couldn't open. To have Jen look at me and know that I'd taken part in killing another human being was more than I could bear.

So I buried it deep, in the hope that it would stay there. In my mind, I kept telling myself that it wasn't me who actually killed him... I was simply defending myself. We all tell ourselves stories to justify our place in events. It's how we live with what we've done.

A couple of weeks later I heard a knock at my front door. I was still milking my few remaining sick days, dreading the inevitable fuss I'd face when I returned to the newsroom. I was terrified by the prospects of trotting out my cover story over and over again to a room of investigative journalists. Jen was at work, and King was sniffing at the crack at the bottom of the door by the time I got there. I opened the door and saw Shaky standing on the threshold.

"Stubby wants to talk to you."

"He could have just called," I said.

"He doesn't trust the phone these days."

In front of our duplex was a Cadillac, with Stubby sitting in the passenger seat, his right arm in a sling. He was wearing his good suit and his hair slicked back. He motioned for me to climb in the back. *Shit, am I a loose end he was looking to tie up?*

We drove in relative silence, exchanging all the formal niceties, but steering clear of the elephant in the car. At a small parking area overlooking Cowansville's Lake, Shaky parked and got out without saying a word. He sat on the hood of the car, smoking, while Stubby and I talked.

"So, you figured it out about your dad," Stubby said.

"Yes. How did you know?"

"He talked to me the other night. He talks to me sometimes."

"We talked when I was in the hospital. Just dreams."

"Yeah, I don't know what the hell to call it. He's been dead for over twenty years, but he's haunted me steady ever since. Kept leaning on me to either leave you alone, protect you or do whatever he thought he should do if he'd been around."

"Is that why you let me believe you killed Frank McConnell? To protect me?"

"More or less... but it's not as simple as that. It never is. Your old man was as good as it gets. He kept me out of jail more than once, but towards the end everything he did went wrong.

The bank was talking about taking the farm and I could see him start to unravel. He drank too much and said he couldn't sleep. Then McConnell showed up, started slapping me around and pulled a gun on us. Your dad handled him pretty quick. Saved my life, but it cost him his own."

A part of me wanted details, but a bigger part of me had heard enough.

"All you gotta know is that he saved me... and you know the rest."

"So now what?"

"Get on with your life. It's yours, not his, and it doesn't have to be anything other than what you want it to be. Stick to your 'borderline truths' and be good to that woman of yours. I heard her talking with the others at your bedside. You're lucky, you've got some amazing women in your life. There's your good fortune right there."

"I thought you didn't like my mom."

"I liked her a lot back in the day; maybe more than I should have. But she was with your dad, so I kept my distance and let her think I was the bad influence. When you've got a friend as good as Slippers, you'll take that hit for him.

"We talked a bit at the hospital, your mother and me," Booker continued. "Mended some fences. I tried to give her some peace. She's carried a lot with her over the years."

He lowered the electric window. "Shaky, we gotta go."

And with that, he drove away, leaving me alone with my thoughts as I walked the few blocks back to the apartment. The fall air was crisp, with a hint of the cold months to come. It felt good to breathe and revel in the sensations of being alive, come what may.

* * *

Charlie McKiernan didn't give Junior's name to the cops. He kept it simple, and told them that some local hood tried to rob the place. This, despite taking a bullet that shattered his collarbone and very nearly caused him to bleed to death. As soon as he regained consciousness, Ted filled him in on what had happened. *Junior wasn't going to be a problem to anyone ever again.*

It was a Wednesday afternoon, and McKiernan was wiping down the bar with his good arm. He still tired easily, but the doctors assured him that he'd be fine once his blood levels stabilized.

"How's Diane taking things?" Charlie asked Ted, who'd made a rare trip in from the country.

"It was hard. She loved that kid," he replied, taking a deep sip of his Molson Export and tomato juice cocktail. "He was a hard worker and he was good to us." Charlie smiled, knowing that "hard worker" was just about the highest compliment his partner could ever pay to someone.

Lost in thought, Ted stared at his beer glass. He'd left out the part about how Junior had been a good kid until he learned about his past, and how that past had consumed him. No point in saying it, since both men already knew.

"That's how it had to be, you know. It's just business," Charlie said.

"I know. I just want to get out. I'm too old and too tired. Diane and I just want to live out the rest of our days in peace."

"You are out, and it's all good. You did a lot of good work for me over the years, so here's a little something for your retirement," Charlie said, sliding an envelope across the bar to Ted, who took it and put it in his pocket without looking. Plenty of time for that later. "And this is to cover your car," Charlie added, handing over a second envelope.

"Thanks, Charlie."

When the door to Charlie's tavern opened, Ellwood turned and instinctively reached for the pistol in his pocket. McKiernan saw who it was and waved him aside.

"Good day, Stubby, welcome to my little establishment," Charlie said. "I'd shake your hand, but it's out of commission right now."

"I've got a bum wing myself," Stubby said.

"Pretty sure we got winged by the same guy," Charlie said

with a slight smile. "Thanks for taking care of that for me."

"I'd say it was no trouble, but that would be bullshit," Stubby said. He reached into his breast pocket and pulled out an Old Port cigar. McKiernan obliged with a wooden match scratched on the metal edge of the melamine bar table and then lit his own pipe with the remaining flame.

"You play cribbage?"

"Not for years."

"You're sharp. It'll come back to you soon enough. Soon enough to lose gracefully."

"Don't worry. In the end, I'll win. I always do." Stubby said with a grin. He took a long haul from his cigar, then leaned back to blow the smoke towards the ceiling.

"I know. That's why I want to do business with you."

The End

About the Author

Born and raised in Quebec's Eastern Townships, Canada, Maurice J.O. Crossfield spent nearly 15 years as a daily newspaper reporter at the *Sherbrooke Record*. He then spent several years as a professional writer, translator and editor-in-chief at *Harrowsmith*. Not content with a single career path, he has worked as an auto mechanic, handyman, forestry worker, organic gardener, and most recently as a gravel truck driver. He lives in the quiet hamlet of West Brome with his wife, musician Sarah Biggs, and a selection of cats and dogs